LINK

WILD NATURE

Ballines, Joaquin Ignacio

Serie: Link - Libro N°: 1
Title: Salvaje Naturaleza
Pages: 276; 15,24 x 22,86

ISBN: 9798694968430
Seal: Independently published

Ilustration:
Cover: Ramon Bunge
Inside: Joaquín Ballines

 @laleyendadelinklibro
 @jib_link
✉ joaquin.ballines@bue.edu.ar

J. I. BALLINES

LINK

WILD NATURE

This book is dedicated to my mother, Ana Maria,
who took upon herself the chore of correcting it,
and also to my father, Francisco,
thank you both for accompanying me throughout my life.
Also, I'd like to dedicate this book to the rest of my family, friends and,
specially, to Gabriel A. Marcovecchio, my reader, critic and corrector friend;
my friend, companion, girlfriend and advisor, Ayelen R. Pingitore
and Adrian D. Gianni, who took upon himself the translation
of this book to the English language.
To all of them, with all my love and thankfulness.

.

LETTER TO THE READER

Dear lovers of adventure and fiction,

If you're reading this, it's because you've got a sample of "Link". My name is Joaquin Ignacio Ballines and I'm the author of this book.

I believe this letter to be a nice way to clear some doubts that may have appeared about this novel, but, before we talk about it, I'd like you to know a little bit about myself.

I was born on March the 25th of 1987. I grew up, and still live, in one of the many neighborhoods in the Ciudad Autonoma de Buenos Aires, in Argentina. Once I finished high school, I started a career in gymnastics and, later on, I graduated as a Red Cross Lifeguard.

As I worked in schools and clubs, I added some extra degrees to my resume. I became a Lic. In physical education and I earned a degree in Swimming.

By the time I wrote this letter, I'm still working as a teacher in the city of Buenos Aires (CABA), constantly updating my resume and my knowledge through courses provided by the Ministry of Education.

Literature seems to be quite distant to my area of expertise, which rises the question: How did this book came to be?

I guess that one of my most important qualities is to be thankful. So, I can't avoid saying that, while I do dedicate myself to what is my dream job, throughout my life I was accompanied by the different enterprises that make video-games, another hobby of mine. Memories like those provided by games as "Star Fox", "Kirbyland" and different releases of "Pokemon" will forever remain in my mind, being those moments, perhaps, the ones that influenced me in my new literary creativity.

Probably, the creators of those games think of me as one more number amongst the enormous number of followers they have, but for me, those memories, many of which come from the "The Legend of Zelda" saga which I enjoyed deeply, still remain and contributed to the added value that makes me who I am today.

For the creation of this book, I got inspired in certain moments and random events from many different games, most of which come from the aforementioned saga. Nonetheless, the personalities of the characters are of my own creation and based on family and friends.

It's not my intention to make money with the fame of the company which created said games, still, obviously, fans will find similitudes.

In any case, there is no need to have played any of the saga's games to be able to understand and enjoy the plot that unravels in these pages.

It is my hope that this story gets translated and spread throughout the world, until it reaches the hands of video-games developers and they see it as an attractive one to be turned into one of their games.

I believe that Video-games are, in many opportunities, an interactive learning tool should you set your mind into it. Many times, I've been able to tie together the world of fiction with my work, creating new and fun activities to work with my students.

Video-games are capable to tell a story as the literary genres do in novels, tales or poems while adding the audio-visual element which could be found in a song, painting or movie. In other words, to me, a video-game is a work of art. Still, I believe that technology can generate an addiction and sometimes an unhealthy dependance.

Many times I've heard people saying "Video-games rot your head", "Those who play video-games become addicted", "you lose social skills by playing video-games" and other phrases that tend to blame gaming in order to avoid accepting the responsibility the grown-ups have to set limits and balance the time their kids spend playing.

One of my main motivations for publishing this book, using the names of the characters created by Nintendo, besides paying tribute or homage, was to prove, in a way, how someone who spent many hours of his childhood and adolescence playing video-games, can be as competitive as anyone else. I'd like for people to think "He played video-games, has a lot of friends, a girlfriend, a rich social life, academic education and also wrote a book which told a story that more than one person considered moving,".

That's why, the objective of this tale, besides entertain, is to link ideas and expand horizons, both for those who aren't keen on video-games, or find it hard to enjoy reading a book, as those who frequently let themselves get carried away in imaginary voyages, whichever the means may be.

On this book, words interact in a way that keeps the dynamic of a video-game, which, from my point of view, make for an easy and fun read.

I hope that you feel the same pleasure while reading this story as I felt while writing it, knowing that it won't be the last one, but the beginning of a larger adventure. I wish that, through your imagination, you can appreciate the fantastic scenarios and submerge yourself in the emotions of the characters.

Without further ado, I invite you to discover, and enjoy, the wonderful tale of Link, the hero of time.

J.I.Ballines

PROLOGUE

The adventure genre is, without a doubt, one of my favourites. It never discriminates anyone by their age and, if we're willing, it lets us live experiences which would be impossible in any other way. When we're kids, it helps us daydream about what we would like to be. When we're adults, it allows us to remember what it felt like to be a kid. But not only that, it takes us to other worlds, to unknown places where not only can we defy every notion of known, conventional or natural law, but also fully experiment those values which we hold dear and rarely are able to witness in all their glory, such as gallantry or camaraderie.

And that is what this book offers: A voyage filled with emotions, dangers and laughter in which we can dive into and carelessly wonder for some good few hours and, once we're finished, close the book and feel a little more daring and a little more fantastical.

When my dear friend asked my help with a prologue for his novel, I immediately accepted. Nonetheless, as days went by, it became harder to find the right wordplay to kickstart this little introduction in order to ease the reader into the adventure with even higher expectation and not bore him with personal experiences or extensive descriptions that lead nowhere. Every idea that came to my mind seemed equally good and bad. I'm not a writer, nor an essayist, critic or editor and, as I had to play the part, even if for some brief lines, it made me realize the incredible weight that one feels when writing for others, to put our ideas into paper and let them exposed to the interpretation and judgement of everyone and, I have to admit that, as short as these paragraphs might seem to you, they brought a terrible headache to me.

Finally, as I'm getting close to the deadline set to me for this endeavor, I sat in front of my computer and decided to write about the two things that seemed really important to point out, which are; a few lines about this novel; and why, I believe, anyone who enjoys the genre is going to find it deeply enjoyable.

I opened with one of those goals in mind, with a mention to what I think about the adventure tales and, as I pointed out before, that's exactly what this book is, a chance for us to be the heroes in perpetual quest for good; to fight the forces of evil with sword and shield; to, once again, save the world. Through the pages that are about to come, you'll be able to verify what I just told you as you submerge yourselves into the reading and fight your own battles, making new friends along the way and discovering, with every step and jump, a wide and amazing world in which action will never fail you, keeping you on edge from the first to the last chapter.

The regular adventure reader will be able to find all those things that build this genre: Suspense, romance, the odyssey, the quick succession of events that forces us to keep on reading one chapter after another, eager to see how the plot, which by now has u caught up like a spider-web, unravels, the plot that deepens by every sentence we read and with every new event that occurs and that forces us to keep on reading.

Lastly, it's my personal desire that you can enjoy this story in the same way that I did when I read it. That you can enter the world presented to you and, as one more character, partake in every chapter, with an epic of your own.

Morkos

This is the story that will take place "a long time ago" and that already happened "after". It's the tale that begins at its end and finishes at the beginning. It's the adventure of who was a hero in a distant future and will be so in the past. This, is the journey of **Link de Hyrule**.

CHAPTER 1

A HAPPY ENDING?

In a farm, south of Hyrule, was a little house beside a stream coming from lake Hylia and to the other side, a little fence with many birds. The cuccos where clucking y pecking the ground, searching for worms, the ground was fertile after a week of heavy rains. The sun was high and a few spongy clouds could be seen, which foretold a lovely weather. A nice, warm, breeze was blowing from the north, caressing the grass of the lively plain. The trees seemed to whisper the peace and calm that comes after the storm.

"The weather is perfect! Wish I could stay a little longer," said a little man of some age while he scratched his grayed beard and watched the farm's horses through the window.

"Me too…" answered a lady, barely shorter than him, blonde with many gray hairs. She had a lovely straight hair, which allowed her pointy ears show through the sides.

Both smiled and besides their eyes, small wrinkles appeared. Marks that joyful times left in their skin and came after many years of happiness. There was no trace of fear in their faces, only hope.

Nevertheless, there was some shed of worrying in the young man, a bit taller than the couple. He was sitting at the end of a narrow, squeaking walnut set of stairs, that led to the cellar of the house.

The old man turned to the young lad, "Don't be worried, we all know you'll give your best. And don't be afraid of being wrong, because that's how you'll learn," the old, wise, man made a short pause and looked to the side of the youngster, "Besides, you've become really proficient with that," he added while he pointed to a bow made with wood, coming from the very same "Deku", a legendary tree, guardian of the kokiris's woods, whose bark was as strong as Oak and flexible as willow.

This fine weapon was joined by the ends with a cord rather thin, but sturdy, "Even more, you've improved my arrow's design,"

The young lad smiled, "If it wasn't by the blade that you received from the gerudo, that you later gave me, I wouldn't be able to make any worthwhile arrow,"

"Nonetheless, I didn't give you the imagination to create them, so you can't deny your own merit," answered the old man as scratched his beard, as if it was a normal gesture of his, "If you'd seen WHY the gerudo gave it to me, you'd be surprised. Also, the effort and practice of all these years only strengthen your worth," he added, while giving him a pat on his back "We'll do just fine, there's no need to worry, it's in your nature, you'll see we'll have fun,".

He smiled and whispered "you might even get a girlfriend!", although it was heard by everyone, and started laughing. The youngster smiled shyly and the old woman crossed her arms while casting a scolding glare, filled with sympathy to the old man.

Both the old man and the youngster were wearing long hooded robes. The eldest one's robe was a dark shade of grey, although it seemed like it used to be black. The young lad's robe was deep brown. Both of them were straight with no details, the best way to go unnoticed if you happened to be a traveler that needed to hide in plain sight. They both had bulky rucksacks, they contained from clothing to leather pouches with tools. In between the robe and rucksack, close to their back each man carried a shield that seemed light yet firm and sturdy. The old man's shield had an infinity of scratches made by claws, swords, arrows, spears, axes and as many sharp and pointy things as one could imagine. The youngster's one shone bright as if it was brand new. Barely a few bumps, made while training. From both man's belts hanged all sorts of trinkets. The young lad was carrying a vial given to him by the old man that very same day, filled with a yellowish, rather thick, liquid, an empty flask, a fabric bag, filled with what seemed to be some shiny, colorful, stones and an old sword; the old man had a sword, a lamp, an empty flask and two fabric pouches, one empty, as if it was a pocket, and one full.

While checking the empty pouch, the old man looked at the lad and asked "How many rupees are you carrying?"

"Fourteen greens, four blues, two yellows, a red and a purple one," he replied.

"Excellent, so you're carrying..." said the old man while adding up the values.

"One hundred and twenty-four green rupees," interrupted the young one.

"More than enough, in case of an emergency," conjectured the old one.

Rupees were what the merchants from Hyrule used to exercise commerce with neighboring villages and to set a price to almost everything in town. Since there were many rupee colors, they established a value to each one depending on how rare and hard the rupee was rather than considering it size, since it was a gemstone that fractured when in contact with air and, almost every time, they had the same sizes.

The most common ones are the green rupees, they aren't hard to find, since they're usually found in the surface and it's why the base value is based on these ones. Next are the blue ones, which are five times as valuable as the green ones. The yellow ones are worth twice as a blue one and the red ones also twice as the yellow ones. Finally, the purple ones are worth exactly fifty green rupees.

The young lad had once or twice seen rupees in other colors, such as orange and silver but was ignorant of their values, although he sensed they would be worth a few hundreds of green ones, given their rarity.

The old man, who was holding a portrait on his left hand, turned to it and observed it.

"What's best of this is that I'll see the guys again and, no matter what, we'll be free once more..." he exclaimed, filled with hope.

"Even more, if everything goes ok, I'll put together a banquet as soon as I come back… and might even invite someone," said with sarcasm while laughing hard, watching the old woman, who laughed with him. The lad also laughed and his tension and nervousness lightened up a bit.

"That's more like it, kid, it's time to laugh! Soon we'll be feasting," and while caressing his beard he continued, "Look, if you do good, I'll make you one of those egg tarts you like so much. But you're getting the eggs from the cuccos…" he added, looking through the window to a corral filled with these birds.

"I wouldn't get in there for all the rupees in the world… I don't like those birds, they have a reputation of being aggressive," and once again, bursted to laughter.

Although he didn't show, it could be said that the old man was as nervous as the kid, but it wasn't the time to cower and even less to make the youngster feel worried about it, that's why the old man hid it up and showed himself calm and collected.

"Well, it's about time, I'm going to miss you darling" said the old man, hugging the woman, "but I trust in the lad, he's going to bring me back, I know… I can feel it. At last, we'll be free of it all… especially from that damn stone with holes.".

The old woman hugged the man back and rested her chin on his shoulder and the old man whispered "Do you see it?"

"What?" she asked.

"A happy ending," replied the old man, so quietly that was almost silent.

"A happy ending?" repeated the woman. She smiled and with her sight wandering in a window behind the man she said louder, so that the young lad sitting at the end of the stairs could hear.

"Of course, I can see it, I'm not worried, I know you'll come back safe and sound. You know what? I see it already… Your triumphal return, riding your horse alongside the kid… who is not so much of a kid anymore," and after a brief pause, added "I know you'll miss me, and I know that'll give you strength when you need it most, but I can't say I'll miss you, because I will never

22

be apart from you. What I can tell you is that you have my love and my heart and soul, and wherever you go, wherever you'll be, they will be with you... with both of you," She said while she stopped hugging the old man, to give a hug to the kid "my heart and soul will be with both of you always and hopefully will light your way," A single tear dropped from her eye, the old man noticed it, but the youngster didn't, even as the tear fell on his shoulder. The lady wiped her eyes with her thumb before letting go of the kid.

It seemed as if both of them were hiding their worries from the young lad, but that wasn't a mistake, it was necessary, the only thing that mattered in that moment was to believe. Believe that even if it looked like an impossible situation, it was not. It was risky, yes, but likely, it was achievable even if really hard to.

Was it hard? Yes. But they only needed to follow a path. A narrow, dark, path. But it was not impossible. Follow a path, only one... only that one.

Both men looked at each other, the woman put her hands together and lowered them. The old man grabbed a tiny red chest, with golden edges and from his boot picked a minuscule key. He opened the chest and ironically from it took a bigger key, which had an engraving similar to a skull with horns. Also, beside it was a weird compass which had some strange pointy markings beneath it.

The young lad looked at the old man, "What is that?" he asked, bemused at the object.

The old man smiled and said "This will keep us from getting lost. I'll teach you how to use it on the road, don't worry, you'll learn fast,". The old man removed a rather small rug that was at their feet, which was only big enough to cover a trap-door, with a rather odd lock in it, on the floor. The keyhole was made of stone and hardly would have opened without the key.

"Well kid, follow me carefully. We won't be able to see anything for a while," He used the key and so the door opened. Thanks to the lighting on the room, many of the steps could be seen, but not even ten steps from the top and the light already abandoned them completely.

The old lady watched them walk down the spiral stair and yelled "I'll see you soon, good luck!".

The young lad didn't say a word but thought "I hope so…".

As if the old man would have heard his thought, he said "Everything can be taken from you champ, but hope," and made a noise with his nose, as if he was holding his laughter back.

After what seemed to be like three floors going down in complete darkness, the old man stopped. The kid, who could barely see amidst the dark, slightly bumped his back. Far away, a sound of flapping wings could be heard, which shook the lad.

The old man then talked to him, "We arrived at the entrance. Give me the jar that I told you to bring,".

The kid searched in his belt, pulled it out and gave it to him. "Very well, let's see… how did this work…?" said the old man, talking to himself. Suddenly, the room lit up. The kid realized what did his partner use the jar for, inside it, there was oil and he was pouring it in some kind of lantern while he explained: "The good thing of this lantern is that it lights up immediately with only pouring the oil in and turning this crank," He said while showing the little knob in the artifact to the youngster. "Besides, thanks to the oil we're using, it will burn longer than usual and will guide us through the right path," and with a smile across his face he added "Lovely gift from that Gorons's tribe".

"Sure," said the kid with sarcasm "as if I knew what you're talking about,".

The old man smiled, "The Gorons, who inhabit that mountain that I told you I knew on my youth,".

"And how exactly are they supposed to guide us through this?" enquired the kid.

"Do you see those weird flashes of light on the stones over there?" asked the old man pointing at the wall. The kid nodded, "Well, only the path to the time chamber has that kind of stones. But they only shine like that when lit up with the right light, which is only produced with this special oil,".

The kid fell silent and the man with the grayish man continued, "It was built by the wise men, well, not by them precisely but by some men from many different places and races to protect

24

the wise men, if they ever were in danger… anyway, the danger passed and everything was abandoned. Since I knew this place, I thought it would be a good place to rend-" Suddenly, the wing flapping was heard again, only this time it was much clearer.

The young man opened his eyes wide and wielded his bow.

Smiling, the old man said "It's a good reflex, at the very least you won't be caught with your guard down…" to the boy, who already had tightened the cord and put an arrow on it, "but as I was saying, this abandoned place seemed like a good place to rendezvous with an old friend of mine, in case of emergency…" He wasn't even finished with his phrase when they reached an archway which split the hallway of the room. The room didn't have any door, other than the one for them to go through. In the middle of the round place there was a table and a couple of chairs to sit while waiting. On top of one of the chairs there was a strange bug, the kid couldn't help but show his amusement. It was a mixture of surprise and disgust that could be seen on his face. The old man looked at him and made a gesture, as if he was suggesting to be a little less obvious about his feelings.

"Ucayaya, old friend!!" Yelled the old man.

"I knew you'd be on time… it was always your thing," said the weird creature while smiling.

The young man couldn't stop looking, speechless, that strange creature which was only half a meter tall, standing on its two cucco legs, with half its torso covered in feathers and two little featherless wings and a long neck which ended in an almost human head. It had no ears; its nose was pointy and both eyes pearly red. The nape of the creature was elongated backwards and a couple of pink and turquoise rings were formed almost at the end of it.

The old man turned to the kid "She's Ucayaya. She's an "uca", the race that inhabit Celestia, the aerial islands which can be seen in the skies of Hyrule in certain times of the year,"

"H-He-Hello… Miss?" said the young lad.

"Ma'am, in any case, dear," answered Ucayaya, smiling "For a long time now, sadly," and outlining an even wider smile she added "Even my son is grown up already!"

"About that. How's Ucanene?" enquired the old man.

"As any mother would say, he's big and dumb," and with a proud face she then added "but he's rather good, he helps me a lot and we're really happy. Anyway... Are you ready?" Asked the uca.

"We were born ready," said the old man, nodding with his head and smiling to the kid.

"Let's go then," added the lady, rising her featherless wings.

The old man grabbed one wing with his hand and at the same time, he looked at the young kid while he gestured him to do the same. The kid shyly followed in the footsteps of the older man and held the strange creature by its other wing. His sight started to distort but there was nothing in his eyes. In fact, he could see the uca and the old man quite clearly. It was everything else that seemed to fade away.

Not even five seconds went by when everything started to turn back to normal, although there was something strange going on. The table wasn't there anymore, nor the chairs. In their place there was a big, round, stone with a fabric bag on it. The room seemed sealed tight, not even the archway from which they came was there. The hall had no entrances nor exits, the roof was sealed and so was the floor. The kid felt a slight sensation of imprisonment and the walls seemed to be closing in. The old man noticed this and put a hand in his shoulder "Everything's OK... this room is the wider room in the world. It doesn't take you to where you want to go, but rather when you want to,".

He then closed in to the small central rock which looked like a small altar and, from the bag, pulled a small stone filled with holes and looking towards his friend he said "Thank you, Ucayaya, the ocarina wouldn't have been safe in any other way,".

"Don't even mention it," she answered "I wouldn't be able to repay everything you once did for me..."

The old man interrupted her "As I wouldn't be able to repay your great friendship,".

The uca smiled. "Good luck, but I don't think you're going to need it, after all, the man who goes with you seems to be rather

26

prepared!" exclaimed the uca while casting a trusting glare to the youngster. He smiled and she went on "Good bye friends, you'll see me again soon," and then she once again faded away.

The kid looked at the old man with a worried expression. The only way out of that room had just turned to smoke flapping its wings on its own.

It was at that moment when the old man spoke to the kid again "grab my shoulders," asked the old one while taking the stone to his mouth.

With the palm of his hands and his thumbs he held the ancient and rustic instrument, he swiftly moved his eight remaining fingers as if he was softening his joints and then put them in strategic places, covering some of the holes, then, he started blowing through the only hole that was pointing upwards and a noise came out of from the other end.

Once again, the younger man felt weird. Once again, his vison was blurry, but in a different way, everything was vibrating and suddenly a gigantic rock disappeared from the wall as if it was absorbed by it, opening a really dark tunnel. Meanwhile, the old man kept on blowing and moving his fingers, some pieces of wood that were laying on the floor, which the youngster did not see before, rose up and got stuck in the wall. Some smoke started coming down from nowhere towards one of the wooden pieces and it lit on fire, soon the rest followed and the whole room was illuminated.

Shortly after, a man appeared, he entered the room walking backwards. Everything was incredibly strange and the kid could not comprehend what was going on, it was like if he was watching the world go in reverse. Then, in a split second, the man stopped walking backwards and turned to start moving his lips, as if he was talking to them.

The old man stopped blowing and the young kid heard the deep voice of the man standing in front of them "About time, follow me," he said.

The old man started following him, without hesitation. The younger one simply went along, what else could he do…

"we'll soon be there, I hope those robes you're wearing will keep you warm, we have a few steps before reaching the cabin, outside it's pouring and the wind is blowing rather hardly," Looking sideways to his new companions, the strange man added "Also, it's the middle of the night and the temperature has dropped heavily today,".

The old man smiled, firmly put one of his hands on his shoulder and, while still walking, he answered "Thank you Astor, there's no way of repaying what you've done for my family, for Hyrule… and even more, for me,"

The strange man laughed silently while his smile was visible and said "You've already done it… or have you forgotten the amount of cucco's eggs I've made you bring me?"

Both burst to laughter, that echoed through the barely enlightened stone hallway.

The youngster, who was paying close attention, focused his sight on the strange man, this so called "Astor" whom the old man was speaking with. He was heavily dressed, it was difficult to tell if he was a bit chummy or stocky, either way, no-one would be able to walk beside him in that hallway. He was carrying a lantern identical to the one they used to go down the stairs, before gathering with Ucayaya, as if he also knew which stones to follow, as a matter of fact, the place wasn't the same but the way to navigate through it surely seemed to be. Although the kid couldn't see Astor's face clearly, he could tell he was carrying a rucksack, a kind of male brown leather purse that hanged just at his waist.

His thoughts were briefly interrupted when Astor turned to him.

"What's wrong with this kid?" And steering his glare to the old man he continued "don't you tell me that you also put him to gather cucco's eggs and they ate his tongue!" Astor smiled and again put his sight on the young kid as if he was waiting for this one to say something.

The youngster smiled shyly and answered "Sorry sir, greetings… my name is…"

"I know who you are boy!" Interrupted Astor "When you bought your first trousers, I had already turned them in shorts!" he said, bursting to laughter "Besides, you have no reason to apologize, I was just pulling your leg," he stopped for a second and then went on " I guess you're still amused by your little trip… I understand that not many can travel as you have. I imagine that you must be tired… Don't worry, as soon as we get to the hut, you'll be able to sleep soundly,".

"will it be too long 'till we can do that?" enquired the boy, just to continue with the chat.

"No, actually we're at the end of this part of the road. We should get out through here," he said as he pointed to a circular tunnel with a rope ladder above their heads. "But you're going first, if I get stuck someone will have to pull from above," he explained as he laughed.

The old man went up first, followed by the kid and lastly Astor. As they came out, the youngster realized they had exited from a well that seemed abandoned. From afar, a cabin, a hovel and, a bit retired from the previous two, a barn could be seen. The three men headed that way on the double.

"Straight towards the cabin," said the stocky owner, looking back, with his bushy moustache soaked in rain water.

The three hurried up and soon they were inside the hut. While the elder men were hanging their robes in a coat rack and taking off their boots, the youngster was contemplating the inside of the cabin. It was illuminated with many candles which exposed the lovely oaken brown of the walls and roof. The furniture was shiny, extremely well-polished. To the side of the young man, there was a drawer with many horse-shoes. To his feet, a square rug that run across the whole room. In front of him, to the end of the house, a chimney with many logs that were burning inside it and a little table, surrounded with low, cushy, armchairs. Everything in there was comforting.

Astor, who already had made himself comfortable and was sporting a couple of loafers that let his toes exposed for everyone to see, once again interrupted his thoughts "Are you going to hang that? Or do you want to sleep while wearing that soaked robe?" said the owner while smiling and stretching his arm to reach for the youngster's coat.

"Oh, yes… I mean, no!... I mean, yes, I want to hang this and no, I don't want to sleep wearing a soaked robe," The youngster started laughing due to his confusion.

The old man, who's been quiet seemed expectant. Suddenly, without giving much importance to it, he said, like telling a secret "He's not coming, is he?" talking about a fourth person.

"No, I gave him the night off," Astor answered "and if he happened to come, he wouldn't come here… Probably, he would head to the hovel next door, it's been a long time since he started sleeping there as if that was his home instead of this one,"

"Well… eventually we all grow up," ascertained the old man "time is not something we can control lightly," he added as he tightened his grip on his left pocket, feeling for the little holey stone "besides, that doesn't mean he doesn't love you, believe me, I know him better than anyone,".

Astor came close and held the old man tightly. The young man thought he saw Astor's eyes fill with tears but his moustache was so big and bushy that it was distracting him and didn't let the youngster appreciate the rest of his factions. In any case, he already realized that his previous doubt was already solved… he was half "a bit chummy" and half "really stocky".

"Well! This is the beginning of an adventure, so before you start scheming plans, strategies and star talking about really boring stuff we should toast with this fine wine I just made with my own two feet," Astor exclaimed as he moved the toes in his feet.

It was at that moment that the young lad realized that Astor's feet had the size of his forearms.

"And also, I have a little delicacy from the last cucco that dared to peck me," Astor laughed and poured three cups of wine as he served some slices of cucco's breast and some goat cheese over the little table that was next to the fire in the chimney.

The trio sat down on the couches next to the table, they made a toast and the contemplated the fire. After several seconds in absolute silence, the old man started talking to the youngster "Well, that whole backpack you brought, filled with stuff, will be useful on due time, so, I'm going to explain, with every detail, how we will manage to accomplish what will probably be the biggest feat in the history of Hyrule,". The young man nodded and started listening, paying close attention.

Outside, the rain was pouring heavily. The cuccos were well protected in what seemed to be a miniature house, the cows, goats and horses were all under refuge in the barn. Despite the storm, the night seemed really safe and, inside the cabin, what was likely to become the most important of tales about Hyrule was being schemed as a well-played game of chess.

32

CHAPTER 2

FAR FROM THE GOAL

It was a full moon night and the real ground of Hyrule was engulfed in flames and destruction. The houses had been uninhabited for a long time. Some were even used from time to time by risky travelers, who used this town to spend the night and continue on their way. However, tonight they had all fled with the onset of battle. It was the third time the Hylian people had tried to retake their home that year, and it was the third time Vaati's troops had driven them out at swordpoint. Although this battle had been different, its results had been the worst and the best at the same time. The worst, because they had never lost so many Hylian lives. The best, because they had never come so close to the castle. A group of Hylians experienced in the art of infiltration found themselves outside the castle, hiding behind two destroyed carriages.

"We're trapped," the leader of the group said seriously but without despair.

"What will we do?" asked a young woman from the group.

"It would be best if we split up. This way some of us could distract the guards and others could enter into the castle," answered the leader.

"Pericleo, I know the castle, I volunteer to enter and achieve our goal," said another man. This, along with the leader were the two oldest and most experienced.

"Okay Leonardo," said Pericleo, agreeing, "but you won't do it alone. Adrian, you'll go with him," he said to a young man in his mid-twenties, stocky, six feet tall, with a serious look under his prominent forehead.

He nodded without saying a word.

"Salma, Jasper and I will head out that way and take care of those guards," he said, pointing a finger at a group of soldiers guarding the south entrance to the main garden. Lucke and Roger will take care of that other group," he added, pointing to other guards covering the entrance to the library.

They all nodded.

"When we finish off those guards, the ones inside will come out. When that starts we'll flee to the settlement. Leonardo and Adrian, at that moment you will be able to enter the castle, but you will be alone. Stick to the plan. Our target is the stone, nothing else," Pericleo said. "I want to see them alive, if the goal is unattainable, give up. We'll regroup and try again another time".

"We hope it won't be necessary," Leonardo said, extending his hand to greet Pericleous, who returned the greeting.

They all agreed and very stealthily attacked. He had managed to reduce the vast majority when one of the guards gave notice before he perished. A few soldiers came out alerted and ready for battle. Pericleo, seeing Leonardo and Adrian slip through a window into the castle, gave the order to retreat and the rest of the group fled in the direction of the abandoned citadel.

«Good luck» Pericleo thought, escaping as well.

Despite its abandoned appearance, Hyrule Castle was more alive than ever. Soldiers ran through the halls, their armor rattling as they went. From time to time a stray arrow entered through the long windows, showering the carpets with glass. These were not in their best moment either, torn and stained showed the decadence of that building that at one time had been so prosperous.

"If he's not in the throne room, where is he?" Adrian asked.

"He must be in the dungeon past the garden," said Leonardo, the other man, a little older but smaller in stature and not so muscular.

"And how do we get there?" asked the first.

"I don't know, Adrian, I need to see the map and think. We've already run into an endless number of blocked doors" answered Leonardo looking at a door behind him.

"Careful, Leonardo," Adrian said, pulling from his shoulder and hiding next to him behind a column.

At that moment, three men in Hylian armor trotted past in the direction of the castle's main gate.

"Thanks. I almost got caught," said Leonardo. "Come, let's see what's beyond this door".

Leonardo and Adrian opened the door and found themselves in an empty room with the windows boarded up.

"No one could see anything in here," Adrian said, walking over to the window.

"Better that way," Leonardo said, lighting a candle.

The light let them appreciate the size of that room. It was extremely small and some items such as buckets and brooms made them understand that it was the cleaning room.

Leonardo knelt on the floor and unfolded a map of the castle.

"Here we are," he said, pointing to a place on the map. "Here we must go," he said, pointing to another. "This access is blocked, this one too and this one too," added by marking on the map.

"Didn't Zelda say something about 'a path under the throne'?" Adrian asked.

"Yes. Of course," said Leonardo, reminding and searching his pockets. Then, he took out a piece of paper folded in four and with a reinforced iron key inside it. "She gave me this," he added.

"Let me see," said Adrian. "Well, according to this, the key allows you to move the throne forward and, below it, there is a ladder," said Adrian.

"Let's see if it is true," Leonardo said.

They both looked at a possible route and memorized it. After a few seconds they left the cleaning room. They stealthily ran to the throne and hid behind it, looking for the lock.

"Here," Adrian pointed out, showing a small hole wrapped in the elaborate carving on the back of the throne.

Leonardo put the key in and turned. Just from the noise, they deduced that something had happened. The men peered over the back of the throne to see that no one was around. Checking their loneliness, they counted to three on their fingers and pushed the king's seat forward. A wooden door with wrought iron was revealed. Adrian pulled up on the handle and they saw a spiral staircase that descended a few floors.

Outside the castle and several kilometers away, a bloody battle took place. The massacre had reached a large settlement. Hylian soldiers had been fighting against other Hylian soldiers. The only way to recognize both sides in battle was through what little skin was visible between their armor. One could say that one side had living skin and the other dead. Hundreds of tents were on fire. Screams of pain, tears and despair tore at the ears of a young girl with golden hair.

"Miss Zelda, we must retreat. The next wave will be here soon!" a soldier told the young woman in the distance, drawing his sword from the enemy's chest.

"I know, Cooker!" she answered, "where's Gracielle?"

"Here, princess!" said a woman in Hylian armor taking away from her back a dead enemy.

"Thank the Goddesses. For a moment I feared the worst," Zelda answered.

The young Hylian princess looked at the castle with tears in her eyes. "So close...so close to getting it back we were this time. How the hell does Vaati manage to bend us like this?" she said, clutching her head helplessly. Then, looking down, behind a wall of trees, a group of people came running and made their way to the princess.

"Breathe Pericleo and then tell me the news," Zelda said.

The man took a deep breath and still with some difficulty in his voice he said, "We must run. On the way here we have seen a horde ready to attack and I don't think we have the numeric advantage.

"Leonardo and Adrian are...?" Zelda asked fearing the worst.

"We don't know, but I hope not." They managed to enter the castle. If there is any opportunity it depends on them.

The princess sighed in relief.

"Even so we must flee, we cannot wait for them." I'm sure they'll meet us. When they don't see us here they'll track us down to wherever we are," Pericleo said.

"Okay, we'll get further away from the castle," Zelda said with tears in her eyes.

"Do you know where we could go to hide from Vaati or do you want any suggestions? Pericleo said.

"Tell me the options," Zelda said.

"To the west is Gerudia, we don't want to go there. To the east is the Kokiri Forest, but I doubt our survivors can easily adapt to the forest. My recommendation is to travel south. We are a month of journey to the great Lake Hylia, but halfway there is a plains area with quarries and rivers that could be good to regroup"

"Of Course," Salma said. "We were there once. Do you remember, Zelda?

"Actually, yes. There is a very special grotto for me in that place," replied the princess and, looking down as if reviewing her memory, she murmured: "Is it possible that...?

"Miss?" Pericleo asked, expecting an answer.

"How many years has it been since the battle of bitter victory?" Zelda asked.

"What?" said Pericleo, surprised. "Seven and something, more or less," he added, answering the question.

"Then it must not be a coincidence. We will go there and set up camp. Give the order Pericleous," Zelda said.

The man nodded and ran to give notice. Soon the horns sounded and the Hylian people began to break camp.

A light of hope had once again appeared on Zelda's face, and murmuring, she repeated to herself: «It can't be a coincidence. That is the place where we will meet. That is the place where I will see you again, Link».

Inside the castle, the infiltrated Hylians had gone down the stairs below the throne, which at the end led to a dark corridor. They went through it blind. In that silence a few dropping leaks resonated amplified and the echo of these propagated from one end to the other. Some side stairs appeared from time to time along the corridor, some went up others went down even lower. The man crouched down to look at the map once more.

"We're right below the exit," Leonardo said.

They both went up the stairs and came to a dead end.

"And now?" Adrian asked.

Leonardo ran his hand along the wall, brushing away the cobwebs and blowing the dust off below what appeared to be a torch holder and discovering a strange engraving.

"And what does that mean?" Adrian asked.

"PULL," answered Leonardo, pulling down the torch holder.

The ceiling above them shifted, showering them with dust. Coughing as quietly as possible, they went outside. In doing so, they noticed that what was once their roof was actually the base of a statue. They found themselves in a garden of dry leaves and overgrown grass.

"It's over there," Leonardo said.

"Wait," Adrian said, pointing to a soldier in Hylian garb who stood guard at the door.

"I'll go for his right," Leonardo said.

"Okay, I'll take care of him," Adrian said.

The men separated and covered by the dark shadows that the statues drew in that bright night went to their objective.

"I'm so sorry, friend, in a few seconds you'll be free," Leonardo told the guard, taking him by surprise.

This one had red eyes and dry skin. "What?!" he asked in a voice from beyond the grave, squeezing the hilt of his sword.

Leonardo didn't have to answer him. A sword came out of the guard's chest. Adrian had taken him from behind and while he covered his mouth to silence him, his blade had pierced him from side to side. The man rolled his eyes up, jerked a bit, and coughed up some black blood that ran through Adrian's fingers. Before he died his eyes lowered again and an expression of freedom flooded his face which, though bruised, seemed grateful.

"You're welcome," Adrian said.

The men went through the no more guarded door and up another spiral staircase, stopping in front of a half-open wooden door. Leonardo stuck his head out and then passed his whole body. Crouched down, the men approached and hid behind a sideboard. The room was dimly lit by a few candles, placed far away on a table.

"You see something?" Adrian whispered.

"Shhh," hushed Leonardo, since at that precise moment, the slim silhouette of what looked like a man approached a shelf full of books located a few meters from the infiltrators. The man picked up a jar and placed it on the table. With chalk he drew something that neither Leonardo nor Adrian could see. Then he walked over to a showcase and gathered up a few more vials. Opening them neatly he poured the contents into a giant goblet. Finally, he pricked his finger with a dagger, dropped a drop of blood, and began to recite words in a language unknown to men.

"What is he saying?" Adrian asked, in an almost inaudible tone of voice.

"I don't know, but he seems to be conjuring up something. Stick to the plan. We will act when he has already used the stone. When that happens he will be in a state of temporary weakness. That's our window," Leonardo murmured.

The scrawny necromancer picked up an empty flask and continued to recite. Suddenly the wide-mouthed metal cup turned red as when iron is exposed to fire. The contents inside began to burn engulfed in flames expelling a dense and dark smoke. The alchemist seemed to control the smoke with his words, forming a small levitating cloud above the chalice. Finally, the man took a small stone out of his pocket and held it in one hand. Holding the empty flask in his other hand, he recited other words. The stone began to glow and the smoke drifted away into the flask. The necromancer covered the wide-mouthed jar with a large cork and propped it on the table with some force. It looked like he was going to pass out. He staggered a little, put both hands on the table and breathed heavily. The stone was right next to his hand.

"We could kill him," Adrian whispered.

"Our goal is the stone," Leonard replied.

"Yes, we can kill him and take the stone with us," Adrian said.

"First let's get the stone, that's our goal," Leonardo said seriously. Wait here.

Leonardo crouched close to the table. He now was a few inches from the stone. At that moment, the necromancer walked in the direction where Adrian was to take a potion from the sideboard.

Without being discovered and only moving his lips, Adrian told Leonardo «I can kill him now» pulling a dagger from his belt.

«No» Leonardo told him without making a sound.

But Adrian was already in position and the opportunity was perfect. He jumped up next to the necromancer and plunged his dagger into his back.

Leonardo froze for a second and Adrian kicked the emaciated wizard who was bleeding from the side of his chest. He fell onto the table and rolled to the floor.

Adrian moved closer to finish him off but the necromancer let out a laugh.

"If you had aimed better you might have succeeded," he said in his gravelly voice from beyond the grave.

Adrian was surprised and looked at the table. The stone was gone. The sorcerer had it in his hands and reciting a few words, it glowed and Adrian went flying backwards, breaking the sideboard that had probably covered them before. The necromancer felt the presence of someone else. Turning around, he saw a figure in the shadow but before he could recite anything else, that figure had released a smoke bomb towards the floor flooding the room and nullifying the vision of anyone. Leonardo kicked the table hitting the sorcerer but without getting him to drop the stone. Adrian felt free of the invisible bonds that had earlier pulled him back and stood up.

"Let's go!" Leonardo shouted, grabbing Adrian by the jacket and dragging him with him.

Adrian stumbled a bit at first, but managed to follow Leonardo down the stairs.

"I screwed up, I'm an idiot!" Adrian said.

"Now worry about getting out alive," Leonardo said.

Making their way past the garden full of statues they had seen earlier, they tried to reach the entrance to the corridor under the large statue, but four guards were around the place. Leonardo saw them and tried to stop, slipping a bit.

"There they are!" one of the guards yelled, starting the chase.

Adrian grabbed Leonardo's arm to change direction on the run. Soon they came to a wall, precisely to a collapsed part, lower than the rest.

"Fast! Here!" Adrian said, putting his back against the wall and his hands in the shape of a step so that Leonardo would jump.

Instinctively he put one foot in the hands of his partner and managed to climb the wall but, once up, he noticed that Adrian had no intention of climbing.

"What are you doing?!" Leonard yelled.

"I'll keep them entertained!" said Adrian.

"Are you crazy?!" Leonard asked, surprised.

"I won't let you pay for my mistakes!" Adrian said, looking at the guards approaching.

"What are you talking about?! Come on up here!" Leonard ordered.

But Leonardo's effort was useless. Adrian was already running in another direction.

"Hey! Idiots! Here!" he yelled at the guards walking away.

Undetected, Leonardo watched them pass and walked over the wall until he found a place to climb down to outside. In silence he walked away from the castle and the royal field. Soon, he found himself alone and he hid in an empty house near the Hyrule's border so he decided to stop for a minute to recover his breath. Reaching into one of the pockets which hung from his belt he pulled out a flask. Inside it was a cloud of black smoke that, from time to time, hit in vain the glass walls of his prison. Leonardo looked at the big cork carefully. A pentagram star with runic symbols was etched into the surface.

"We may not have gotten the stone, but I'm not going to waste your sacrifice" he whispered as if Adrian were there. "Perhaps the mission wasn't a complete failure after all," he said, studying the flask. "I'll make sure of it".

44

CHAPTER 3

DIRTY, DRUNK AND DIZZY

Two young man, almost the same age and not even four inches different in height were walking uphill. Behind them, to their left, the sun was setting under a nearby low hill. Slowly, the clear day was turning reddish and the clouds were less visible as time went by, not because the sky was clearing up but because it was getting darker and darker. Some holes in between the clouds let see the first stars, shining non-stop and giving walker a brittle light to go on their way.

The dew was starting to get the grass wet, "I love the smell of wet grass," said the taller of the men.

"Well, it makes two of us then," answered his partner "it gets me nostalgic… even if I can't remember anything of my childhood," he added.

"That's amazing. Isn't it? How smells get stuck in your brain, even for you, who lost his memory in that battle, it gets you back in time," said the taller looking at the sky.

"How incredible is time, it seems only one, always so linear, but it becomes malleable thanks to memories," the shorter man said.

Both men seemed to be Hyrule regulars, though they were not wearing the classic garments nor armor. To a bystander, they would seem to be two soldiers on their day off.

"My friend, we're almost there," assured the tall man.

"Really?" said his friend cheerfully, "I thought you had no idea of where we were going. After walking for almost two hours I supposed you had gotten lost and didn't want to admit it," he went on.

"Ja… ja… ja…" Laughed, ironically, the first one and added "Have I ever steered you wrong?".

"I don't know if wrong is the way to put it, champ," said the shorty kindly "but you've taken me down some rough roads. And even if I can't remember it, I know I met you when we were kids, so more than one rough road tie us together,".

"Well, champ," replied the tall man, imitating his friend with a hint of sarcasm on his voice "when you became a soldier of Hyrule you knew you were going to hit many bumps in your way," he added, as if he was taking importance from their adventures together. "Anyways, we're really close now, see that light in that little hut over there? That's where we're heading,".

The shorter man nodded and asked "And who are we supposed to meet there?".

"For now, we're not meeting anyone, well, probably some local drunkards, after all this is a pretty famous bar. I might even invite you a beer. I still have some rupees left from our previous trip," laughed the tall man, while checking his pocket, "Later, and old friend of mine will meet us and give us some instructions. Depending on what he tells us, we'll see what we do. Anyhow I'm sure you'll be surprised,".

"Well, that's rich... so if this old friend of yours doesn't show up, we're screwed. Because I see you have no clue of how our trip continues. That's some planning on your part, genius," the short man jokingly mocked his friend, but something interrupted the chattering.

"Wait a minute, I know this place,"

"So, your short-term memory is still intact, I thought that the alcohol here might have affected it," added the taller man while bursting to laughter.

"Ja... Ja... Ja..." the short man laughed ironically this time, "It's possible that alcohol may have blurred my memory a couple of times," and, while smiling fiendishly, he added "but I've come more times to this bar than those that I've forgotten... it's just that I've never gotten here through that road. In fact, I've never entered through the back door,".

"Well, it's as they say: "There's a first time for everything","" replied the tall guy.

"As long as it's not the last one... after all, this is a bar for real men," answered the shorter man, before being interrupted.

"Oh, come on! The things I have to listen to! Stop pretending to be a tough man," said the tall man sarcastically, "You think that the fact that you can stay a week without taking a bath makes you tougher than me? It doesn't make you manlier, it only makes you dirtier,".

"Well, excuse me, miss i-never-burp-because-i-don't-know-how-to," said the short man mockingly.

"I do know how to burp, but you won't listen to it because I don't think it's appropriate to do it in public," explained the taller of them.

"Smells like a lie to me... it's like the tale of the tree that fell on the forest without anyone near to listen to it. Did it actually make noise? Well, no one knows, because no-one was there to listen to it," the short man paused and then went on "Are you burping for me today?" he said while looking at his friend as if it was a romantic scene and then burst to laughter.

Both men entered the bar, the tallest asked for two beers at the counter and they sat down at a table in the back of the bar which the light refused to reach.

That night was their free night. For a while, they could forget about their problems that struck, strike and will go on striking Hyrule. That night, they could be just two friends sharing a couple beers at the bar. Laughing, as hard as it was then, for someone compromised with the cause, remembering old tales, as difficult as it was to remember some good old tales at those times.

Despite the lighting at the young man table wasn't all that good, the rest of the bar looked all lit up and joyful. The walls had seen their fair share of years, several holes could be seen on them, plugged with lime and stone. The counter of the bar had all the stuff you could find at any bar in Hyrule: Some ashtrays, filled with burnt tobacco from the pipes; little bowls with peanuts; many round markings from the liquids in the glasses that were there a moment ago; and the usual drunkards, who were always there.

At the far end of the bar, there were two "Loop" table, an ancient and well-known game in the region. They were circular tables, 2 mts wide, lined with cow's leather painted black and with a little protrusion in the center, as if it was a bump in the table, with a hole in the center, and thirteen pearls the size of a fist, which came from the giant oysters from the bottom of The Great Bay, a familiar place for Hyruleans. One of the pearls still retained its characteristic whitish color, from the twelve remaining ones, six where shiny golden and six where silver. The paint used was a special one, given that you could still see the pearls opalescence. It seemed to be a really attractive game for the tall man sitting in the back of the bar.

"Care to join me for a round?" said the short man. "I don't know how to play," answered his friend, disheartened. "Come on, it's really easy. See those sticks over there?" Insisted the first one. "Yes," the tall man replied. The short man then continued to explain the rules "Well, using those sticks, you have to hit the white pearl to make it crash against one of the colored ones and sink that one in the hole in bump on the middle of the table,".

"The bump?" the tall man asked. "Yes, bump, that's how it's called that protrusion in the center and it has a hole on it. See that the pearls are around that bump? That's how the game begins. You hit one and if you sink one, whichever color it is, that's your color. Then, the pearls will move around the table and the first one to sink all of the pearls of his color wins," the short man was getting overexcited as he explained the rules. It's been a long time since he last played.

"And when does the other participant play?" asked his friend.

"If you sink one, you keep going. If you don't, it's the other player turn; If you miss and don't even hit a pearl, that's two hits for the other player; If you hit the other player's color it's three shots for him; and if you sink the white pearl, you lose. Come on, you'll see that you'll learn faster as we go," said the short man while standing up.

Both men got near the table, with a hand gesture, the one with more experience let know to the barman that they wanted to play a round. The barman's aid came close and, with a little key, he pulled the pearls from a drawer where they fell after being sunk in the central hole. Together, the three of them put the pearls in position over the table and the aid close the drawer back after which, with an amicable gesture of his hand he said "If you gentlemen need anything, please let me know. Ok?". Both men nodded and thanked the aid.

Five rounds, two beers, nine toasts and many jokes and laughs went by. The matches were getting longer and longer, since the accuracy of their hits diminished as the amount of drinks they had augmented. After the eleventh toast and once they finished the last drop from their jar, they decided to go and sit back to their dark corner.

"This man is taking far too long," said the taller man. "Who?" asked the short one, with his eyes almost closed. "The one I told you we were meeting with," replied the taller, as best as he could, due to the alcohol. "Oh, right, we were waiting for someone," remembered the short one.

They both begun laughing again but suddenly, a voice, coming from a silhouette standing in the absolute dark of the corner, crept from behind them.

"It's good that you're having fun, but... Was it necessary the state you're both in? In the end it seems that every soldier in Hyrule's royal court are cut from the same cloth," The man was frowning while speaking, but it seemed faked and in his voice a note of mockery could be sensed.

Both men turned around, the shorter opened his eyes and mouth wide, but couldn't make a sound. The other one stuttered while trying to speak. "N-n-no, w-we're not drunk. It's just that... we kind of... drank... a bit. We were... I... And he... And i..." The taller man was moving his arms, without managing to express the faintest idea.

"Easy champ, I'm not here to scold you," laughed the old man, while coming out of hiding. "Take this papyrus, it has the instructions for your next mission. You're doing great and I commend you for it. It makes me glad and it puts me at ease seeing you two making such a good team,"

The previously stuttering man managed to articulate. "Hey, y-you… When you go… I'd like to tell you that…"

The old man, put a hand over his shoulder, comforting him. "Don't worry about it. What you're trying to tell me isn't probably something new. Your only mission tonight is to enjoy. Tomorrow you'll read the parchment and you'll know what to do. Meanwhile, I have to deal with the new guy," He said, while pointing to the front door which opened, letting in a dirty, drunk and dizzy lad.

The three man observed the entrance of the reeking man.

Stumbling and dragging a leg he managed to reach the counter and put a put a fabric bag on it. He stuck his hand into it and pulled a blue rupee. This meant he could spend the whole night drinking and keep it going throughout the day. He made a gesture to the barman and crossed his arms over the counter and dropped his head over them. His hair was made a mess, all dry and filled with mud. His beard and moustache weren't any luckier either. His eyes irritated, now closed while his forehead was over his arms.

He was wearing a shirt that once, probably, used to be white but now sported a patchy brown. His trousers and boots were a disaster, and it seemed as if his hands would have been working the land for years and years. He was a complete waste of a human being and it was probable that he's been kicked form another bar recently.

The barman and his aid where talking between them. It looked like they had no intention of allowing the man to keep on drinking, no matter how many rupees he had. Then, the barman collected himself and went near the man. "Sir, I'm afraid that we cannot accept your payment, nor serve you any more alcohol,".

The man, who seemed to be young, but was in such a poor state that made it impossible to guess at his age, rose his head, squinted, as to better see the barman, and said. "Why? Are my rupees not good enough? Did I mishear, or are you telling me that you won't sell me a drink?".

"I'm afraid that you already have inside you more than enough of the stuff we sell," answered the barman, bartering with the man "can I offer you something to eat, perhaps?".

"I think I'll know when I had enough… And right now, I have enough rupees to pay for another drink," Insisted the drunk man.

"Believe me sir, I have no qualms with you. I'm just doing this for your own good," said the barman, while stretching the neck of his shirt, looking for some fresh air.

"Listen, good man, it's not been what could be called "a good day", don't make it worse… it wouldn't be good for you," said the drunken one, while losing his patience.

The barman went on, "I'm sorry sir, but I feel as if you were threateni…" but he couldn't even finish his sentence and the drunkard threw himself over the counter, grabbed the barman from his shirt and between tight teeth he spewed. "It's PRECISELY what I'm doing you bast…".

But now, it was the drunkard who couldn't get to finish his line before finding himself lying on the floor. It happened incredibly fast, so fast actually, that the drunkard didn't even realize how he got to the floor.

The old man was standing right next to him, but no one saw him get near. In his hand, he had a loop stick which he used to sweep away the drunkard's stool.

The bar was in complete silence and expecting the obvious fight to come. The barman straightened his shirt while making himself scarce and the drunkard, who had regained some degree of consciousness, looked at the old man and furiously got up. "What's the problem with you, old man!!" he screamed.

"The same as everyone else's in this bar. Your presence," he said. The tone on the old man's voice was calm, unwavering. The bar was frozen; not even a fly dared to fly. One could smell the impending skirmish from miles away.

"Well everyone can leave if it bothers them," said the drunk man. He grabbed the stool and, before setting it down, he added "you're lucky that, out of respect, I'm not going to hit an elder man," and then he put the stool, once again, near the bar.

The old man, stick in hand, moved the stool away from the drunkard just as he was about to sit. He, once again hit the floor hard as the old man answered him "it's a shame that you're not lucky enough for me to have any trouble hitting someone younger,".

The rugged man rose from the ground, like a bursting volcano, fist clenched straight towards the elder's chin. He dodged it, without even flinching, and, with the tip of the same stick that he used to move the stool, hit the ankles of the drunken lad. Throwing him for a third time to the ground.

The people in the bar, who until now was dead silent, started bursting in laughter. The young drunk, completely dizzied out, stood up with his other fist heading towards the old man's belly and, again, he missed the target. Regardless, he kept on trying; one, two, three, four more punches. None of them landed on the old man who, after the fourth blow, was in a perfect position to push the drunk lad from behind. The drunk and the floor seemed to be as one. The people were laughing non-stop.

One last time, the young man, now devoid of strength, rose from the ground to counter-strike but this time the elder had no mercy. He let go of the stick and went to strike with his bare fists: One blow to the stomach and another in his face, right under his left cheek. The drunk lad closed his eyes and fell, defeated, to the ground.

Before anyone could laugh again, the old man spoke up and said "I hope all of you can excuse the misbehavior of this young man, today he has lost a loved one,".

The people in the bar looked at the old man in shock. They couldn't believe they knew each other after the beating the elder gave the lad.

The old man called the two soldiers in the back and, with a gesture, instructed them to take the young one out of the place. Then, he approached the counter and apologized for the inconvenient and left a red rupee to make amends of any broken propriety.

The barman and his aid opened their eyes wide and accepted with a nod of their heads. The old man came out of the bar and met with the three youngsters, the soldiers were carrying the beat-up drunken by his arms and legs.

"Please lads, get him on the horse," asked the old man to them.

"Yessir," answered the taller. "I hope his bruises won't be sore tomorrow," he said, with a smile on his face, while looking at the drunkard, now lying on the back of the horse.

"I can assure you he won't be sore, not even this very night," added the short one. "I have received hits like those and I know the old man has the right medicine to heal them," the short soldier started laughing, his friend and the old man soon joined him.

"Don't worry, I've also gotten myself beat up pretty bad," said the elder as they laugh, and added "but sometimes, it's the only way to learn,".

"Don't get me started!" answered the taller lad, grabbing his head as if he was remembering a past time when he got a nasty hit there.

A brief silence overcame them and the three of them stared at each other. The old man turned around and in a single, rather skilled for his age, movement he hopped on the horse where the drunken lad was sleeping soundly.

As he put his mount in movement with a slight kick and a sound from his mouth, the smaller soldier tried to speak up again, "What I meant to say at the bar…!".

"Is something that I don't care about," answered the old man laughing, "You can tell me some other time,".

"I hope we get one," muttered the young lad, but the elder couldn't hear him anymore. So, he simply looked at his partner who was holding the piece of parchment on his left hand. They looked at each other, looked at the parchment and went into the bar again.

In the night, only the gallop of the horse the elder and his companion were riding could be heard. It was a dark night, but warm despite the autumn was reaching its end and a refreshing dew was pouring. The old man let the droplets hit his face, the fainted man he was carrying couldn't avoid it.

The old man was riding calmly, making way through some grass fields and jumping the eventual log in the way while splashing when passing over the puddles he was never even going to try to avoid. Soon, they reached a little hut, near a cabin. A man came from inside it and approached the elder's horse, which was now standing near a gate. The old man unmounted and greeted said man.

"Do we get him down?" the man asked.

"Yes, Astor. For tonight, we're going to leave him in the hut," answered the elder.

Together, they put him off the horse and brought him into the hut. They hurled him with a certain degree of care into a bed that was near a chimney and Astor lit the fire. The old man sat on a little seat and sighed.

"It's been a while since last I had some activity," he said, while caressing his knuckles. "I think that, in a certain way, I was missing it," he smiled.

"I'm glad you're having fun," answered Astor while kindling the fire and approached to it a little kettle with water for it to heat up.

A little time went by and Astor offered a tea to the old man, they were both contemplating the ragged youngster who moved a little from time to time.

"I think it's time to go to sleep," said the old man.

"I... think I'll stay for a while to see if he needs something..." said Astor, before being interrupted.

"I don't need anything, uncle,". The young man was awake and sitting in the bed he was lying before. With his thumb and index, he was applying pressure to the high part of his nose, right between his eyebrows. It was still hard for him to gather his thoughts, he opened his hand, still covering his eyes, and the fingers that were pressuring his nose were now up on his temple.

"Who is this guy?... How did I get here?... How is it that you know each other?" asked the lad, without caring which question got answered first.

The old man stood up and headed to the fire, while passing through the young lad's side, he stepped away, a reflex, no doubt, due to the beating he received previously by the man now standing twenty centimeters away. The elder kept going to the fire and poured more water into his cup, he took a handful of herbs from the recipient that was in the small table near Astor and threw them into the cup. Lastly, he grabbed a little bottle with a shiny blue, rather thick, liquid in it and poured a few drops into the cup of the he just made. Astor outstretched his arm and offered a spoon he was holding. The elder took it and mixed the contents of the cup.

"Here, Link, this is going to make you feel better,".

The young lad, in shock, grabbed the cup. "It surprises me that you know my name, even more so because no one calls me that way…" he sipped from the cup and went on "Anyways, it doesn't surprise me more than everything else I just asked, I mean, if you two know each other, it's no wonder you know my name," the youngster took another sip, this time, looking at the cup. There was something strange in it. What was that blue liquid? The elder went back to his seat, without saying a word.

The lad rose his sight from the cup and added "Though, giving it a second thought, it's been a while since people only call me hoarder or blacksmith's nephew… but I've told everyone who asked my name that it was Neil, at least as far as I can remember… which is not much, given that-".

"You lost your memory after that fight a good matter of years back," said the old man, finishing his sentence. The kid opened his eyes wide and then looked at his uncle, as if asking, with his stare, if it was him who told the elder the story.

The old man kept talking. "You see, Link, you're not the only one who lost his memory in that battle… as a matter of fact, in the bar you were today, there were at least three people, including you, with the same problem," the old man made a pause to reflect on his words. "For the time being, you won't get all the answers as you want them, but in time your curiosity will be satiated almost completely,".

Link had drunk half the contents of his cup, his hangover was nearly imperceptible, the headache and the bruises where less painful by the minute. The youngster couldn't decide which of the things that were going on was the strangest. In his mind, he was going over the events from that night, quickly burning the most important ones into his memory.

The old man started talking again. "I'm Hood; I'm the one who brought you here. I've known your uncle from a lifelong and, starting tomorrow, I'll be looking after you. That's what you need to know, for now," the elder sank deeper into his seat and closed his eyes. The lad heard that last thing and thought about fighting back, but he kept his mouth shut when the beating came to his mind. He finished his cup of tea and looked upon himself. It seemed as if he had never had a drink in his whole life. The aches where gone, not only those produced by the old man, but also those he got from working the fields. What on earth was that drink the old man gave him that got him better than ever? And… Why did he give it to him?

Link kept on thinking, silently, for a few more minutes. He looked at his uncle who met his gaze, then he looked at Hood. The old man was sleeping soundly, as if there were no enemies in the room, but it wasn't even three hours ago that both of them were skirmishing in the bar. That's if you can call a fight to one person beating the other one to a pulp without batting an eyelash and not even getting a scratch.

Astor put his hands near the fire, Link once again laid back and whispered to his uncle. "It's a shame you didn't introduce him earlier," and then went on to speak to the old man. "That blue thing you put in my tea would have been really useful throughout my life…" he smiled and closed his eyes. Astor looked at Link and then at Hood, a prideful smile got drawn across his face. He waited a couple of minutes and then got up. He grabbed three blankets that where hanging from a piece of furniture and headed towards Link. He covered him with one of them and whispered. "Soon you'll become one hell of a hero, Link. Soon, Zelda will be protected again,".

He then went towards Hood and covered him with other of the blankets. The old man spoke as if he wasn't really asleep. "Zelda never was nor will be unprotected, Astor, I will see it that way. The same way you took care of me when it was necessary,".

Astor sat down, brandishing a satisfied smile and eyes wet with emotion. He covered himself with the third blanket and closed his eyes.

CHAPTER 4

ALL IN DUE TIME

Un golpe contundente despertó a Link de un sobresalto. Hood había tirado un paquete mullido sobre su estómago. Link se incorporó poco a poco y miró al viejo que estaba en el umbral de la puerta, por donde el sol entraba resplandeciente.

—U A heavy strike woke Link up all of a sudden. Hood had thrown a cushy package over his lap. Link slowly sat up and looked at the old man who was standing under the door's threshold, through which the sun was shining bright.

"Is it too much to ask for a good morning?" asked Link, ironically.

"Get up, there's no time to waste. Take that package into your rucksack," the old man was ready to depart. He was wearing a long, dark green, coat with short sleeves made in, what seemed to be, reptile leather. He also had a pair of dark trousers and brown leather boots. His gloves, made with the same material as the boots, were long but his fingers could be seen.

The elder had already brought two horses with him up to the door. "Where are we going in such a hurry?" asked link.

"For starters, I'm going to make a man out of you. A proper one. Then, we'll have breakfast with your uncle. And after that… well, you'll see," the old man walked up to his horse and got up.

Link could have refused, but he had so many questions unanswered, so many doubts, so much curiosity… they were reason enough to follow him. Besides, the old man said they would be back for breakfast, so there was no reason to believe that he would be giving him another beating. So, Link took his uncle's rucksack, put the package in it, got out of the house, glared at the clear skies, caressed the horse Hood brought him and got up.

Hood looked at him, his eyes filled with a spark of youthful mischief, and said. "Think you can keep up with this old man?".

Before Link could answer, Hood spurred his horse and it went off full speed, rising up what little dust there was since the ground was still moist from the night before.

"Yah!!" Link shouted. His horse also blasted full speed ahead, soon catching up to the old man's, which seemed to have slowed down a little.

They were speeding through one of the huge outskirt plains of Hyrule. Hood avoided some trees while Link was hopping through bushes, stones, puddles and everything that crossed his way. They looked like two brothers running a race. Hood took a tight road and barely missed a low branch from a tree which leaves hit Link in his face.

The elder laughed at the sight of this. "You didn't see that one coming, did you boy?" he teased him.

"I did, old man, it's just that I don't mind some little twigs hitting me," lied link after spitting a pair of leaves that were stuck in his mouth.

"That's true, seems like the only hits you can't take are those of an old man in a bar!" joked Hood.

"Punching a drunk is easy. Care to try now? We'll see if you're as lucky," asked Link defyingly. Although inside he preferred that the old man didn't unmount and asked again.

The old man laughed and went on "we're nearly there. Let's follow that creek,"

Link could see the narrow creek a few meters up ahead.

Both started following the stream which grew larger little by little. Link watched how the old man was looking upwards, he seemed to really enjoy the horse-ride. And suddenly a chill went down his spine.

"Sir..." called Link.

"You can call me Hood," the old man answered.

"You and I... Are we related somehow? I mean, I see some things in you that remind me of myself and, since I can't remember my childhood, I was wondering..." but then He was interrupted.

"Sorry Link, trust me I really am, but I'm not your father," answered Hood before Link could finish his question. An awkward silence followed shortly, but Hood continued "Although, if you let me speak my mind, your father was a great man... In due time you might find out more about him but it won't come from me...".

Link swallowed hard "thank you," he muttered.

"For what?" Hood asked. "For remembering my father like that, even if I can't. Actually, I should thank you for many things, like bringing me back home, giving me the healing tea... though I'm afraid to ask what was it made from," Link said jokingly.

"Don't worry, nothing foul was in it, matter of fact, it wouldn't hurt to have some more right now. Shame it's so hard to find... However, I'm not speaking about that now, so don't push on it. Got it?"

"I guess... don't understand why so much suspense all the time but I guess you'll have your reasons," Link answered "Anyway, thanks for everything. You know... I'm not like this..." he started apologizing.

"Like this how?" The old man asked.

"Like yesterday... it's just that yesterday..."

"I know about Epona... Beautiful beast. But she wasn't killed, only sold. And that's not excuse to drink the way you did," the old man talked about the issue as if he knew every detail of a story that was never told. "Besides, that mare needed some training... even more so if it's going to go with you throughout your long journey,".

Link's jaw was hanging wide but no sound was coming out of it. Epona was his lifelong mare, he saw her birth and upbringing. The fondness that he had for her was like father and daughter.

"Did you buy her?" Link asked

"Do you see me riding your majestic horse right now?" retorted Hood ironically.

"If you didn't... how come you know so much about what happened?" Enquired Link, as if it was the winning question of the argument.

"You know that your uncle is a really good friend of mine, don't you?" spat back Hood, crushing down the lad's wild ideas.

Link crossed his arms and stared right at him, thinking that there was something amiss somewhere in his tale. They weren't galloping anymore; it was more like a soft trot besides the water stream which by now had turned into a river. The y went on until the old man stopped besides some bushes. Part of the river went under those bushes and the other part went downhill.

"Come, Link, it's this way," The old man moved aside a few branches and went on by foot while pulling from the horse's reins. Link followed closely and, no more than ten steps ahead, they found themselves at the foot of a big rock where the river transformed into a little waterfall. In its base a somewhat deep lagoon had formed. The old man tied the horse's reins to a tree, put down his backpack and leapt head first into the pond.

"You afraid of water?" he screamed to Link.

He, who was bemused by the beauty of the place, left the rucksack on the ground, tied his horse to a tree, removed his boots and shirt and threw himself into the water.

"I thought that reeking shirt was part of your skin," the old man mocked Link.

"Well… it's been a couple of days since I last took it off… so I think I should have burnt it…" both men laughed.

Soon, Hood came out of the water and approached the backpack. Took out some kind of soap and threw it to Link.

"Use it. You smell horrible, then come back up… I have to make a little something," said Hood while going through his backpack. "YES! Here you are my old friend," and took out of it three pieces of cane, some cord and a hook. He put the pieces together and made a huge fishing-rod and then put a little piece of bread in the hook as bait.

Once everything was ready, Link, who had finished his bath, went towards the old man, who stuck the rod in the ground and put a stone in front of it.

"Sit there, kid," said the old man signaling to a log.

"As you wish," he said, shaking his head as he was drying his hair.

The old man rumbled through the backpack and took out a thick blanket.

62

"Here, dry yourself," he threw it to him and went on looking for something else.

Link cleaned his face and when he removed the blanket the old man wasn't there anymore. A hand fell heavy on his shoulder and a blade, sharp enough to cut the air was around his neck.

"If you move, it's likely that I'll cut your throat. The blade in this dagger is rather sharp," said the old man, from behind him.

"Wha- WHAT ARE YOU DOING?!" enquired a worried Link.

"What does it look like?" said Hood "I'm going to fix the unworthy looks you're sporting. You can't go on like this with that horrible beard and hair... I don't understand how you're not itchy all over,"

Link breathed relieved. "Well... you get used to it over time,"

"To the beard?" Hood asked.

"No, to the itch!" said Link laughing.

The veteran also laughed and said "Anyways, shortly there will be no more beard to itch you.

Link could have denied, probably without success, but could have initially refused, however, something inside himself told him that it could be a good opportunity to get some more data from the old man, anything that Hood could say about his youth, Epona, the relation with his uncle... anything was more interesting that denying to the "trimming" of his beard. After all, it wasn't so bad and, perhaps, he even needed it.

"I can ask you something?" asked Link

"you're already doing it" joked Hood, "go on, ask away,".

"Why did you take me to my uncle's after the way I behaved last night?" Link enquired.

Hood Sighed and answered "Well, here we go again... Look Link, I know you aren't a bad person, that don't drink in excess and I understand that Epona..."

"Yes, I know that it's no excuse for my behavior," interrupted Link, "but it's not only about Epona... Lately, the iron for the horseshoes that my uncle gets from the mines is getting increasingly expensive... since Ganondorf and his troops took the citadels near Hyrule, all has gone downhill," Link's face grew dark with hopelessness, "The harvests aren't enough, the cattle dies of hunger…".

"Believe me, I understand your situation perfectly. You don't have an idea about all I know about this matter, but you'll get nothing hurting yourself in such a way. I need you on your feet to strike-back…" Explained the old man.

"Strike-back?" Link said, moving the old man's hand away from his left cheek, which was being shaved at that very moment, "I don't know what you have in mind, but I'm only a farmer,".

The old man got up and walked towards the horse in which he hanged his rucksack and, from it, took out an arrow. Besides the rucksack there was a rudimentary bow. He went back to where Link was seated and said to him "See that gap in the tree ahead?" While signaling an Ombú tree located just across the lagoon.

"Yes…" Answered Link.

"I want you to put this arrow in that hole," said Hood.

"What?! You're kidding? It's impossible!!! The gap isn't bigger than my fist! and this far away? No, I can't, you'd be wasting an arrow…"

The old gave him the bow and arrow, stood behind him and muttered silently, as if he was his consciousness, "Imagine that the gap is the small and corrupt heart of Ganondorf. And that branch, the sword he'll use to kill your uncle `All will die, Link, you can't do anything at all to stop me. Astor will be the first of many and you will witness it all, while I take all their lives´" said Hood mimicking Ganondorfs voice.

"No!" Link's mind went blank.

Submerged in the brief tale he just listened, he aimed and let loose. The arrow cut the air, silent, sharp and precise. Now it lied in the centre of the gap, that completed its task as target. When Link came to his senses, he could not believe what happened. Still trembling due to the heat of the moment, he shouted "I can't believe it! I never shot an arrow in my life, but your voice… and that phrase…".

"Not that you remember," said the old man, while gesturing him to sit back on the tree lump to continue shaving him.

"What did I use to do before losing my memory?" asked Link to the old man.

"I'm sorry kid, that's something that you'll discover over time," He took the bow and left it on the floor, "For now, I've got to retrain you, so that your body regains strength with skills that you used to know,".

Hood kept on shaving Link and afterwards, fixed his hair. From time to time, he checked the fishing rod, to see if something bit. They continued chatting about nothing and everything throughout the "Hair Saloon" session, and once the old man was finished, Link looked like a new man.

"Open the package I gave you before coming out of the house," said Hood, signalling Link's rucksack.

"What is it?" asked Link.

"If you don't open it, you'll never Kno-" Hood could not finish his sentence because a fish had taken the bait, "Holy…! It seems big!".

Link left the package and ran to help Hood. Together, they took out a fish that was the size of the old man's arm.

"Well, today we'll have some good lunch!" affirmed Hood while examining the catch, now in his hands.

Link nodded and went back to where he left the package, picked it up, and opened it.

"Wow! Is this for me?" He asked.

"If it fits you…" answered the old man, as nonchalant as he could.

Link had now on his hands a white t-shirt whit round short neck and long sleeves, that fit perfectly, as if it adapted to his body. He wore it and, from the package, took out a pair of sturdy, clear brown, mounting trousers of very good quality.

"Awesome!" Exclaimed Link, "HEY! Watch elsewhere!" He

shouted to Hood, although didn't matter much to him. There was something in this old man that seemed fatherly to him and, as such, Link didn't care if Hood saw him in undergarments.

"Sorry Link, but I do already have someone special in my life…" answered the old man Jokingly.

"Ja, ja, ja," Laughed, ironically, Link, "How do I look?".

"I guess it's ok," said Hood without paying much attention.

Link, with the package still on his hands, took out two more items: a spiky cap, quite warm and an enclosed jacket. It was moss-green, like the cap, with short sleeves. Both items were made from the same cloth. Link lingered a while, watching his new attire.

"It's warm in winter and fresh in summer," said Hood, describing the attire, "It's a rare cloth, rather hard to get,".

"I don't think I can pay for this…".

"I think you can… or will," smiled Hood, "Consider it an advance payment, for your coming services to the community of Hyrule,".

"And what will I be doing for Hyrule precisely?" asked Link, moving the hand in circles, signaling Hood to continue with his tale.

All in due time, my boy," answered Hood taking the reins of his horse, "for now, let's go back to your uncle for breakfast. Afterwards I'll begin to explain you some things about your training…"

"Training?" questioned Link, raising an eyebrow.

"Yes mister, all hero need training. After that, we'll do a quick pause to have lunch," added Hood as he tied the fish they caught to the saddle of the horse, "and finally… some more training,".

"Won't it be a lot of training?" Joked Link.

"look id, what you did with that arrow wasn't luck. You have potential, but if we don't reinforce it, you'll hardly repeat it," Hood mounted his horse and rallied it, with a little kick and a noise from his mouth.

Link still had the clothing given to him in his hands. Quickly, he put them on and jumped on the horse. In a few seconds he caught up to the old man. Both rode near the skirts of the river. They chatted of several, irrelevant subjects, kidding and laughing. That level of understanding was not the same as the one at the tavern, some hours before.

In spite of them just getting to know each other and had an age difference of no less than twenty-something years, they seemed to be lifelong friends.

Soon they diverted from the river and followed the road up-hill. As they arrived, they saw Astor moving away from a cow towards the house. In his left hand he carried a bucket filled with freshly gathered milk. He saw them approach, waved at them with his free hand and went into the house. Hood and Link unmounted and put away all the stuff they were carrying in the stable. Hood put some hay in the food container of the horses while Link pumped some fresh water to leave them to drink. When going out of the stable, Link hastily collected six eggs that there were near him. Fortunately, the cuccos were distracted and didn't notice him. When they went into the house, they found Astor with an apron that seemed tiny in contrast with his huge body.

"Hood, where did you leave Link? Who is this elegant young man?" asked Astor sarcastically when seeing youngster's new appearance. Link did a grimace of satisfaction and puffed his chest. Without expecting an answer to his questions, he went on, "I see that you brought lunch," added the robust man, signaling with his eyes the fish that Hood held in his hands.

"I see that you're wearing the perfect clothes to cook it," quickly joked Hood.

"Very funny. It's not my fault that there are no more clothing shops for real, robust, men," claimed Astor.

"It's either that or you're looking for clothes in women shops," Link told him, jokingly.

"Oh, look who deigned to speak, if it's no other than the moss-green princess!" answered back Astor, "If you've already fini-shed mocking my apron, you can seat at the table. In a minute I'll bring a couple of hot cocoa cups,"

"Hot cocoa?", repeated Hood thrilled "It's been ages since I drank some! It seems that winter is coming... How I missed your hospitality, my dear Astor,".

"You don't say," said Astor ironically, "but I never threw you out. You left by yourself, no? Well, not by yourself, I understand that you were in very good company," laughed Astor.

"And when did this happened?" asked Link as if he didn't really care to know.

"You think that we go to walk into that one so easily? It'll take much more than that to catch me with my guard down," said the old man, laughing, "I repeat, all in due time. Soon you'll understand some of it,"

Link seated without the strength to keep on questioning anymore. The secret they were keeping didn't seem to be something bad, so he didn't have to worry about it. Besides, his preoccupation laid with the coming training, which he totally ignored. He kept thinking on this, with his sight stray in the flames of the small fire that heated the pot with milk.

Hood and Astor were remembering an anecdote of a cold winter day in which, after a lot of heavy work, they sat to drink a cup of hot cocoa. To Link, this story seemed familiar, but he wasn't paying much attention. Maybe his uncle had told it to him before, he thought. Maybe, it was his imagination.

Soon the milk was hot enough as to melt the cocoa bars Astor had thrown in it. The uncle served three big cups and some bread with peach jam. Link and Hood took the cup with both hands, to heat them. Although the day was sunny and had dawned somewhat warm, the temperature was beginning to drop.

The farm was found very south of Hyrule, in a small town called Ordon. It was one of the southernmost towns of the continent and the world, together with the sheikah territory to the west. Throughout the course of the morning, the wind shifted from nor'-east to southwest. Thus, a drop in the temperature was expected. In short, the first day of winter was right upon them.

"I Already spoke with Braulio so that Link can begin training according to your plans, Hood," commented Astor while whipping some milk leftovers from his moustache.

"Well then, once we finish breakfast, we'll head his way," said Hood, happily.

"Braulio? The goatherd?" asked Link.

"The very same, my kid," said Hood smiling even wider than before.

Link was about to ask what for, but he guessed the old man would tell him "all in due time" or something like that, so, he went back to his cup of hot cocoa and kept on drinking.

Hood Noticed this and then claimed, "I See that you're starting to understand how does this work,".

The three continued with their breakfast by the side of the barely lit fire in the chimney. The hot coals that heated the milk had consumed almost entirely. Link was the first to finish, followed by Astor. Hood took a little longer, he seemed to be taking his time to enjoy himself.

As the old man put the cup on the table, he got up and begun stretching noisily, raising both arms above his head. Astor observed with contempt, but smiled.

"Nobody could, can or will be able to correct some bad manners..."

Link laughed and added, "I see that I am not the only one who gets scold over these things, uncle,".

"Well, off we go!" said Hood, walking towards the door, "We are quite near, so we're going on foot. It won't take us more than a couple hours, Astor,".

"All right, don't worry. The fish will be ready by then," —said the man with the moustache.

Hood Opened the door and gestured Link to move out. When passing through his side, Hood whispered to him, "Ladies and boys first,".

Once outside of the house, Link answered "it seems tom me that I am sufficiently big to not be considered a boy," while showing a grimace of satisfaction in his face, the same someone would have when winning an argument.

Hood Did exactly the same gesture and answered "You may be too big to be a boy, but not beardy enough to be a man," and burst to laughter.

"That's unfair! You were the one who shaved me!!" retorted Link.

Both laughed and walked through a path of dry earth.

While exiting the farm, Hood headed to the stable, the night before, he left some things in his rucksack beside his horse. Amongst them there was a short-sword, quite beaten-up, an old shield and a bow with some arrows.

They walked for around ten minutes through the dusty path until reaching a granary, where someone was waiting for them by the door.

CHAPTER 5

THE HERO'S TRAINING

As they arrived, Hood approached and greeted the man that was expecting them at the door of the barn.

A peasant of good physic, product of the field labor he did. The guy had a slightly darker tone of skin than Link, with brown hair and rounded ears, classic of the inhabitants of Ordon, in contrast with the typical pointy ears of the majority of the hylians. He was wearing a couple of high boots, covered in mud, and a clear brown gardener with a belt filled with farm tools.

"Braulio dearest, it's been a while!" said Hood as he embraced the man.

"A while?" you must be joking," smiled Braulio, "How are you doing, Link? your uncle told me that you were going to do some unorthodox training…".

"Well, I guess so…. The truth is that I don't have the least idea of what I came to do," Link answered, while looking at Hood, who then said, "Braulio is one of the few in the village that knows my true name. He's a trustworthy person although I'm sure that you already know that and therefore that's why we're here?

The three men were heading towards the barn and Link said to Braulio, "This old geezer showed up yesterday in the tavern, struck me, carried me home, threw me on a bed, healed me, woke me up with a blow, gifted me clothes… Truth is that each good deed that he has done for me, is followed by a bad one, and then again, another good… so, if I keep track," — Link looked upwards and to the left, as thinking in something and kept on — "if the last that thing he did was to give me clothes… then I suppose that now comes something bad,". The three laughed.

Hood put a hand on Link's shoulder, "Nothing is good neither bad, it just depends on the value that we give to the things, as to comprehend a reason behind them,". Hood was sporting an intellectual look, as if that sentence was a philosophical reflection of dire importance, and then added "But this we'll do here... might not seem good for you at the beginning," smiled Jokingly.

The guys continued walking until they arrived at a wooden wall.

"Well, here we are," said Braulio.

"Thank you, Braulio," answered Hood.

"I'm sorry I don't have any goats to offer to you" — regretted Braulio — "If only things weren't so bad... I fear for the times that near us, fear for Hyrule and its people,"

"Times will be difficult, Braulio, but if we are here today, it's because we still believe that there's hope, right?" added Hood letting a slight smile through.

"I suppose you're right" smiled Braulio, "I leave you two alone, if you need anything, I'll be at the cabin,".

"All right, and thanks again, Braulio," said Hood.

Braulio moved away doing a gesture with his hand, as saying "don't worry about it".

Hood and Link found themselves in front of a pen, that contained eight wild but groomed animals. Link contemplated the beasts that were eating near him. They were big and strong enough as to be mounted. Those were the goats of Hyrule's meadows, some majestic quadrupeds with huge and dangerous horns that coiled around their heads and joined at the ends. Link stopped looking at them and realized that he was, with Hood, really near of these goats... and some training was expected. His face transformed, his gesture of contemplation became a gesture of doubt and worry. Then, he asked "Just to know... What are we supposed to be doing here?".

"We're putting these goats in that stable at the back," answered Hood.

"Right... Either you're crazy, or death seems to be the solution to Hyrule's problems," Link said.

"Crazy? Me? Nooo... Well... I mean... Well... Maybe... Maybe a bit," kidded Hood.

"These animals become more docile at night. Even so, this job gets hard even to Braulio, who's very prepared to perform this task… and these goats know and trust him!!! If we go in, they're going to destroy us. Besides, we didn't bring any tool, nor horses, anything at all!" said Link.

"Yeah… Anyway, it's not my training, so I won't be the one who gets in there,".

"Ohh… I got it," said Link sarcastically, "At a very young age, you struck your head and were left a bit dumb! now, you expect me to get in there and try to put these eight tiny little goats in that stable so that I'm left just as dumb as you!" kidded Link, with his face filled with fear, "There aren't enough rupees in the world to make me go and do something that stupid!" and then, link stopped speaking to take a deep breath, then he went on,

"It was a long time ago… I was playing with my boomerang, I think… and it fell inside a pen, identical to this one," said Link hesitatingly, as he was doing a big effort to remember, "Right then, I didn't know this kind of goats that well and went into it, to fetch it. I had no idea of how territorial these animals were. I don't know why I keep this memory, since it's of my childhood, i suppose it's because, it was then that I learnt that, by no circumstances, i had to go into a closed space, filled of goats," told Link, while getting those thoughts off his chest.

"And how did you get out of there? I mean, if you're telling me this, it's because you got out alive,".

"A young man, a bit higher than us… can't remember his face, nor his name…" said Link frowning, "I can only remember that he went in, jumping the fence, and ran between the goats. He raised me and took me out of there. It was incredibly fast, he seemed to have feline reflexes. It was awesome, it's a shame that I can't remember him…".

"Yes, it is. But if we look at it from another point of view, we at least have something to learn from him. I mean, we already know that it's possible to get out of a pen, filled with coats, alive, no matter how territorial they are," Concluded Hood.

"Yeah, you might be right, but even so, it's too risky for someone who never did it. I repeat, you won't get me in there, not even for all the rupees of the world.

73

"Link…" Hood started to speak "I'll share with you something that I learnt by myself and was proven right time and time again,".

Link had his sight set in the goats as if he was calculating what would happen if he tried to get in. He then looked at the old man sideways and listened to him.

"Today, it's possible that we end up working in something else, other than your skills," affirmed Hood, "The day that your rescuer saved your life, he had as much fear as you have now,".

"Wait… Do you know the man who saved me?" interrupted Link.

"For now, I will only say that you know him also," said Hood, bringing to a halt any possibility of derailing from the subject.

Link opened his eyes as wide as he could. "Anyway, the youngster that saved you had as much fear as you have and, like you, he had never set a foot in a pen full of wild goats. However, he went in and took you out. What do you think made him do that?"

"I don't know…. He became crazy, maybe?" said Link sporting a shy smile.

"No, two things made him. For one, fear. Fear that you couldn't get out alone, and you would get injured. Fear that happen something very grave would happen if he didn't take you out," The veteran paused but Link didn't ask anything, it seemed that he wanted Hood to say which was the other thing before interrupting again.

Then the old continued "And also, his attitude. He knew that he could. He believed it. That was all he needed to know to make it happen.

Hood Stroked his beard and looked at the goats.

"Link, is not a bad thing to be afraid, on the contrary, it's very good. Fear is what tells us "how far we can go". Without fear, we would act without prudence and not being careful isn't brave, it's stupid.

Link smiled; this time it was more evident. He began to look at the goats in another way, calculating their height and estimating their weight. Hood went on.

74

"I call THAT: "healthy fear". It's the fear that follows you around, it prevents you from doing stupidities. The fear that's beside you, counseling you," explained the veteran, "And right in front of you, I mean you and your fear, it's the attitude. which knows how to move and foresees all, so that you can get the best possible outcome. The one that anticipates everything. The attitude, Link, is vital. Without it you can turn around and head back to your uncle's until Ganondorf decides what to do with you all," said Hood extending his arm in the direction from which they arrived.

"What do I have to do with the goats?" asked Link, now taking things seriously.

Hood Smiled, satisfied, "I knew you had a hero in you! Your mission is simply to put those goats in the stable behind, by running between them and dodging before they hit you. Which means, you make them chase you all the way to that ramp and once there, move out of the way. This ramp works like a seesaw, when the goat steps on it will get stuck on the other side and won't be able to go back out.

Link climbed the pen's door and looked back.

"I hope this is worth it old man!" He jumped inside and faced towards the first goat, "Hey, you, come on!" He shouted to the animal as if it understood him.

The goat saw Link and began to run towards him. The other animals snorted and began to become unrest.

Link ran to the ramp, but had to slow down, since the goat chasing him was not precisely the youngest one. When it was about to reach him, Link sped up in direction to the ramp and went straight through it, into the stable with goat and everything.

"Well, it didn't go as expected. I think I'll have to improvise..." said Link in out loud, although nobody heard him. He was able to easily dodge the goat, which was pretty tired already, and jump the wall outside the stable.

"That went well..." Link said to himself.

"Very well, seven to go!" shouted Hood from the other side of the wall which surrounded the pen.

"Ha... ha... ha...!" laughed Link ironically.

Then, Link saw two goats approach at full speed, breathing strongly and venting steam through their snouts. He ran parallel to the stable, straight to the ramp. The nearest animal was closer than a second to reach him, Link jumped the ramp by its side and the animal went straight through, stepping on the ramp and going into the stable.

A lot of dust was raised, due to the dry earth that was on the way, and the goat which was left behind went into the cloud of dust facing straight to the ramp and into the stable.

Almost without realizing, Link had put three of them inside the stable.

"Five to go!" shouted Hood, encouraging him.

Link didn't pay attention to that. He had two mor beasts approaching him from both sides in front of him. It took him two seconds to think what his course of action was going to be and began to run straight forward. In his brain, the adrenaline made everything seem to move slowly and he could see the animals move gracefully towards him.

Less than a second away from both animals crushing him, Link threw himself to the floor, sliding about three meters. Behind him, the goats had bumped each other. They both collapsed and remained stunned on the ground.

Hood Laughed loudly and said "You Have to put them away, not knock 'em out!".

"At least this buys me some time!!" answered Link. "I've got an idea!!..." he thought while running to one of the two knocked goats, which was getting back up.

"What are you going to do? Piggy ride it? shouted the old man, sarcastically, when he saw the boy heading directly to the animal.

Link jumped on the back of the goat and took it by the horns. It got up and tried to shake him off.

The others beast observed cautiously, then Link spurred it softly as if it was a horse. "YEEEHAWWW!" he shouted instinctively, and curiously enough; the goat began to run forwards.

Held firmly by its two horns, Link rode towards the others, shouting in such a way that it wasn't noticeably which was more aggressive, if the goat or the enraged youngster.

The boy seemed to be possessed and his attitude played in his favor. With a bit of skill and luck, he managed to corner three of the goats against the stable. Link pulled from one horn to the other to make the goat go from side to side.

The cornered beasts were backing to the ramp and one by one fell inside the stable. As the last of the three goats went in, Link noticed that his own goat, had two hooves on the ramp and, taking advantage of the opportunity, he jumped backwards making it step forwards and enter the stable.

"Very well boy, only one more to go!" shouted Hood euphorically.

Just one goat remained, the fiercest and maybe, since it didn't fall for any of the previous schemes, the most cunning one. The goat's brown and somewhat reddish eyes met the young boy's clear brown eyes, challenging him, but Link gazed back, focused, cold and calculator. The situation was so tense that it seemed as if sparks would start flying between them. The goat struck the floor twice with it's forward left hoof and charged at full speed. Link, could have headed towards the ramp, since he was somewhat near twenty meters away from it, while the animal was at least fifty meters away from him. Then the youngster sported a somewhat fearful smirk and decided to run, but towards the goat. Forty meters, thirty, twenty, ten. Link threw himself to the ground, rolling to his right and the goat barely scrapped him. It took about ten meters to the animal to stop its thrust. The boy ran towards the goat again, shouting frantically, this didn't scare it, but it didn't advance either. It simply lowered its' horns, bracing for impact. Link was already one step away; he took it by the horns pushing it back a few centimeters. The animal held its ground, began to make the young boy fall back and, with a sudden shake of its horns, threw Link to the ground. As he fell, Link remembered how afraid he was and his strong and brave attitude abandoned suddenly abandoned him.

"Running is no longer an option, it would reach me," Link thought quickly, "moving slowly is also a bad idea, his snout won't stop blowing off steam,".

Completely surrendered, Link closed his eyes, preparing for the pain to come… BOOM!!! A deaf noise was heard in the field. Link found himself on the ground, the goat lying beside him and Hood standing tall in front of both of them.

The beast tried to raise up before something else happened, but it was too late, Hood was already on its back.

"Yah!" Shouted the old man, riding the goat, which was now heading hatefully towards the ramp.

Link was speechless and thoughtless. He only watched the old man ride the animal, as if he was some kind of professional horse rider.

The goat didn't seem to slow down and was already twenty meters away from the ramp.

"Watch out! It'll take you inside with the other beasts!" shouted Link, but the old man ignored him.

"Go on! Faster!" shouted the old man, barely ten meters away from the ramp.

The goat stepped onto the ramp with enough strength as to jump into the pen. Hood Quickly stepped on the animal's back and just as the goat left the ramp, the old jumped upwards.

Link couldn't believe it. Hood Found himself hanging from one of the stables beams.

Swinging a bit, he pulled himself up and walked through the beam towards a solid, high surface in the granary which was used to feed the animals. Then, he descended calmly through a set of stairs that led outside.

"Well, I didn't expect this," said Link how was a few meters away from the staircase.

"Very well, boy!" said Hood, "You've done it great!".

"You're kidding me, right? I couldn't do it… I was one goat short,".

"Look, Link, in my opinion seven out of eight is not a miss, but seven rights," declared the old man, smiling, "You have to start seeing the positive side of things, I mean, give it your best shot, but don't expect everything to go your way. Otherwise, when things go wrong you'll panic, as you did with the last goat,".

The old man hit the nail on the head. Link had surrendered in the last moment, because fear had taken hold of him.

"Don't be broken-hearted," said Hood patting Link's back, "Let's recap today training,".

"What?" asked the youngster.

"Yes, yes. Let's see… What can you tell me of the attitude?" asked the old man.

"Eh?" doubted Link.

"Come on, play along boy," asked Hood as they began to walk back.

"Well… The attitude… I think it helped me a lot. I felt very alive and, when I ran toward the goats, I thought that I could do it… mainly with the one which I mounted successfully,".

"And the fear?"

"At the beginning it helped me, I guess. It kept me from being reckless and allowed me to think over the ideas that came to my head at great speed. But then, something changed and I think I lost control,"

"So, we could say that it would've been impossible for you to survive without fear," reaffirmed Hood.

"Yes, we could say that," answered Link, smiling.

"Very well! Then I would call this a very positive training!" concluded the old man satisfied, "Besides, I think you learnt something else, that right now you're forgetting,"

"Oh yeah?" inquired, thoughtful, link, "And what is that?".

"That with your fifty-five, maybe barely sixty kilograms, you can't face a creature with four legs and over a hundred and fifty kilograms of weight!" —affirmed the old man, laughing, "Unless you have a pair of goronian boots, that is".

"A pair of what now? asked Link without understanding the last part.

"Goronian boots," repeated Hood, "I call them that because a fellow goron made me a pair a long time ago,".

"You mean the gorons from the mountains?" asked the youngster, surprised.

"Yes, those," the old man answered.

"Well I regret to tell you that, if any goron remains after Ganondorf's advance through the arid mountains, It must to be scared, hidden and waiting for his kind to extinguish," said Link disheartened.

"They are many and their numbers are rising once more. Sadly, as Ganondorf razed through the arid mountains, very important lives were lost, but these lives had young descendants which now are adults and are willing to fight against Ganondorf," said Hood with a big, satisfied, smile. He paused and went on, "They only need a hero to guide them,".

I feel that you're referring to me. Please tell me that I'm wrong," asked Link.

"Link, I won't lie to you." said the old and went on walking, silently.

"You won't lie to me… but you don't say anything at all!"

Hood smiled, "Figure it out yourself, genius,".

"So then you are referring to me," thought Link out loud, grabbing his head, "I think I'm going to panic again,".

"Well… take advantage of what you learnt today," finished Hood smiling.

They walked somewhat about ten steps in silence and Braulio showed at the door.

"Where done, Braulio, see you soon!" shouted Hood, raising a hand.

"No problem! Whenever you want to!" answered Braulio, greeting from the door.

Link didn't say anything at all, he greeted with his hand, smiling. Although, once Braulio went in, he ceased to smile.

"What I don't understand… "said Link, "Is that everyone knows that after the tragic events in the arid mountains, the gorons closed up the road, blocking it with enormous stones. Today, if you're really careful, since the whole area is taken by Ganondorf's troops, and get close enough, you can see the gigantic rocks…" In this moment Link was interrupted by Hood.

"What everyone knows is what everyone has to know…" The old man smiled and scratched his beard, looking upwards, reflexive, "I'll tell you a small, real, tale about that day, my young friend. After all, we have to speak about something on the way back to the house of your uncle, if not, it would be a very boring trip,"

Link nodded, but didn't say anything at all and then Hood began to speak.

"Shortly before that battle, information leaked about a big part of Ganondorf's army would head through the base of the arid hills. Darunia, king of the gorons, had managed to gather a big group of ready to battle adults to fight against this unstoppable troops. The plan was brilliant, taking advantage of their physical appearance, since goron skin looks rocky and, when they hold still and hid, they seem like big stones, the king ordered his men to scattered throughout the area, crouching in groups of three or four, covering their axes and hammers, classical goronian weapons,".

Link, surprised, couldn't help asking "But really? Just like that? Only them and their weapons?".

"As strange as that may seem to you, young Link, it was just like that and, at the beginning, it worked quite well. Although you didn't let me finish the tale," the old man made a quick pause, and went on "They weren't just lying around there, they had something indispensable. The most important thing in a battle and to which more than a victory is attributed throughout history; It was, my dear friend, the surprise factor! Never forget it Link, the one who hits first, hits twice. I am not the kind of man that tries to resolve problems by means of violence and I would say to you that, if you could avoid it, you should. But Ganondorf is ruthless, the only thing that matters to him is his own gain and his troops are alike.

"am I ruthless?" asked Link smiling.

"What? Why?" asked Hood, very surprised.

Link put a hand in the shoulder of the old man.

"I don't remember you trying to speak with me in a peaceful way in the bar," said Link jokingly and both started to laughed.

—I don't think you would have understated me in that state of drunkenness," answered Hood.

"Well," said Link "and then, what happened with the gorons? They were all scattered by the pass of the arid mountains and you even say that it worked… at the beginning? What worked?".

Hood Looked upwards, to his temple, a sign of being remembering the battle such as it happened.

"Darunia was sitting, legs crossed, in the middle of the way, with his hammer on his knees. The famous hammer "Megaton" which was forged by his ancestor, when he was the patriarch, which he used to force Volvagia, a great red dragon of quite a… particular behavior, to remain incarcerated in the volcanic caves, north of the arid hills.

"You say it as if you were there," said Link.

Hood remained quiet.

Link opened the mouth but no word came out of it. He began to babble something, but Hood interrupted him "It could be said that my family and I have seen closely more than one fight," the old man laughed heroically and went on, "Anyway, there he was, Darunia, seated down, when the troops arrived and found him. Nobody approached him initially, but they surrounded him, so that he couldn't escape. As if Darunia was going to do anything like that!" added Hood, offended, "Once surrounded, a soldier approached him, in truth, I don't know who he was. I assume it must've been the commander of that troop... Anyway, it didn't last long, for Darunia, as heavy as he seemed, moved faster that an arrow. He rose up, wielding his war-hammer and the poor soldier didn't stand a chance. He must have been sent flying something like five, or maybe six, meters away. Darunia Took advantage of the shock caused sound the horn he was carrying around his robust neck. A thundering sound came out of it and hundreds of rocks came to life. The gorons came from all sides and, in a few minutes, thousands of servants of Ganondorf perished. A few survived and broke ranks, but sorely, it wasn't a withdrawal. The gorons chased after them, but as they crossed the first hill, they found thousands of enemies awaiting there,".

Link lowered his head and sadness was all over his face, "A typical tactic of Ganondorf. I imagine that he purposefully leaked the information so that it reached Darunia,"

Hood Affirmed mildly with the head.

"For some reason, I think Likewise, but we'll never know. Anyway, hundreds of gorons fell defeated. Darunia Shouted "withdrawal!" A few times. His son found himself cornered and Darunia was on the ground, defending himself as much as he could with his hammer,".

Link swallowed hardly and asked, "That was when he and his son died?".

Hood Doubted before answering, "No, it was then when two mysterious outlanders mingled in, perfectly coordinated. Their arrows reached the heads of several enemies and with shield and sword made way until they reached the patriarch. From the floor, the goron leader shouted: "No, don't't come for me! Save my son!". Then raising euphoric, five of Ganondorf soldiers went out flying. The brave strangers saw the goron youngling, son of the leader, and headed towards him, reaching him shortly after, although afterwards, they found themselves surrounded. The three fought back admirably. Tens of enemies fell to their feet, but that wouldn't last long…" Hood stopped the tale to open the gate, since they already had arrived to Astor's house.

Link perceived the smell of roasted fish, his lungs flooded with the exquisite smell that came from the spices that his uncle usually used, but, although Link was hungry, the history that I lood was telling was his priority at the moment. And so, he grabbed the old man from his shoulder, stopping him on his steps, and demanded him to finish the tale, "And then, what happened? Did they managed to escape?".

Hood Contemplated Link's distressed expression, "You know the end, know that Darunia is a very iconic martyr of the goron resistance and, regretfully, one does not turn into martyr precisely by… well, you know…"

Link hurried to speak, "Yes, I know, but the son and the two strangers, did they escape?

Hood, already with a hand in the doorknob of the house's door, looked at him, "Well... it's a pitty, but the past is sometimes as uncertain as the future. What do you think happened?".

"I believe they escaped" answered Link and added "If not, this talk would've been senseless,".

"If you think that the sense of the tale is in the outcome of it, then you have to learn something more. Not always the end is the most important part of a story. Sometimes, you must understand its development to be able to learn and appreciate more essential things. Don't underestimate the power of the details, because they are the big workers in histories. Only when you can be attentive to the details, you'll be able to reason in an absolute and objective way.

"They survived?", asked Link, praying for an answer.

"That's a detail, and it's answer you will find over time," answered Hood, in a serious way.

Link swallowed hard and understood that Hood wouldn't give him an answer. In the short time he had spent with him he deduced that Hood, whoever he was, was here to mentor him. Moreover, he was the one who would decide which things Link had to know and which not. In conclusion, the boy assented seriously with his head and waited for Hood to open the door.

Hood turned over and, before opening the door, let see a slight smile of satisfaction through the left side of his mouth. He turned the doorknob and went in.

CHAPTER 6

CUCCOS & DEMONS

Time passed by and Winter came over the plainlands outside Hyrule. The green pastures were covered in a thin white layer of ice, which was nothing else than the morning dew, frozen over by the cold of the previous night. Nevertheless, Astor was happier than ever. Hood and Link were working a lot. Every morning, they helped him at the farm and, in the afternoon, they dedicated themselves to train.

Some days it was combat oriented training, which ranged from bow and arch, maybe spear or sword and shield, or two-handed sword, hammer and a wide array of axes, even the blowgun had a place from time to time.

Other times, Hood applied more physical training, using what nature provided. Climbing up trees, jumping fences, swimming in a small pond near Orton's farm which, by the way, was incredibly cold at the time. Goats were also a subject for training, together with other animals, like horses, faithful allies in battle, and Cuccos, famous by their pecking.

"Very well, today we train with the cuccos!" said Hood, as soon as they finished lunch.

"What?! No... not again... Can't we do something else?" Objected Link, pretending to be terribly scared.

"Come on Link, don't be a crybaby, it's not THAT bad," Commented Astor, while picking up the dishes to start the clean-up.

"I'd rather take another bath in the pond," said Link, making short notice of the pond-bath, which was one of his worst cold-related experiences.

"Nope, today it's cuccos. Last time you saved yourself when it started snowing, but today is a lovely, sunny day and, even though the winter's cold weather, it's nice over the sun," Answered Hood.

The old man rose up and Link followed after. Both men exited the lodge and walked towards the housing of the most feared birds in Hyrule. Link jumped into it and asked "Like last time?".

Hood took out a small sand-watch from his pocket "Yes, let's begin with one. You have thirty seconds to put it into that little cage," he said as he pointed towards a little pen next to where Link was.

Link moved his knees in little circles and hopped three times on the spot, as a warm-up of sorts. He lay low and moved his fingers as he got ready, "Well, whenever you say...".

Then Hood turned the watch over... "GO!"

Link swiftly jumped over and grabbed the nearest bird. The animal Clucked and pecked a bit at his fingers but, in less than ten seconds, Link had attained his goal. "Easy-peasy old man!" he claimed as he released a cucco into the little pen.

"Very well, and so we arrive at today's first lesson: When the objective is one, and is clear, the result is, usually, much more favorable than expected,". Said Hood, as he turned over the sand-watch and waited until it emptied itself on one side.

"Sure, whatever," replied Link with a satisfied smile and a smug face.

Hood ignored this attitude and added, "Are you ready for round two?".

"Pfff... I was BORN ready," answered the young one.

"You've got one minute to catch three of them," said the old one.

"If it took me ten seconds to catch one, I'll barely need thirty seconds to catch three... but whatever, you're the one that calls the time," Link answered, without a shred of modesty.

"Ready, set, go!" shouted Hood without even paying attention to what the boy was saying.

Link jumped over the nearest bird and grabbed it, alarming the rest of them. Threw the finger-pecking bird into the pen and, in a split-second, ran towards another one. This one was a bit harder, but nonetheless, Link managed to catch it. He left it in the pen and by the side of the eye managed to catch a glance at Hood turning over the watch, which took thirty seconds to empty itself, which meant that he had only thirty seconds to go.

Under a bit of pressure, link threw himself over a cucco but it slipped through his fingers. Luckily for him, another one, a bit distracted, passed running by. From the ground, Link caught one of the bird's legs and, after receiving his fair share of pecking through his body, he put the bird into the pen second away from the time-up.

Hood didn't speak… he just waited. Link, knowing that Hood would say something like "Wasn't thirty seconds more than enough?" hurried up and commented, "Just in time! Well, what's next?".

The old man, without changing his expression let out "Five in two minutes,".

This time Link didn't make any comment about it. He just readied himself, caught a deep breath and waited for the go.

Hood turned the watch over and screamed "GO!".

Ling started running and managed to catch the first bird, dropped it and went on to the second prey. He jumped over it, crushing it a bit while it pecked at his nose, and threw it into the pen without breaking his rhythm. As he massaged his face, he went after the third one. He lunged over it, managing to grab it from its legs and got pecked at his head for it.

"Only two to go…" he said to himself, while he dropped the third one into the little pen where the other two awaited. He run, unsuccessfully, other two nearby cuccos. Then he jumped over another one, without any luck. After that he managed to corner one and grabbed its wings from behind, this one couldn't peck at him.

"Yeah! That was a good one!" He said out loud, talking to no-one. Hood didn't even flinch.

Link jumped over a cucco, but it slipped away. Two other run him over and Link tried to catch them, but no luck there. In a split second he got up and headed towards another bird, but then…

"Time's up!" Shouted Hood, signaling the watch with all its sand on the lower side.

Link, who was on the ground, got up angrily but recognized his error.

"All right, don't even say it, I boasted way to much and made a fool out of myself," he said.

"Care to know which is the second lesson of the day or no?" said Hood in a serious tone, "Ye-Yeah of course," he admitted bitterly.

"Very well, but… Do you remember which the first lesson was?" asked the old man.

Link looked up, "Yes, yes. The lesser the objectives, the better," he summed up.

"Well, that's not how I put it, but I guess you got the point," said Hood, rising both eyebrows, "And how do we get to have lesser objectives?".

Link started to answer, "Well you can't if you have to catch five of those cucco-" and Hood interrupted "Wrong! You're taking the cuccos as individual targets and that keeps you from making an effective strategy," replied the old man as he passed the birds from the pen to the bird house, "which leads us to the second lesson: If the objectives are many, go from easiest to hardest. That way you'll manage one objective that get them all,".

Link was scratching his head as he said "Ok… now I'm confused,".

The old man went on, "Look, let's say that the objective is getting every cucco in the pen and we compare it to saving Hyrule,".

"I wish saving Hyrule was that easy!" laughed out Link.

The old man rose an eyebrow, "Easy or not, you didn't make it… So, it's the same,". Link whipped out the smile from his face and the old man continued, "Then, locking every cucco is as saving Hyrule. Each cucco is a demon, but demons, as cuccos, are not all the same," Link was silent and Hood asked, "To save Hyrule, would you start by killing Ganondorf?".

"I would if I could…" answered Link.

But you can't, why?" asked the old man.

"Because he's got helpers and demons everywhere," deducted Link as if it was obvious.

"Then we should start whit his minions and then get to the king, right?" ask Hood, as if he was trying to lead to the answer.

"Well… yeah. I would start with those who are easiest to beat," concluded Link.

Hood then, began to explain his weird but simple enough idea.

"This is just the same Link, not every cuckoo is an easy catch. Some will be easier than others… Look, those two were fighting amongst them; That has a blind eye, and that, is limping. Those are easier prey than the others," Pointed out Hood, "That one has an injured wing and, when he starts running, he'll do so in a circle. Just by standing in the right spot you'll have an advantage… just like in a fight," explained hood as he went on, "That one in the corner; he seems to be the leader of the pack. Male cuccos are prone to have a certain number of females following them. Is said male is captured, the females become way more vulnerable… What I mean Link is that you need to plan a strategy, focusing on your virtues and defects, else you'll be starting on the wrong foot,".

Link nodded and started to observe the cuccos in a more focused way.

"want to give it another go?" Asked Hood, and a cheerful Link replied "Of course! You don't think I'd give up so easily… After all, the destiny of all Hyrule depends on this," Jokes aside, he was a bit right.

Hood grabbed the clock… "Ready? Set… GO!"

This time, Link was focused. It took him only two second to choose his target. He went after the most oblivious bird and grabbed it from behind, it didn't have time to even try to peck at him before it was put into the little cage. Link went to one of the sides, flanking the cucco that could only see with one eye and swiftly grabbed him and carefully threw it into the cage.

"Well done young friend, now you're using your head. You've got a lot of time ahead of you and only three left," Said Hood while clapping loudly with both hands.

Link found the limping bird, curiously enough it didn't fight back, since the boy approached calmly and held it softly and likewise put it into the cage, without earning any pecking from it.

After seeing this, Hood smiled and said "Well done lad, better use brains rather than brawn. Only two more to go and you still have a whole minute of time. Take it slow,".

Link saw the bird with the broken wing. He scared it and, as expected, it started running in a circle which led directly to where Link was standing and to its obvious capture. Though it didn't go down quietly since it managed to peck at the boy a couple of times, but only his hands. Link put it into the cage and went after his last prey; though none of them seemed an easy target. So, the boy started screaming wildly and started walking towards the cuccos, cornering them. Suddenly one of them clucked and turned around. Link grabbed it and, to his surprise, it had laid three eggs! The young fellow put the animal into the cage, managing his objective at last.

"Congratulations! You passed with flying colors… and with a bonus!" Said Hood cheerfully as he pointed towards the freshly laid eggs, "Now we have something for tomorrow's lunch!" he then added.

Link laughed relieved at his achievement and the release of his prior frustration. The old man, who seem to have noticed that, said "Something else that you can learn from all of this is to be tolerant with frustration. A good leader has to be able to bear to be defeated," Hood did a small pause to ponder on his words and as he scratched his beard he added "He who never loses will never be the better rival. On the contrary, he's the most vulnerable one. He doesn't know the bitterness of defeat and how to cope with it. Losing many times makes us stronger and being able to bear that makes you a better leader. You should keep that in mind young man, you won't always win throughout your life,".

"I think I've lost enough… I've never met my parents, I don't even know who they are; I've lost my memories and it hasn't been that long since I've lost my dearest Epona," said link a bit disheartened and, looking up, he added "I believe it's time I win some! I don't pretend to be selfish, obviously,".

Hood shared his point of view and said "If you say so, it's time… Should we go on with today's training?".

"Of course!" answered the animated youngster as he freed the birds from the cage.

"You've got to catch ten in five minutes," and as he grabbed the clock he said "Ready? Set, go!".

Link started to apply strategy to his hunting. One by one the animals were going into the cage. Hood kept track of the time and encouraged him from outside the pen. Soon, the ten cuccos were into the little cage. Then, Hood asked for fifteen in eight minutes, which Link managed with almost a minute to spare.

"Well… last one. How many cuccos are there? Two… four… and those three make seven… plus those five… and then its fourteen… sixteen plus those four…" and rising his voice said "TWENTY! You have to catch the twenty of them!".

"Cool! How long do I have?" Asked the boy.

"As long as it takes… I don't care. Take it as an extra lesson. Sometimes, things don't take a set amount of time. In those cases, time is not important. Just the better you do it, the better it is,".

"And how do I know when I'm getting better if I have no timeframe?" asked the boy.

"This time, I guess the number of pecks you receive should do. The less you take, the better you are," answered a smiley Hood "Anyway, I'll take your timings and when we do this again, we'll see if you're getting faster or not. But, as you learnt on our first day the importance of the balance between fear and stupidity, attitude and recklessness, today you'll learn the importance of balance between time and efficiency,".

Link listened attentive, the old spoke so seriously and at the same time his words were so precise, so easy to understand. The ability he had to turn his thoughts to simple words was incredible. It showed that Hood was a born teacher.

"It is important that do it fast, but you don't have to risk it going wrong for doing it fast. That's where balance is. As effective as possible, in the least time possible... That is, Link, what I'm asking you to achieve... Are you ready?". Asked the old man.

The youngster hopped a couple of times in place, swinging his arms and feet a bit.

"I'm ready," he said.

"Perfect, then... Set, GO!" answered the old man.

Link trained for an extra two hours that afternoon. He took nine minutes and a half on the first try and from there, his times improved. Nine minutes twenty five seconds, nine minutes twenty... Nine twelve... Nine eight... Nine three... Eight minutes fifty five seconds... Eight fifty two.

"Eight minutes and fifty seconds... Time to leave. You're already tired, from here on you'll only get worse timings and that would be pointless," said the old man while he observed the watch, "it would bring you down and the times wouldn't show your true potential. So, this is it. Today, your best record was twenty cuccos in eight minutes and fifty seconds. An excellent mark!" claimed Hood while patting the back of the youngster who was slowly recovering his breath. He thanked the old man with a thumb up.

They were both on the way back to the hut when suddenly...

"Can you smell that?" asked the young lad.

The old man, as he heard the boy, started to pay attention to what his nose was telling him.

"Sulfur... They're here," said Hood as his face turned "Link, this is what we'll do, I need you to trust me and do what I ask, as I ask you to do it. You can't doubt me for one second. Can I trust you?" told the old man to the youngling.

Link still trying to catch on with what was going on answered "I don't understand, what's going on? What...".

"No, Link, No questions now. Can I trust you'll do whatever I ask you to?". Interrupted the old man.

92

He nodded and so Hood explained what they would do.

"You'll go in through the back window. Search my backpack for a little dagger with a cerulean sphere in its center. Grab it and wait for my go. I'll storm the front door, pretending not to know what's going on and buy you some time,".

Link was pale, but trusted the old man.

"I'll do as you ask," he answered, eyes wide open.

"I wouldn't ask you to do anything bad for anyone. Trust me, even if it seems that way. I'll explain later in detail," said the old man, calming the kid down.

With a slight nod, both men got moving. The younger when behind the house and the elder stayed near the front door. Another nod was their "ready" sign and…

"ASTOR!!! My friend! I'm home!! Link went on his own to se Braulio!" Hood stormed into the hut.

In the room, two beings were holding Link's uncle hostage and stood there, watching the old man. One of them held Astor by his back with a knife at his throat. The other, was standing right beside them with his blade sheeted and his hand over it.

"If you don't want him to die, give us the stone," said the decrepit thug who held the sturdy man with the mustache, popping out from behind, showing his red eyes and a bit of his face.

Their skin was dry and opaque and they both looked rather skinny.

"Stone? I don't know what you're talking about…" said Hood as he slowly moved towards the corner where a sword was hanging on the wall.

"We know you've got the Ocarina, hand it over," interrupted the other one.

Link was hiding behind the bedroom's door, which led directly to the room with the men, listening carefully while he waited for his time to act.

Hood continued "I don't have an Ocarina. I don't know what you're talking about, we're only farmers,".

The old man had the sword right behind him.

The demon that was holding Astor smiled, "If you won't tell me, you'll tell him," and right then, he bit the neck of Astor, sinking his teeth in. Both men eyes where white and started shaking.

Hood didn't waste the chance, grabbed the sword and lounged towards the other demon as he screamed "NOW Link! Stick the dagger in Astor's arm!".

Link heard this, he doubted for a moment and, though he knew he couldn't, he wanted to ask the old man if he was crazy. But he only had time to react. So, he trusted the old man and did what he asked, sinking the dagger in Astor's left arm as he asked him to forgive him while doing so.

Meanwhile, Hood had managed to reduce the other demon which was now lying on the floor and was now heading towards his friends.

Link observed how Astor and the demon stopped shaking. The dagger's gem went from cerulean to black, as if someone dropped ink in a bowl of clear water.

The body of the demon who attacked the blacksmith fell to the ground and both men held Astor, to stop him from falling too.

"Bring me some bandages and a wet cloth," said in a calm tone the old man.

Link hurried to fetch what was required from him. At his return, the old man grabbed the dagger and removed it from Astor's arm. "Quickly Link, wrap the wound with the cloth," he said.

Link tended to his uncle and he opened his eyes.

"Sorry, I almost ruin everything," said a weakened Astor.

Hood couldn't stay silent "Are you mad? Why are you asking for forgiveness? Everything went well. Let's put you on the bed,".

With Link's help, Hood put Astor onto a more comforting place.

"Don't touch the dagger boy, it still has a demon in it," said the old man as soon as he saw the young lad observing the sharp blade up close.

"Ok Hood, now I'm going to need an explanation," said Link, eyes fixed on the old man.

"And you'll get them, but first…" said Hood as he headed towards Astor and began healing his arm, "for starters, thanks for not doubting me and not asking questions,".

"It's not like I didn't want to," answered Link.

"I know, but you didn't," said Hood with a smile wide across his face "Astor. Do you thing you can handle this yourself while we deal with that?" he asked while pointing towards the two dead demon bodies.

Astor replied "Go… and while you're at it, explain everything to the kid," and started to bandage his own arm.

Hood headed to the door, and turned around "Come with me Link,".

He went after him, quietly, and they walked to the granary. Hood seemed to be thinking about what happened. How to explain everything that was going on.

Link was simply waiting for the old man to say something.

"Grab that shovel and follow me," said Hood. Link complied without hesitation, "Here. We must dig a hole, not too deep. We won't need to bury them, the hole is for burning them,".

Hood seemed distant, as if talking about things that were never alive to begin with. Nonetheless, the kid started digging while going over what happened in the hut in his head. That's when Hood started talking.

"What a shame those poor people… If only they didn't become so vulnerable,".

Link heard him and without understanding his words let out a shy "Beg your pardon?".

And the old man replied "You see, Link, those people died a long time ago. What we saw were demons. Those posses the weaker ones. Not physically, of course, but spiritually… When faced with extremely frightful situations the spirit is left weakened and it's easy to lose control of the body if a demon posses it," Hood paused, while wiping his forehead and went on as he shoveled dirt "For a while, the spirit is trapped inside the body and the demon torments it. Then, the demon takes full control and there's no turning back. If the demon dies, so does the person he possessed,".

Link rose his head and asked "Is that why Astor was possessed?".

Hood nodded "Astor was worried about you; me; risking the plan; the ocarina and who knows what other kind of worries he had going on… That made him an easy target,".

"I don't know what the ocarina is, but tell me something, how is it that the dagger helped him?" asked Link.

"That dagger is a special one that I got a long time ago and, in due time, you'll get your own one. For now, it's the only one we've got and what it does is absorb the demon out of whoever you stab with it. If it didn't consume too much of the person possessed, then it's possible to save him, if you stab him in a non-lethal place, that is," said the old man as he kept on shoveling dirt out of the hole. "If the demon has full control over the person, we'll get to trap the demon and take it out of the possessed body, releasing the trapped spirit while doing so but, obviously, the person would die as well,".

The young lad was trying to comprehend how the whole deal worked, though it seemed to be confusing.

"Also, a body that was possessed can be possessed again. The thing is, there are two kind of demons; dead ones and oppressed. The oppressed are those that you just saw. The dead demons are those which possess a body AFTER it has died. Not every dead person can be possessed, only those that have been possessed while they were alive,".

As soon as he heard this, Link dropped everything and rushed towards the hut.

"Easy boy! Come back here!" screamed Hood.

A frightened Link replied "But my uncle is in there with two monsters that could come back any minute now!".

"I promise that nothing will happen, let me finish my explanation and grab that shovel, this hole will not dig itself," said Hood, while pointing towards the muddy shovel on the ground

"As I was saying, only those possessed while alive can be possessed once they're dead. But only by the same demon that did before. When a demon dies it is sent to another dimension, which is really hard to escape from… It's almost impossible for a "dead" demon to come back to life. Anyway, and out of respect for the persons they once were, we burn the bodies, so that they cannot be possessed once again,".

"And why are we digging? I mean, isn't enough with burning them?" asked the young boy.

"We will, my friend. But we won't do it in the open. We don't want some curios fellow coming close. Imagine, not even the sanest person would be at peace if we say something like "don't worry, we're just burning demons" don't you think?" said the old man.

"Oh, I get it. We dig the hole, cover with leaves, burn the bodies and cover them with dirt," deduced Link.

Both men finished digging the hole, brought the bodies, covered them with leaves…

"I can do this, if you're not ready," said Hood.

"No. Sooner or later I'll have to gather the courage," said Link unwavering.

The kid grabbed a stick, damped it in oil to make a torch out of it, lit it on fire and threw it into the hole.

"May the spirit of the woods be with you," said the old man, standing next to the pyre.

Both watched the fire burn. Not saying another word, they finished up, covering the ashy hole with dirt and went into the hut. Silence reigned supreme in the room, Astor was making dinner but only the sound of utensils and cooking pots was sounding. Hood was sitting in front of the fire, brooding. Link just like Hood, but at the window, sight lost in the pile of dirt a few meters away from the hut.

Then, the boy broke the ice. "So what's up with the dagger?".

Hood answered without turning his sight from the fire, as if he was expecting that question "Wherever you stab that dagger,

97

while containing a demon, is where the demon will head to. If you stick it into a piece of wood, it will rot, but the demon will be trapped in it. And if then you burn that wood, the demon will burn with it. Just like it's doing the one that attacked your uncle,".

Link turned from the window and observed that Hood wasn't lost in the fire. He had his eyes set on one particular log, which burned with a blue flame that came from the sulfur that was burning.

"But if you burn it… can it come back?" asked Link.

"Just like good spirits are immortal, so are the bad ones. They're energy. Some stick to the light out of their own choice. Others, try to escape the darkness," said Hood and then, as he turned towards Link, he went on "A lot of sacrifices, fear and black magic is needed to bring demons to this dimension… And that is precisely what Ganondorf is doing. It took him long enough, but it seems that this kind of demons will be more frequent with time,".

"Well, that's enough for today. Now we eat and think of other, more positive, stuff. If it's all the same to you,". Said the Stocky uncle.

"Of course, Astor. You had enough for today," said Hood scratching his head and standing up to help lay the table.

"Sorry uncle. Let's talk about tomorrow's training," said link switching subjects "Are we going to throw assassin watermelons? Shave rabid Sheep? Walk over hot coal?" Added Link mocking the old man as his laughter lifted the moods.

"No, tomorrow we'll ride for a while," answered Hood smiling back at the boy with a mysterious look on his face.

CHAPTER 7

THE YOUNG ARCHER

The following day, Link got woken up by the house's noice. Eyes squinted, he could see Hood moving from one side to the other, packing up stuff. Astor was cooking, as usual, but it seemed to be a lot of cooking, way too much for just breakfast. So, the youngster sat up quickly if not a bit worried.

"Everything cool here?" He asked.

"Yep, don't worry, as soon as you're fully awake, start packing up your stuff. No need to hurry though, but we're leaving for a while," Answered Hood without paying much attention.

"We're leaving? But… Where to?" enquired the young man.

"We're setting off to Hyrule, my young friend. Or, at least, towards where most of the hylians are. If we stay too long in one place, we'll become easy targets. Soon they'll find out that those sent for the ocarina are not coming back. Those ignorant are looking for something I can't give them," explained the man with the grey beard, "and, once that happen and they come looking, we won't be here anymore," he added, while blinking an eye at the boy.

Link threw himself back and stretched loudly. Still lying in the bed, he cracked his fingers and claimed loudly "Well! Time to get up!" speaking to himself.

He went towards the water pump with the big empty bowl under it, cranked the lever a couple of times and the water started pouring out. At the beginning, it was brownish, but eventually it became clear. The youngster stuck both hands under the stream and threw a huge handful of water onto his face.

"I have to go empty the tanks," said while pointing to the door with his thumb. He headed out and made his way to the latrine which was near the granary. Once he went back into the hut, he claimed "Ahhh!!! Now I feel like I was born again!".

The old man didn't seem to care, but Astor muttered loudly

enough so that everyone could hear him "Couldn't be any more of an animal,". Hearing this, Link let a little smile out and started to pack up.

Hood pat Astor in the back as he passed by "I'm going to bring the horses. Need anything from over there?".

As he dried his hands with his apron he answered "I've already secured two horses to the carriage that was into the granary and left a couple little cages to put some cuccos into them. We still need to put the seats onto the other two horses, tie the goat to the carriage and lastly choose which cuccos we're not eating to hand over to Braulio,".

"Excellent, then I'm off to complete those chores," offered Hood and then turned over to speak to Link "Once you're done packing, come help me with the horses. I'm going to take the remaining cuccos to Braulio first. I think you'll be done here by the time I get back,".

"Got it, no problem, I wrap this up and be right there with you," said the lad as he signaled towards his backpack with his head.

The old man lef the hut, went on his way to the cuccos pen and, carefully, put half of the birds into a cage with wheels that looked kind of like a cart with bars. Enjoying the morning sun and despite the cold, usual in winter, Hood heads calmly to the house of the owner of the wild goats. The old man seemed nostalgic, like he was remembering old times. He watched the trees, the fields of grass, the fences that separated each property and every animal that was moving around. Soon, he was at Braulio's door.

He knocked twice and immediately Braulio was checking through the door's portkey. He came out and invited the old man in. He rejected kindly such invitation, explaining the reason for their hasty departure. Briefly told him about the previous day events and also let him know about where they would be heading, without much detail, of course. After this, they both shook hands, both gentlemen greeted goodbye and the grey bearded man returned to the hut.

Once there, Link greeted him with a smile.

"I hope you don't mind that I started without you," said the lad while showing him that one of the horses had the saddle on and the other one was halfway through.

"Of course not, boy," answered the old man as he pat his back, "I'll bring the goat and tie it to the carriage," he added as he left.

Once back, he tied the animal to the back of the carriage using a threaded rope. Then, he got into the carriage and pulled a package, "Here, Link. I know that it's a bit rustic, but I believe it can become useful in today's training,".

The young man took the package, but before opening it, he couldn't avoid asking "Today's training?".

"Yes, and also, here's your own quiver," said the old man, pointing to the package, still closed.

"Thank you, Hood," said the lad, hugging the old man.

"You're welcome. But in fact, I'm giving you this because in the last two months of training we might had used the bow two… three times at most. And we always used mine… I'm tired of having to borrow it to you!" Joked the old man.

Both men laughed and Link couldn't keep his curiosity at bay.

"And… how are we going to do today's training?" he asked.

To what the old man answered "On horseback. I'll tell you which are the targets and you'll try to shoot them down as we go. Some of them while trotting other galloping and some at full blown race. You'll see how fun that is!".

"Ok… but, what if I lose the arrows?" Link asked.

The old man looked at him… and only smiled.

"Good thing about arrows… you can almost always go for them and get them back… Probably, some of them will break, but I hopefully not all of them. They should last until we can restock," said the old man.

Link thought about what Hood told him and answered "you're right about that," and turning towards the hut's door screamed "Uncle!! Look at what Hood gave me!".

At that time, Astor came out of the hut. He wasn't wearing his apron, but a garment similar to the one Hood gave Link the day after they met. The only difference was the color and, obviously, the size. Instead of moss green it was almond brown and on top of it all, a big tunic, the same color, but a couple shades darker that covered him from head to toes. From his belt many fabric balls were hanging. He held a package in one hand, full of what seemed to be food for about a week and in the other, tied together with a piece of cloth, three swords.

"We have to be ready for anything, no?" said Astor as he headed towards the carriage.

"You mean the swords or the food? Because last time I checked, the last station of Hyrule's big encampment is less than a week away…" Said Hood, laughing.

"Thing is, he eats as much as three persons!" joked Link.

"It's good that you're not hungry. More for me," said Astor with a smile wide across his face.

"Don't be like that. We were teasing you," said Hood.

"Please uncle! Don't starve us to death!!" begged Link on his knees and hands together, enacting a praying man.

"Mmm…. I don't know. I'll think about it," answered the stocky man as he tossed both packages into the carriage.

"Very well… it's time," claimed the old man "I'm going to get my backpack. Someone has something that want to get from the hut? We won't be seeing it for a long time…".

"Not me. I already got everything out," answered Link.

"I'm all set, but check if I didn't leave anything that can rot in the pantry. In time, I want to come back home and wouldn't like to see it filled with rats and flies," said Astor.

"Don't be exaggerated! I'll go get my stuff and check out while I'm at it," answered Hood, as he entered the hut.

It wasn't even two minutes before he was out, but once he did, Link was already on a Horse, equipped with his bow and quiver strapped to his back. Astor was sitting onto the carriage's little bench, reins in hand. Hood, who was holding a linen sack on his hand, closed the door, put a lock in it and walked to the young lad.

"Here Link, this is for you," said the old man.

"But… it's empty," he claimed, surprised.

"For now," answered the old man, with a malicious grin on his face.

"I don't like how this looks… and even less with the face he made," commented Link, as he put the sack as a backpack, since it had a handle that went though it's side.

The old man went to his horse and, with a slight hop he managed to get onto it without a fuss.

"Not bad for a man my age, right?" the old man flattered himself, and with a slight kick to the horses back he added "Let's get moving people," and the horse started it's walk.

The three man rode for a while without speaking. They all seemed to be thinking about everything that happened. Suddenly, as always, the young lad broke the silence.

"Is it going to be a quiet ride or will we cross some other guys like those from yesterday?" said Link.

"Good question. Honestly Link, it's a possibility, but I think that we shouldn't worry. After all, now we're ready to defend ourselves," said the old man reaching to his dagger which hanged from his belt "and, since we're speaking of readiness, don't you think we should start today's training session? Today you have to shoot arrows while moving." He added.

"Sure. Why not?" answered Link.

"Great idea! Some training for the trip!" Added a thankful Astor.

"Well, first thing you've got to do is secure the reins to the saddle," started explaining Hood and Link obliged "Nice. Now get a good grip on the bow… remember your lessons and don't forget to put your hands the right way. We'll start with some east targets,".

The lad grabbed his bow with determination and took an arrow and armed. He took a deep breath and focused.

"I want you to hit that pinecone that's hanging from that tree, the one about thirty meters away from you," said Hood as he pointed the pine that was ahead.

Link aimed, held his breath and loosed. The arrow missed for about twenty centimeters.

"Almost," coughed out Astor, mocking him.

Link looked at him, rabid. "Quickly Link, you've got to find the arrow and bring it back. That includes getting down and up again from the horse… and it won't stop moving," said Hood.

He got down from the horse and ran to look for the arrow, as he did, he realized that this training could be tiring after a while and, added the frustration of not hitting the target, it could become the most annoying activity for a trip, not to forget that Astor would make a comment every time he missed a shot.

Right then, while contorting his face, the lad thought "How I wish we were there already…".

It seemed as if the old man could read his mind since he said "Easy boy. Take a couple more seconds to secure the target and remember that overcoming frustration is a quality fitting for a leader,".

Hood words didn't sway Link from being angry at missing the first shot, but they succeeded at preventing Link from wanting to quit training. The lad ran back to the horse, and got onto the saddle with a swift jump.

"Let's try again but with that pinecone over there," said Hood, choosing a new target.

Link stood still; felt the horse's walk and assimilated it into his own swing, to avoid any interference with the arrow's trajectory. Took a deep breath and released the arrow.

"Beginner's luck…" said Astor as the arrow hit the target.

"IN YOUR FACE, MOUSTACHO!" said Link overflowing with happiness.

"I wouldn't claim victory just yet. It was a nice shot, but you still have to recover the arrow," said Hood while he raised his eyebrows and looked at Link sideways "matter of fact, while you're at it, why don't you put that pinecone in the linen sack that I gave you?" smiled ironically the old man.

"You've got to be kidding me. Do I have to gather everything that I hit?" asked the lad, knowing already the answer.

Hood just stared at him.

104

"No, you're not kidding," accepted Link.

"Don't worry, I'll get them for you," said Hood grinning "Of course you'll pick them up. They're your preys, not mine!" concluded the old man.

"This is going to be tough," said Link as he got down from the horse and trotted to his target.

"The hero's mettle doesn't form up in a day. What did you expect three months ago when I told you I was going to train you?" said Hood.

Hours went by, slowly and painfully to Link. The had eaten a few sandwiches barely getting off their horses, since Hood only gave a one-hour break to the lad.

Four days went by, Link kept training, more successfully each day. They all stopped three times a day to eat the meals that were into the carriage. They slept, got up and continued on their way. Soon the sun of the fifth day started to hide amongst the clouds and the tree-tops and sight became difficult. The lad had his sack filled with pinecones of every size. Some earned while trotting, others galloping and also some at full speed. The old man even made him stand on the horse and, in the most extreme cases, once there, jump and shot. Link could only hit one target like this, but that lonely pinecone, acquired with a jumping shot, gave the young man the confidence he needed, the joy that over-came after defeating his frustration. It was only once he got tired of hearing how Link boasted at Astor about his achievement that Hood decided to set a last target.

"I hit it! And Mustacchio can't say a thing!" sang Link filled to the brim with joy with his arrow crossed pinecone in one hand and pointing to his uncle with the other.

"Link…" called Hood

"I hit it, I hit it…" went on the singing lad.

"Link…" insisted the old man.

"How's laughing now eh?" teased the lad who was so close to his uncle that didn't pay attention to the grey bearded man.

"LINK!" yelled Hood, as he made sure that this time the youngster heard him "you're not done yet…".

The lad turned around astonished and jokingly said "Come on man… What do I have to do now? Jump while I do a barrel-roll, eyes closed, and hit an acorn?" he asked, arms wide open "although… I don't think I need to close my eyes since it's gotten really dark since the clouds set in,".

"Last target. It's three times larger than a pinecone and you can do it walking…" said the old man.

"Piece of cake," answered Link.

"Don't be too hasty to celebrate kid. When will that bad habit of yours wash away? Anyway, as I was saying, the target is three times as large and you are on steadier ground, but this time, your target is our dinner," declared Hood.

"What?!" questioned a clearly outraged Astor, "You're going to leave something as important as our food in the hands of a rookie pinecone-hunter?" Now I'm seriously worried about your decision-taking abilities my friend," Joked the stocky man on the carriage.

Hood smiled and went on, "Yes, I'm willing to take that risk,".

"Don't worry, you'll see I'll manage without troubles," replied the confident lad.

"Yeah… for tomorrow's dinner," Astor mocked at him.

"Well Link, soon we'll be arriving at a stream. Once there, we'll look for a place with tall grass and bushes to get some cover from the wind and enough grass for our horses. After that, Astor and I will look for some logs and, with the pinecones in your sack, we'll lit a bonfire to cook whatever you hunt for us. Everyone on board?" Said the old man, as he awaited confirmation.

"Yessir!" Link smiled.

"You're the boss my friend," said Astor.

A couple of minutes went by and the three of them stopped on the shore of a stream. On the horizon, the sun was going down, showing that only a few minutes of daylight were left. Luckily, the sky had cleared from the clouds that were covering so heavily before.

"We'll tie our horses here while you carry out your quest," said Hood to Link while he strapped his horse to a tree and it started to drink a bit of water from the stream.

Astor did the same with the horse that was pulling from the carriage. Link handed his reins over to Hood and took his bow and arrow onto his hands.

"Well… I'm off, got to take advantage of the dying light,". The young man said.

He entered into the wilderness, a few meters away from the road. He went forward with his sight fixed to the ground as he tried to remember some of the stuff that Hood taught him from time to time during lunch time.

"So, I have to move as slow as possible. If I find some animal footprints, I can figure out it's species and approximate size, even if it's running or calmly walking. Little mounts with holes are burrows, I could find a hare or two near them" he went on in his mind.

Around twenty minutes went by when the lad saw, with as little light as remained, a couple of tiny hare footprints. He kneeled and touched them with his fingertips, "They seem fresh," he thought, and started following the set of prints that were lying ahead.

A few minutes went by and in the distance the youngster heard a chilling howl "Wolves? I have to hurry or I'll go from hunter to pray," he said to himself.

Not five minutes after, he saw afar, covered by the roots of a big tree, a gray mane of hair. A big hare was biting on a branch. Link aimed cautiously "Fast and painless," he thought. He didn't wish to see the creature suffer. He let loose and, with a sharp whistle, the arrow cut through the air and hit its target.

"Well… it was easier than I thought," bragged to himself the young man. He walked to his pray and grabbed it.

"Well isn't this my lucky day. I found food and a prisoner all at the same time," said a deep voice.

The youngster rose his sight and, to his surprise, the tip of a sword was not even an inch away from his face.

"On your feet," demanded the skinny man, with pale skin and red, opaque, eyes.

Link slowly got up, prey in hand. Thoughts were rushing into his head. Run away, attack, obey, scream for help or keep silence.

Suddenly, out of thin air, the sharp blade of a sword came from the demon's chest, running it through, as a brown leather glove covered its mouth. The eyes of the demon rolled up and it started to shake wildly. Once it stopped, the possessed man regained some consciousness and, with its last breath, muttered something that Link took as a thanking of sorts.

The body fell on the ground and the young bowman saw a dark shape, which concealed its face with its arm and was covered from head to toes. With a voice that, to Link guess, was forced, it claimed "It's a pity but, believe me, not even your friend's dagger could have saved this one,".

"Who are you?" the words escaped Link's mouth.

"I'm the one who saved your life. That's all I'm saying," answered the mysterious person, "now go. I'll deal with the body. Don't try to follow me,".

Link, once again, words escaping from him said "But..." but he was cut short "Bear with me for a second young archer. You carry a bow, but no arrow, which gives me an edge since we're in close quarters. If I wanted you dead, you would already be. So, I'm not an enemy. I'm just asking that you head back with your hunting party. You'll know who I am eventually and you will realize why I can't tell that to you now,".

The mysterious figure started to walk forward carefully, wielding its sword towards Link, who only managed to take three steps back. It kneeled, grabbed the dead demon body, put it over its shoulder and said "I'll only tell you that our path will cross in many opportunities. After all, it's not the first time, nor the last, that I save the life of Link from Hyrule,". After that, the figure walked away slowly.

Link didn't understand what was going on. His mouth was open but no words were coming out of it. For a few seconds, the lad stood still as a statue. Suddenly he looked down and looked at the hare in his hand. He was in one piece, but in barely three minutes his luck went from good to bad, to good again and, now, uncertain. Still shocked for what happened and with the silent savior still wondering on his mind, Link took a few seconds to start walking again towards the encampment. Once he did, the figure was nowhere to be seen nor heard. Link headed towards where the horses were tied and realized that he had gotten quite far since it took him about fifteen minutes, on a steady rhythm, to reach the stream. On the lad's head there were only questions banging against his skull. "Who the hell was that guy? Why did he save me? How did he know that I had a party with me? When did he save me before? Maybe… was it before I lost my memories? How does he know he'll do it again? He must've been bluffing. Could he be my father? Why did he take the corpse? Did he know the person that was possessed?" were some of the questions running through his mind. But sadly, none of them had any shred of an answer.

"Look who's back!" said Astor in such a loud voice that shook consciousness back into Link's body "And it seems its mission accomplished!".

Hood didn't say anything, he just watched the lad. Link didn't say anything either, but his gaze was lost.

"Wow! Such brooding! Seems you run out of cockiness for today…" said Astor "Are you ok, Link?" he asked as he realized that something odd was going on.

Link's eyes met the old man's and started to suspect that Hood was sniffing something from the get go.

"I don't know, ask Hood. I feel he knows," said Link without beating around the bushes.

An awkward silence took over the place. Link was standing there, hare in hand, serious but no emotions came from his face. Hood, less than three meters away, sitting in front of the fire, gazing back but silent, and it seemed that it was going to keep that way. Astor eyes juggled from one to the other, but none looked back at him. The tension was earth-shattering.

"Well, if the old man isn't going to speak, I will," said Link "The thing is, I caught a hare and a demon came out of nowhere," Link started to walk towards his partners as he spoke "but it doesn't end there, obviously. From the same nowhere it came out, some dude did also. He stabbed the demon right on its heart with a sword. But wait, that's not all, this guy covered his face and told me that he knew me and that I should come back to you guys. How did he know about us? Who was he? Why did he save me? I have no clue, but something tells me that you do!" said Link staring straight into Hood eyes "I could have died for this stupid hare!" he yelled as he threw it on the ground amongst his companions "but, I'm convinced that you knew that I wasn't going to die. That I was going to come back and that I needed to see that," Link did a short pause, as giving up, tired of a situation that goes on and on forever "You know what, hood? What's really bothering me is not that I have to go through these lessons of yours but that, with all your cloak and dagger methods, I believe that you don't trust me at all,"

"Don't you dare think such a stupidity!" the lad was interrupted by Hood, who got up in a split second.

"Even if you don't believe it, I'm putting the life of my friends, my own, even my family's life, into your hands!" said Hood, leaving Link with his mouth wide open, unable to speak.

"I understand that all these uncertainties might bother you and, if I'm hiding some information, it's not because I want to, but because it's necessary. You can't toy lightly with time," right then, Hood stopped and opened his eyes wide as if he had said something he shouldn't have.

In Link's head, his words sounded heavy, leaving one question. What did he mean with "toy with time"?

"Look, Link, hear me out. Let's eat what you hunted, speak about something else, rest up and tomorrow, on out why to Hyrule's encampment, I'll tell you a bit more about your… my… our mission. You see, it's not something that can be explained in a few minutes… I promise I'll fill you in on many useful things, but in return I'll ask for something," said the old man.

110

"What? What do you want?" Asked an anxious and barter ready Link.

"Tomorrow, Link... I'll ask you to trust me on more time. Can you do that?" asked the old man.

"As long as this is not some weird kind of diversion... I guess I can wait for a couple more hours," said the lad, looking upwards, one eyebrow raised, not fully convinced with what he agreed to.

"Well then, let me cook this," said Astor as he grabbed the hare from the ground and then headed towards the stream to clean it up.

Hood patted Link on his shoulder and said "Demon and rescuer business aside... How was the hunt? Did it work out easily?".

"I don't know. Tracking it was the more time-consuming part... But I followed the footprints... Basically I did everything as you taught me," Link answered.

"Well, that seems good enough. As I can see, you only used one arrow, so I believe it was quick and painless," said the old man, as if that was really important.

"As I said, EVERYTHING as you taught me," said Link, a bit annoyed about having to repeat himself, "That includes the ending. Honestly, I don't want the animal to suffer either, Hood,".

The two men, now more relaxed, went near Astor who was spicing the hare, now hanging from some twigs near the fire. He finished up his chore, pulled out some vegetables and, handing a knife to each of his partners, he asked them to cut them. The three teamed-up and in about an hour, they had had dinner already.

"It was really tasty Astor," said Hood.

"Yeah, cooking is really your thing. Didn't you ever think about quitting blacksmithing and opening up a restaurant?" asked Link, laughing as he said it.

The three men laughed about Link's joke. "Maybe once all this Ganondorf and company stuff I will!" answered Astor.

"That's optimistic. Do you think we will be done soon?" asked Link.

"Ganondorf has his days numbered. The best man I've ever known is training the best lad I know," said the man with the big moustache looking towards Hood and Link.

"Seriously, I'd love to know how did you two meet each other," said Link, frustrated as he knew he would not get his answer.

"Rest up, Link. Tomorrow I'll tell you a tale about your ancestors that will give sense to your future… To the future of all of us. Tomorrow, I'll tell you about the Ocarina of Time," said Hood as he lay down to sleep.

Link wanted to ask, but he was exhausted. So, he threw himself back on the ground and stared at the sky. It was a bit clearer than before and a lot of stars could be seen.

The view in the countryside was lovely, but little time did Link have to take it in since he, tired by the long day, closed his eyes and fell in a deep sleep.

CHAPTER 8

THE OCARINA OF TIME

"Wake up nephew, it's time to continue with our journey," said Astor as he shook, subtlety, the young bowman.

"Is it morning already? Boy did I sleep well," replied Link as he sat up.

"Here boy," said Hood while he offered the lad a cup of hot tea and a piece of bread from the carriage supply.

"Thanks Hood... Wow! It's really hot!!" Link said as he had a sip and burned his tongue.

"Well... yes, champ, you should drink the tea while it's hot..." replied Hood, as he kept having his own.

Link slowly drank his tea and ate his piece of bread. He noticed that Hood and Astor had practically packed everything away and were getting ready to move out. Hood was covering the remaining embers with wet soil from the stream's shore and Astor was checking the reins and saddles on the horses and checked that the carriage was in good condition to keep going. Link stood up and helped with the remaining chores. He washed the little pots used for the tea in the stream and put it into the carriage with the rest of the stuff that was used for breakfast and soon the three of them where ready to continue on their way.

"Well, hylians... ready or not, here we go!" said an enthusiastic Hood and, with a little bump at the side of his horse, the march begun.

For a couple of minutes, no-one spoke. Link, who didn't forget about the old man promise from the past day, coughed twice and made some noise with his throat, signaling the old man so that this one would start speaking, as he promised.

"Have you ever heard about the Tri-force, Link?" said the old man, as he noticed his intentions.

"Not that I remember. Though, as you know, there are many things that I don't remember," answered the lad.

"Well then, I'll start from the beginning," replied Hood, and after clearing his throat, he went on "Long ago, three beings, made out of pure energy and known as "goddesses" appeared in this world, molding it. The mythical divinities are known as Din, the goddess of power; Nayru, goddess of wisdom and Farore, goddess of courage,".

"I don't understand why you're telling me this, but let's say that I'm curious about how this ends up in the fact that we're here. So, if you don't mind, I'll make the questions that I deem necessary," said Link, not completely convinced about where all the talk was going.

"Ask whatever you need. I, of course, have the right to not answering, if I don't want to or if I don't know the answer," answered Hood, without paying much attention to the lad's comment.

"Ok then, why goddesses and not gods?" the lad asked.

"That... That's your question? I was expecting something more meaningful... Anyway, it's because those who've seen them, describe them as feminine beings," said Hood, without going in further detail.

"Oh... just wondered. Ok, go on," replied Link.

The old man looked at Link in disbelief for a second and then continued his tale, "Well... It's believed that these goddesses abandoned our world a long time ago, leaving behind these triangular stones known as Tri-forces. As far as we know, each Tri-force gives its wielder a set of skills of the same nature as the goddess that represents it,".

"If what you say is true, I imagine that Ganondorf wants to acquire these Tri-forces," assumed the lad.

"He already has one," claimed the old man.

Link was shocked, frozen in the spot, "What did you say?".

"Can you guess which one it is?" asked the elder, without paying attention to the lad's reaction.

"I... don't. I really don't know what each of them can do," answered Link.

Hood looked at him and explained, "He has the Tri-force of Din, the goddess of power. That's why his army becomes unsto-

114

ppable when he leads them in battle and they wipe the enemy from the field. The tri-force of power gives him this unnatural strength, more than any mortal can have. Besides, his body becomes resistant to extreme temperatures. He can't be frozen nor burned no matter what it's done to him. Imagine what can a man like that be and do... Run non-stop, jump like no other, overcome any obstacle, endure incredible blows... That, my boy, is what makes him unstoppable,".

"But then... it's impossible to stop him. I mean, if he has the Tri-force of power, what chances do we have of defeating him? Asked a disheartened Link.

"You're looking at this the wrong way, Link," Astor, who was listening from the carriage, Interrupted, "The way I see it, if what makes him invincible is the Tri-force, all we need to do is take it from him. Then, he doesn't stand a chance,".

"Exactly, Astor," cut in Hood, "as your uncle says, his power is artificial. Without the Tri-force, he's nothing. That's why our final objective is to steal the stone and use it against him, before he can get the remaining two. Furthermore, the use of a Tri-force comes at a price. Even if he can use it at will, he doesn't, he only reaches for it in moments of need. Otherwise, given how long it's been since he's got it, it wouldn't be illogical that he would have acquired the remaining two stones, defeated any opposing army and we should be dead,".

"Ok, I understand... But what is it exactly that the other stones do? And, where are they?" Link questioned.

Hood smiled, "Now you're making some good questions! Initially, the Tri-force of wisdom was in the hands of a sage. A leader above the rest of the sages. As far as I know, the king of Hyrule decided to split the stone in many pieces. That way, if Ganondorf captured him, he wouldn't get all the tri-force's perks.

"And what perks are these?" wondered the lad.

"Simply put, you can dominate any kind of magic," Hood made a short pause to look at the awed face of the lad, "you see, there are some things that, as mortal beings, we don't understand. Sicknesses, emotions and even death. It's believed that this stone can defeat them,".

"WHAT?! You're saying that the Tri-force of wisdom can prevent death? Because if it's that way, I'd say it's the most powerful one… Who would want to die?" asked the young bowman.

"I wouldn't want to live forever…" said Astor.

"Neither would I," went on the old man, "anyway, there is some truth in what you say. It's possible that it's a very powerful Tri-force. Even more for someone who's well versed on the subject," Hood scratched his beard and continued "Why do I say this? Well, it's because it's believed that one of the pieces of this Tri-force is in the hands of Vaati. A sorcerer that delves, and quite proficiently I may add, the dark magic, necromancy and alchemy and it's transmutations,".

"He seems very famous… and very busy," said Link with a pinch of sarcasm in his voice.

"You see, Link, Vaati is, at this moment, the closest being to Ganondorf and, in some ways, respected by him. We believe that the sorcerer is who's providing Ganondorf with his demons and, in exchange, Ganondorf protects him… But both of them are quite ambitious. I imagine that, if Vaati gets all the pieces of the Tri-force of wisdom, he would try to steal Ganondorf of his stone… and vice versa," explained the old man.

For a brief moment, the lad remained silent. He just wondered; gaze lost in the horizon.

"What would be best… recover a whole Tri-force, or part of one?" he thought.

Link was trying to analyze and compare the options at hand. Search for the remaining pieces of the Tri-force of wisdom or search for the courage one. Right there, he realized he didn't know anything about the last one.

"And what about the Tri-force of courage?" he asked.

"My favorite one, no doubt about it," said the old man, with a joyful glimmer in his eyes "That's the stone of skill. It allows to manipulate anything. This Tri-force is the one in charge of protecting the other two. That's why it's most significant perks do not depend on mysticism and supernatural, but in the enhan-

116

cing of the best qualities of the wielder. With it on your grasp, everything comes easy for you. Decisions are spot-on; The sword moves in your hand as a fine tuned musical instrument; A shield can defend you from anything, even mosquito's bites; Your arrows don't hit a target, they hit them all; Your moves in a battle are so precise that..." Hood was telling, but Link interrupted, pointing at him, filled with awe, like an exited little kid, " I can't believe that you had the Tri-force of courage!".

"What? I didn't say that," answered Hood who, for the first time, was caught by the lad in a moment of weakness.

"Aww come on Hood, I'm not stupid. The way you speak sold you out completely,". Link claimed.

"It seems that, even the more cautious ones can screw up from time to time," Said Astor as he laughed at the old man.

"Ok, ok. It may be true that at some time I perhaps wielded the Tri-force of courage. But it was over twenty years ago, I can barely remember it," accepted Hood.

"Yeah, right..." said Link with a shrew smile on his face, "and what did you do with the stone?" he then asked.

"I used it for what it needed to be used... As will you," the old man replied.

"No! Not again! This will be another one of your mysteries, that will leave me hanging until I'm properly ready, right?" asked the young bowman.

"No, my young friend, it's not," Answered Hood, leaving the lad with his jaw on the floor, "The Tri-force of courage disappeared seven years ago. So, in a not too distant future, you will travel back in time and, together with your own self from the past, will try to find the Tri-force. Believe me, I know,". He added.

The youngster sight shifted from the old man to Astor and to Hood again.

"You sure didn't hit your head today old man? Really...Time travel? What's next, dragons maybe?" asked Link while trying to mock the old man.

"No, Link, that will be first. So, can I finish up what I was saying?" answered the old man.

"I don't know Hood. It all seems out of a fairy-tale. It doesn't make much sense," replied the lad.

"Boy, you speak of fairies as if they were frail. I can assure you they're not so kind when in a bad mood and they don't write tales as memorable as the Minish," said the old man, as if it wasn't anything out of the ordinary.

"It's settled. You suffered food poisoning and now are delirious," said the lad.

"You don't have to believe me If you don't want to. Anyway, I'll finish my tale," said Hood, dismissing the youngster's comments, "As we were, the Tri-forces. The legend says that, if you gather the three of them, you don't only get filled with a supernatural power, but also have the chance to ask for a wish to the highest deity,".

The old man paused while thinking on his words and recapture a rather skeptical Link's attention.

"It's believed that long, long, time ago, before your grandparent's grandparents were born, existed someone that managed to gather the Tri-forces and wished for an object that allowed to dominate or destroy anything, all in his quest to achieve order in his time. I guess he expected something as a magical staff or something of the sorts, but the deity granted him an ocarina, known as the ocarina of time. Technically, the deity wasn't wrong. Imagine you can control time; you can make someone not exist. You just go back in time and avoid his birth or dominate him under the threat that you could do just that," explained the old man.

"It does make sense... Although the story itself lacks credibility," said Link cutting to the chase.

"What would you say if I tell you that this person, near his life's end, wrapped the ocarina in a piece of papyrus and put it in a chest, that he hid afterwards?" Hood asked.

"I would ask if you know about this papyrus existence and what is written in it," answered Link.

"An interesting question, for which I have the right answer," doubled the old man, and went on "it's believed that many years after the chest was buried, it was found by an ancestor of the actual king of Hyrule. He took it to the sages because the writing was ancient and he couldn't read it and they revealed its contents and translated it. In short, the papyrus tales the story of how the ocarina's bearer got a hold of it through the deities and that only him, or a descendant of his bloodline, would be capable of destroying it. But to do this, the Tri-forces should be gathered once again,".

"Oh… Oooooh, right! Now I get it. I understood. Now we only need to find a descendant of the first wielder of the ocarina!" said a sarcastic Link.

Hood, without paying attention to the lad's sarcasm answered "Correct! We just need to find the Tri-forces and the heir to destroy the artefact that Ganondorf so much desires. Because he knows about it's existence,".

Link looked at him in disbelief, rose an eyebrow and asked "Anything more to add to our chore list? Let me recheck, shall I? Three stones of great power, from which, one of them is in the hands of the tyrant of the day; the other one is fragmented, of course a piece of it is in the hands of our enemy's lacky; The last one lost, seven years ago and I should travel back in time to look for it. What else? Oh right! To do this I have to find this musical instrument made of stone that allows it wielder to travel through time. I believe that's simple enough. Who doesn't have one of those in his wardrobe?" said Link as he laughed loudly before continuing "And to top it off, the heir of someone who, for all we know, can be very well dust in the wind!".

The old man looked at him and a smile showed up on his face. Link frowned and the old man said "I do know where the ocarina is… and I know the heir. As I see it, we have two out of the five items on your list. Ganondorf and his minions only have one and a bit of another,".

"What did you say? You KNOW where the ocarina is?" asked Link.

"A very dear ally of us has it," answered the old man.

"And what about the heir? Explain yourself," demanded the lad.

"You see, Link. The papyrus also explained how to recognize the heir, or his mother," explained Hood, leaving Link in even a bigger dismay, "Throughout pregnancy, in the middle of the mother's back, at the same height as her navel, a kind of a mark, bearing three little dots, appears. As the pregnancy evolves, the three dots become triangles and these, in time, form a bigger triangle altogether. This mark passes on to her child and, once he's born, he has the same mark in the back of his wrist, near the palm of the hand,".

Link looked at Astor and then turned back at Hood.

"Tell me, Link. What's underneath the bandage on your left hand?" asked the old man.

Link was frozen on the spot. It even took him a while to be able to make a sound.

"How is it that you know?" asked the lad as he grabbed his wrist, "I never take this bandage off, only my uncle knows that I have it and it was himself who told me to cover it up to avoid letting the wrong people know who I really was," Link stopped talking, reflected for a moment and told his uncle "This is what you meant. You always knew I was someone important," and Astor interrupted him, "Link, I know the legend of the bearers of the deity. In fact, I lived part of it with you. You are a bearer. I know that's a mark that makes you important and sought after at once. I also know that I cannot give you the proper protection nor teach you so that you can protect yourself properly. But I know that he can," said Astor pointing at Hood, "That's why I had to wait for him to arrive, hide you and cover all this business up. I never told you, because I didn't want you to start asking questions that I wouldn't be able to answer. Your father had to flee, obviously, because he also was a bearer of the mark, as did your mother, my sister," Astor stopped talking. Speaking of his sister seemed to be painful for him and his eyes were watery. He swallowed, hardly, and went on, before Link could say anything, "Please, boy, don't be mad at me. I only did what I thought was right to look after you, just as she asked me to... This man is the key to many answers to your questions and I believe in him,

120

more than you can imagine. I won't ask you to do the same, I don't need to. I know you will,".

"I'm sorry uncle, I didn't know that speaking about my mom would hurt you, I guess it's something we have in common,". Link moved his horse near his uncle's carriage and pat his back, "At least we're not alone, we have one another... If you say he's that important, it must be so," he said, while looking at Hood.

The old man smiled and continued with his explanation, "In the end, my young friend, that mark grants you a huge power and, also, a great burden. I know that your parents knew this and, to protect you, they had to leave you with Astor. The way I see it, you have two choices. Either look aside, live your live in hiding and, once you have kids, hide them in the same way that you were hidden. Or face your destiny and free us all from this damned tyranny,".

Link looked forward, "I guess that, if you're here, it's because there really aren't two choices, are they?" he said, smiling sarcastically, "Tell me about your ally. The one with the ocarina... Who is he? And where is he at?".

"Well, his name is Peer and it's not actually where, as it's when," said Hood.

Link looked at him and frowned again, "After all you've said, I'm not even going to be surprised anymore. Just explain yourself better,".

Hood laughed, "I told you he had the ocarina, right? Well, he'll be with you in less than a year, you'll meet him then, but once you do, you will be in for a little surprise,".

Then Link wondered, "And... I mean, if your friend has this powerful artifact with him... Why doesn't he go back in time and kills Ganondorf before he can muster his power? Or even better, why doesn't he go straight to my ancestor and destroys the ocarina at the moment of its creation?".

"Those are great ideas, pretty straightforward surely, but then you realize that time itself is so fragile that you can destroy it all," explained Hood.

Link managed only to look at Hood, eyes clenched, trying to understand what he just said.

"Let's say that you get to speak with your ancestor. To be able to speak comfortably, you ask him to sit down in a chair, where someone else was supposed to be sat, but now it's occupied by your ancestor. Suppose that this young lady, who should have sat down there, was meant to meet your ancestor and later on, be the mother of his children. But now, she won't, because you're there with him. So now you disappear and the conversation with your ancestor would never have happened. Because of that, the time resets itself and everything happens again. Now everyone would be caught up in an infinite temporal loop," explained Hood.

"Ok, my brain just bided you farewell," said Link as he scratched his head, "isn't that a bit of a complex theory?".

"Isn't time a complex construct?" asked back Hood.

"The grey bearded man scores one!" shouted Astor all the way from the carriage.

Link looked back at Astor and teased him before directing once again to Hood, "And couldn't this Peer guy travel back in time with me to the moment when the stones are together and destroy the ocarina?".

Hood took a deep breath and once again spoke, "Well, you could go back and destroy the ocarina, but if you did, you would be stuck there forever. And knowing that, since you're there, you could cause a time loop at any moment… Would you do it all the same?"

Link sighed, "you're right, it does sound risky but… Was that the only time that the Tri-force stones were put together?" he asked.

"They will once again be gathered in a near future," Hood answered.

"And why don't we go to that time?" questioned Link.

"Because if we travel forward, it won't be us who will be holding the Tri-forces," said the old man.

"You mean that it'll be us who manage to get the Tri-forces?" ask the lad.

"With any luck, I hope so," the old man replied.

"And how do you know?" insisted Link.

122

And Hood confessed "Because, in a certain way, I was already there,".

"Wooo, wooo! Hold your horses, let me see if I get this. You were in the future, stones gathered, ocarina in hand and you didn't bring them here for me to destroy them? I mean, we would've finished this ordeal over two month ago! Link wondered.

The old man started to state his answer, "If I've done that, time would have been altered in such a way that, the event that needed to happen, would never have happened and we would be in a..." but Link, cut his speech in half, "A time loop... Bla, bla, bla, bla. I know, thank you," he mocked the old man and once again enquired, "but if you where already there, tell me how the future is. Clear some questions at least,".

Once again, Hood sighed "Stubborn... my god you're stubborn! If I change anything: time-loop! If I tell you anything that might make you change the way you'd do something: time loop! If someone changes anything because of me: TIME. LOOP," Hood grabbed his forehead and went on, "Look, I want this to be over as much as you do, but the only thing I can do is guide you. The decisions will be taken by you. Time is fragile, very fragile and I learnt that there are some things that have to remain the way they are,".

"Well... at least you're at ease. Things will go as they should go," said Link.

"Well... not necessarily. Since the ocarina exists, thousands of time-trails were made and none of them is like the next one," explained Hood.

"And how do you know this?" asked Link.

"That's another story... and a long one at that," answered Hood, "I guess that, eventually, you'll get to hear it, but I doubt that you've got the time to right now since, that thing you see right there, is Hyrule's royal encampment," said Hood pointing at some logs, fashioned in the way of a wall.

The three travelers who were coming from the Ordon plains rode calmly until they reached the wall's gates. The logs were about three meters tall and, at the end of them, they were carved in the shape of a spearhead. This wooden wall continued far enough as to be lost from sight beyond the trees and far into the forest. At each side of the gate, two watch towers stood tall, over two meter above the end of the wall and, into each of them, a handful of archers were mounting guard. One of them descended through a ladder once he saw the three strangers coming. A short while after, this man and a second one climbed back up, the second one seemed to be of a higher rank than the first one, given his uniform. He was the first one to speak.

"Strangers, is there anything I can do for you?" asked out loud and perfectly clear the man.

"Yes, we wish to enter the encampment, sir," answered Hood, just as loudly.

"And who are you, gentlemen, to enter our encampment?" once again enquired the guard.

"My name, good sir, is Hood from Hyrule..." the old man answered.

Link noticed that the other bowmen started doing gestures and mumbling amongst them just as soon as Hood said his name.

And the old man went on, "I'm joined by Astor and his nephew Link, both from Hyrule as well,".

This time they weren't mumbling. Not moving either. They all looked at them with their eyes wide open.

"I believe miss Zelda has been expecting us for quite a while..." said the old man.

The doors opened briefly after. Astor and his carriage were in between of the other two men horses. Link looked at Hood, surprised, and the last one barely looked back at the lad. The old man face was filled with satisfaction and a sense of victory. Then, with a couple of little kicks to his horse, he went into the fort. Astor followed, and finally, Link went in as well. The three men were inside and the door closed behind them. Some of the soldiers and many farmers came near and ensembled a sort of hallway. Many meters of this human pathway led to a big tent set onto a wooden stage that set it about half a meter over the ground, making it noticeable over the rest of them. It was a compound tent, it had an entrance, where two soldiers with halberds were keeping guard, a central hall, square, no less than for meters long on each side, and, to each side of this hall, two more smaller rooms. It seemed like a big, sturdy, fabric-made, castle. Suddenly, a hand came through what seemed to be the door of this castle, and a blonde, long-haired, gal came out. She had her hair braided, in the shape of a crown and had two pointy ears and a pale skin, though somewhat tanned. This fair lady was wearing a garment that was somewhere in between a military and royalty one. It consisted of a tight vest, like a corset and beneath it, a brown shirt with its sleeves rolled up. Her skirt was longer on one side and was also brown, but a darker shade. In her leg, she had a kind of belt on her thigh and a couple of daggers were hanging of it. She was wearing short boots, with no heel, that exposed her true height, a bit shorter than Link. From her waist hanged a belt with a couple of leather bags and a short sheath, which probably was meant to hold a sword.

The young lady descended the four steps from the stage and came close to the travelers, who she gazed upon slowly.

"Good day, Astor," she said.

"Good day, princess," he answered, unable to hide his smile.

"Hood?" asked the lady, looking at the old man

"Correct, miss," the old man answered.

The young lady's eyes filled with tears, she looked to the side, to see the last man of the group and, as if she was unable to wait any longer, she ran off and gave the lad a big hug, "Link! You've came back!".

125

126

CHAPTER 8

VAATI

Somewhere else, not far away, two grim looking people were dragging a third one, held by his arms. Both men sported a sword, which hanged from their belts, a cuirass, two pauldrons and a pair of scout boots. Their light armor exposed their grey, dry and cracked skinned arms. Their hands, both with long fingers and broken nails, held a bruised man, who dragged his knees through a stony road which led to the entrance of a dark castle which, in other time, shone bright when the sun hit its walls. To each side of the stony road, where once green bushes filled with flowers grew, now there was only frozen, spiky, weeds.

The entrance shown the scars of war all the way from its base to the highest point. It had cracks made by huge stones and scratches made by swords and arrows. It was a double decked door, about three meters high, splintered in whichever place you looked at. Beside it, two soldiers with heavy armor were keeping guard. These soldiers' skin was barely visible, although their helms didn't cover their faces and their black and darken eyes could be seen as they watched the poor, dying, prisoner. The guards moved their pole-axes aside and the huge door opened. No one spoke. The scouts entered and their prisoner kept dragging his legs though another pathway. This time, covered in a dirty and torn red carpet. The entrance hall was dim lit, only two candlesticks burned lightly in the huge room. The men turned right and stepped through a door. They crossed an alleyway which led to a garden, where the weed had overtaken almost every possible place. Amongst the thorns and dead grass, many statues of people were standing, haphazardly through the entire courtyard, most of them with an agonic expression. Some of the statues where kneeling, covering their faces with their forearm with their mouth open, as if they were screaming; others, stood as if they tried to run away; and some stood on their feet, looking down, as if they had given up. The dying man barely lifted his head and laid his eyes on some of the stone figures. He didn't even had strength enough to offer some resistance and, with his eyes filled with tears, he looked down once again.

In the middle of the courtyard was set of spiral stairs and the three men descended through it. The prisoner left a bloody trail on his wake, as he went down. They descended about two levels, until they reached a huge room which looked like a library in the middle of a crypt.

"Put him over there," said a ghastly voice.

The greyish soldiers threw the prisoner over a rectangular block of marble, which looked like an altar. The block was covered in seals, engraved in the stone. To its side, there was a wall, with some kind of ring on it also made of stone. It looked like the hole of a watering well. The ring came about twenty centimeters off from the wall and was empty. Only the dark hole was visible and it seemed to go on forever.

On the corner of the room, the man who asked the soldiers to put the prisoner down was sitting at a large desk. He was tall and skinny and wore a dark green robe.

The skinny man was talking to another man. The dim light barely made it possible to see the shape of the other man's shoulder. It was a stocky figure, big in size and covered with a deep scarlet cowl. Only his tanned chin, covered with a short, red beard was visible under it.

As they finished talking in whispers, the skinny man enquired the red bearded one "Very well then. Would you like to try the power of the stone now?".

"Of course, Let's see what you can do with this," he replied as he pulled a leather package from under his robe and threw it on the desk.

The skinny man reached to it with his hand, savoring the moment, but the other man hastily put his hand over the package, "Needles to say that our goals align, isn't it so?".

As he bent over the desk, the light shone on his face and his eyes, red as fire, met the other man's. He had a menacing gaze, which instilled fear in the bravest of soldiers.

"Of course, my lord, not even for a second would I think of betraying you," skillfully answered the skinny man.

The red bearded man moved his hand from over the package and laid back on his seat, returning to the cover of darkness. The skeletal man grabbed it and, from it, pulled a piece of stone that started to glimmer faintly. Then he pulled from his long and ragged robe another stone, made from the same material. He gazed upon both of them, marveled on his possessions and then put them together, as if they were both part of a jigsaw. The glimmer of both the stones went straight to their joint. It shone brighter and then it faded away. After this, the skinny man let go of one of the stones and it became evident that both pieces were now soldered. It had two clear cut sides and a ragged one, as if some of it was still missing.

The man put the stone in his pocket and started to explain, "As you already know, my lord, there's not only demons in the underworld. There's also the beasts that walk amongst them," the man moved his hand towards the ring in the wall and started to pronounce some words in an unknown language. The seals etched in the mysterious ring started to shine. It was a greenish light that came out of them and a vibrant sound rumbled into the ring. The sound grew louder until a thick smoke poured like a liquid from the darkness into the surface of the stone ring until it was filled with it.

On the smoke, human like faces were forming. The red bearded man, was looking with enthusiasm and a bit of impatience, hands clasp together and elbows firmly put onto his seat's arms. The skinny man, took the stone from his pocket and held it with both his hands over his head as he spoke in an incomprehensible and ancient language. His sleeves rolled back and his bony arms were exposed. For quite a long time, he kept repeating the same phrase over and over again. Suddenly, a monstrous figure came out of the smoke and floated near the skinny alchemist for a brief moment. He then spoke some other phrase, pointing the stone towards the smoking figure with one hand and the body that laid on the marble altar with the other.

The man lying there could barely breathe. His body was broken wherever it was looked at. An infinity of bruises and cuts covered him completely. He could only observe what was about to happen, but couldn't do anything to avoid it.

The smoking monster headed his way. It floated over him for a few moments and then forcefully entered him through his mouth. The man was tense as if he was receiving a huge electric shock. His lower back was arched and lifted from the altar and his neck exposed every vein and tendon about to burst. As the smoke went into him, the man started to transform. His muscles got swollen and, even if the man looked tough, he looked even tougher now. His skin got dehydrated and both it's color and brightness faded away. Most of his clothing couldn't stand the man's body expansion and got ripped, mainly his sleeves and trousers. Once the smoke finished entering him, the man was completely changed. He now had his eyes blood shot; his pupils dilated; his nose wider. Even his hair was now longer and color-less. The monstrous man was now sitting in the altar. Then he put one foot on the floor and the other followed. Slowly, like if he was waking from a long slumber, he took two steps towards the wizard and growled, showing his teeth and most of his gum.

"Welcome to the world of the living, beast," said the skinny necromancer looking up to its face since, even if the wizard was tall indeed, the monster was half a body taller than him, "I know that your poor consciousness and tiny, damaged, brain don't allow you to comprehend too much but, as you know, I am the one who brought you here and I am who can send you back. That is why I am the one who controls you. I own you and you will obey me… And whoever I tell you to," he clarified, as he noticed that the man in the darkness was fondling his knuckles, "you will refer to me as Master Vaati. Was I clear?" he asked at last.

The beast growled something that resembled a "yes".

"Yes… what?" Asked Vaati, without a shred of fear while moving the stone in his hand as a token of authority.

"Yes, master Vaati," the huge demon answered.

"That's what I like… Respect!" said the skinny man, smiling.

"Respect based on fear," added the red bearded man, sitting on the back.

"Is there any other form of respect?" asked Vaati sarcastically while smiling in a malicious way.

"Not that I know of," answered the red bearded man, "You are a valious ally, wizard. I hope you remain to be so. I wouldn't like to have to end your life,".

"Of course, my lord. Your trust is well founded," answered the wizard, who seemed to respect the other man.

The red bearded man stood up, but didn't come into the light. He was keeping himself in the shadows, as if he was comfortable there. He put a hand on a column and asked, "With how many of these demons can I count for my army?".

Vaati, fearful, answered "You see, my lord. That's a complex question which I cannot answer even if I wanted to," and then hurried to back his words, "The problem is that not every human can host this kind of demon… How can I explain it?" he said as he looked around, searching for something to exemplify. Then he saw the wrapping of the stone over the desk, "Let's say that you have this pouch that can hold one kilogram of stones. You try to forcefully put two kilograms in it. Obviously, the pouch will break spilling the stones everywhere. Well, with people it's the same thing… If the demon is too large to fit into the vessel, it will break. In that case, it would be set loose and, in that state, It's dangerous to anyone that's near it,".

"And what makes that vessel capable of housing such demon?" asked the hooded man.

"Many factors, my lord," answered Vaati, "physical condition for once. The vessel must be strong enough to be able to fight the demon, but weaken enough so that the demon can posses it," both man started to walk towards the exit, leaving the beast behind with many other demons putting it on chains, "Besides, to be able to tolerate the demon, the vessel must posses great courage,". They headed out of the room and climbed up the stairs, "As you might imagine, these persons couldn't be able to bare such a demon into them," said Vaati, signaling to the fearful statues.

Both men shared an evil grimace and kept walking to the castle's door.

"I see that my efforts to gather the pieces of this stone had bare fruit," said the bulk man, referring to the stone in the necromancer's pocket, "and I expect the favorable results to keep coming. I'll put a whole troop of my soldiers on your command to capture Hyrule soldiers… as alive as possible,".

"Of course, they will have access to the whole castle, since it'll be them who'll keep me posted of your progress," said the red bearded man, skillfully letting the necromancer know that he would be constantly watched.

"Of course, my lord," He accepted, albeit regretfully.

"Also, I need some of these demons ready as soon as possible," pushed the red bearded man, "I'm planning an attack. Something a bit stronger that what's already heading towards the settlements near Hyrule. It would be useful to count with some units that strike a bit more of fear than the usual," he said as he kept moving, "I don't comprehend why these stupid survivors of Hyrule keep rising against me… I haven't left them anything… not even hope!" said the tyrant clenching his fist.

"Sanity is somewhat scarce these days, my lord," said the wizard, trying to get on his good side.

"Never mind. I'll return in a couple of days to see my… investments," went on the bulk man, as he mounted his horse. It was dark as the night, equipped with a metallic armor covered in diabolical markings which sounded in the dark of the night as he rode away from the deteriorated fortification.

The wizard turned around and headed towards the castle.

"What are you looking at?" he asked to a demon that was at the door.

"Nothing, my lord," the demon answered as he lowered his head.

Then the necromancer stood in front of the demon and spoke again.

"Do I know you? I don't remember having seen you around here…" claimed Vaati as he tried to remember where this demon came from.

132

"I've been here for not longer than a couple of months, my lord. I'm just learning the ropes, sir. The human I'm possessing used to serve in this castle. The demon-commander thought that it would be useful to keep me inside the castle, my lord," said the demon, still with his head down.

"All right… I guess that's what we have slaves for. Do you know the name of the person you've possessed?" asked Vaati, as he examined him.

The demon answered "Yes, my lord. Leonardo, my lord,".

134

CHAPTER 10

THE HYLIAN PRINCESS

Link could not believe the receiving he was getting from the total stranger. A beautiful young lady, similar to those who run away from him at a glance of his poorly kept looks a while back. Besides, as it turned out, she was the princess, despite her warrior-like garments, and was in charge of the encampment.

"He... Hello," said the young bowman.

"I can't believe it... after so long... I knew you'd come back. I knew it," said the girl.

"Excuse me, miss, but i..." started going Link, but was cut short by the girl "Have no idea of who I am,".

"Precisely..." he answered as he smiled in a weird and forced way, not knowing how to react.

The princess let out a subtle laugh given the odd situation and the expression of the perplexed Link.

"Don't worry Link. I do know you. It seems as if it was yesterday that we were only kids. Well of course you're now... bigger," she said as she examined Link from head to feet, "not so much in height, but this is new," she went on as she pressed one of her fingers against the arm of the boy while looking at Hood and Astor, as if she knew they were the ones responsible for Link's changes, "I guess you've already been told. My name is Zelda, I'm the princess of Hyrule. Regretfully, my father is uncapable to rule his kingdom right now, that is why I'm in charge of everything,".

Link was astounded. He looked at the young girl and then swiped sideways with his sight to his partners, who started laughing at his expression.

Noticing that the young man was unable to speak, Zelda said "Well now, gentlemen, if you'd follow me please," and the four of them started walking.

Link and Zelda were in the lead and Hood and Astor followed behind. Two guards rushed to escort them, "thank you, but it won't be necessary," said Zelda to the guards, "believe me when I tell you that these men would sacrifice anything for me. Actually, one of them already did so with his memories,". The guards nodded, did a kind of flourished bow and went back to their posts at the sides of the tent.

"I am the one who sacrificed his memories, right?" asked Link

"Yes, Link. You are," answered Zelda.

Hood gestured, as if he was to add something, but in second thought preferred to keep quiet.

"And... how? I mean... When...? where? Why do you say that I did it for you?" Asked Link, hoping for the answers that Hood was keeping from him.

"Mmm.... I should not answer to so many things at once," said Zelda, "I guess that, in time, you'll understand,".

Link opened his mouth but no sound came out. After a short while, he started talking "I can't believe it! You're just like him!" he claimed as he pointed at Hood, "Won't anyone tell me about my own life?" he asked, offended.

"I can't, Link. I'm not allowed to," answered Zelda.

Astor scratched his nose and, while covering his mouth as he did so, he smiled. Hood noticed this and also held back a slight smile, covering with his mouth and biting his lips once he couldn't do so anymore.

"Would you be so kind to, my lady, to tell me who forbade you from telling me such things?" said the lad with a fair degree of demeanor in his voice.

"Well of course I can. You did," replied Zelda, without beating around the bushes.

The other two men couldn't hold back any longer and bursted into laughter. The young lad turned around in a split second straight to them with a mixed look of surprise and disbelief on his face.

"I can't believe it! Not even you let yourself know anything!" Said Hood while laughing profusely.

Link sent them a killer glare… but did not speak. After a few seconds, and realizing that they wouldn't stop laughing he decided to join them.

Once he calmed down, he went back to speak to Zelda, who also was caught in the funny situation, and said "It really is a surprise, and funny and actually quite ironic, but, are you sure it wasn't this old man who forbade you from speaking about those things?" he asked as he pointed at Hood.

"I don't know, maybe he had something to do with it, but it was you who said Zelda, when you see me again, it's important that you don't tell me anything about my past. I know that a few minor things will be let out, but you must try not to say anything about what happened here. It might be troublesome for me, but I will understand. After all, I will be used to it," rephrased the princess.

"I said all that?" asked Link.

"Yes, Link. I've held that line in my head for a long time, waiting to see you again," She answered.

"Awww… *cough* lame *cough*" joked Hood.

This time, it was Zelda who turned around and looked at Hood with fire in her eyes. While it's true that she was the princess of every hylian, Hood didn't seem to mind about ranks, but that time, her glare made him take his comment back.

"Sorry, sorry, pretend I didn't say anything," he cowered back.

Astor waited until Zelda turned around and then silently mocked Hood, straight in his face. The old man didn't miss this chance to signal out to the stocky man how hot tempered the princess was.

Link didn't pay attention to Hood's comment and went on his way besides the princess. Soon they were far from the settlement and had reached a rocky place, where a little stream had formed a cute little waterfall.

"Okay Link, I have a gift for you. But you'll have to get it from inside that cave," said Zelda as she led him to the waterfall.

"Which cave?" asked Link.

"I see that your memory was seriously damaged," said the princess "behind the waterfall there's a cave. We used to come here often when we were kids. You loved to swim in the little ponds that are inside and climb the walls,".

"Should we go in then?" asked the lad.

"You two go in, Astor and I will mount guard out here," Hood claimed. Without waiting for anyone's opinion.

The princess put one foot in the water, the other one on a rock and jumped into the waterfall, passing through completely.

Astor looked at Link "you shouldn't keep a lady waiting… Good luck," and giving him a little push, he threw Link through the waterfall and into the cave. Link tripped with Zelda as he passed through and they both ended up on the floor. Link's reflexes allowed him to put himself under the princess and break her fall with his own body. They were both lying on the floor, noses not even five centimeters from one another. Zelda blushed and quickly got up. Link didn't get to the point of blushing, but right then and there he realized how incredibly beautiful the princess was.

That short moment was enough to make him, even if only for a second, forget about how he was supposed to save Hyrule, Ganondorf, the Ocarina, the Tri-force and anything that was going on in his mind. Even his forgotten past.

"I… I'm really sorry! Astor… Astor pushed me through and I lost my balance and then…" stuttered Link

"It's ok, don't worry," answered a still blushed Zelda, "Come, it's this way," she then added, leading Link through a path inside the cave.

"Sure, yeah, Lead the way," answered Link "Although it's somewhat dark in here… Don't you think? We might trip again," and just as he said it, Link realized that this sentence seemed to insinuate a different situation. Right at that moment he tried to fix his mistake "I MEAN! I wouldn't want to fall over you… it's just that I wouldn't want you to get hurt. Not that it bothered me that you fell over me… But no, I mean, what I want to say is…" Link babbled as he tried, unsuccessfully, of course, to clarify

138

and try to make the situation less awkward, nevertheless, Zelda seemed to secretly enjoy the young man babbling. In any case, she pulled out a yellowish sphere from one of her fabric pouches, gave it a little shake, and it started to shine, lighting up the path.

Link took this chance to put the previous subject, and the embarrassing situation, behind them "Unbelievable! It seems that the princess has more than one trick under her sleeve," he said.

Zelda Laughed, "You also forgot that I was one of the top students in school, didn't you? Well, at least in the theorical subjects, that is,".

"We went to school together? I went to school?" asked Link, surprised with this news.

Educational tuition was expensive and not anyone could afford it. Only a few lucky hyrulians, who came from somewhat wealthy families, had the chance to attend to the only school in Hyrule.

"Yes, Link. I believe that it wouldn't hurt you to know that. I used to be really good at theorical subjects. But as any royalty kid, had trouble with combat and hunting skills. Although I had a... Partner/Private-teacher of sorts that helped me tremendously with those. He was really lazy with the subjects I preferred, such as ancient reading, chemistry and alchemy..." then Zelda stopped talking as she reached a ledge, "We'll need to swim and dive a bit to reach the other side of this path," she claimed as she pointed the way forward.

"AWESOME!" Answered Link, who loved to swim.

They both jumped into the water mirror and swam forward. Once they reached a wall, Zelda stopped.

"I doubt you can't do this, but we'll need to dive here," the princess paused, as she tried to remember something and added "Once you taught me that rocks and ledges could be used to obtain an impulse and swim faster underwater. I guess that your own advice can be useful for you through this part of the way,". Zelda submerged and Link followed for about twenty meters. As they went on, Link followed the princess, holding on to the ledges she used to impulse herself. The little light that was there, came from the sphere in the princess pouch. The shiny sphere was dimmed, but still some light shone through.

Zelda reached a certain place and stopped again. She signaled Link to ascend. Link obeyed and they both got their head out of the water into what seemed to be a small cavity. It was an air pocket that some underwater caves have, filled with moss which provides it with constant clear air. Zelda used this opportunity to breathe in and explain a little of the way forward.

"Now, the path is going to get narrower and the walls have a few sharp shells sticking to them. Don't get to close or you'll end with a lot of cuts," she explained.

Link nodded and then Zelda submerged again. They both were really careful from that point on. Link could see the sharp shells and, regretfully, could feel one of them in his forearm which made a little cut.

Zelda emerged in what seemed to be another air pocket, quite smaller that the previous one. Link followed her and emerged, and once again, their noses where almost touching. This time, they both blushed a bit.

"Well then… last checkpoint. Do you have a dagger on you?" asked Zelda.

"Yeah. I mean, not here, but in the carriage there's a…" Kink tried to explain, but was cut short, "we can't go back to the carriage now Link," laughed the young princess, "Here, I have a spare one," she said, as she pulled a couple of daggers from the hilt in her left thigh, "Don't lose it, it's a souvenir," she said, smiling, "Now, we're going to pass through some algae-filled path. It's normal the get a bit entangled in them, so don't panic. Just cut them with the dagger. Don't worry, it's really sharp,".

"Cut the seaweed, no problem." Replied Link.

They both submerged and, once again, Link followed Zelda. She quickly cut through but, as it was to be expected, Link's foot got entangled in the algae. Without worrying too much, Link reached his foot, all caught up in the squishy thing, and took the dagger on his free hand to cut the damn thing, but as he was about to, he felt a strong sting on his head, which brought back a memory. A really old image. He was younger and he could see his hands cutting the alga, but it wasn't wrapped around his foot but in someone else's. He was freeing another person.

His vison was interrupted when his lungs reminded him that he wasn't precisely an aquatic being and he still needed fresh air to survive. He then cut the seaweed and rushed to reach Zelda, who had already emerged.

"You took your sweet time," mocked the girl, "problems with the algae?".

"No… not too many. But you did have problem with them and you almost end up dead," said Link, looking at the princess straight in the eyes.

"Link… have you recovered your memories?" wondered the girl, eyes wide open.

"No, it was only an instant," he answered, "but I felt it… just like when it happened. The desperation… I wasn't scared for my life, it was worse than that… Zelda, I start to believe that you were more important for me than any other citizen of Hyrule… I don't think I cared about your royal status… I think I'm getting near something that I worry a bit about remembering," deducted the young man out loud.

"Maybe so, Link, but don't rush it," asked Zelda, "let's move on… right this way," she then added as she leaded the way.

They both continued through, surrounded by an awkward silence, until Zelda let out a scream that echoed throughout the whole cave, "Ahhh!! No, no, no, no, no!! I hate them!! Get out!! Shoo, shoo!!".

Link didn't understand what was going on, but he had his dagger grasped tightly and run straight to her. Once he reached the princess he started looking where the danger was coming from. He then saw a spider that, while it wasn't exactly huge, it was, at least, the size of a fist.

He looked at Zelda, and asked, with an expression of disbelief, "really? The princess of Hyrule, commander of the great hyrulean army? The warrior who…" he couldn't finish the

141

sentence, since the spider jumped over him. Link turned around hastily and Zelda saw how the spider climbed through his back to his shoulder, leaving on his trail a thick silk. Link tried to hit it with his hand, but it was too agile and descended through his torso to his legs, tying him up with the thick silk. The young man kept trying to squash the spider, but the more he tried the more tied up he ended. Then the princess took the luminous sphere from the fabric pouch and shook it harder. The spider fell back, blinded by it's light and Link seized the moment and, with the hand that still remained barely free, skewered it with his dagger. The swift arachnid contorted and it's eight legs joined in its center.

"Is it dead?" asked Link.

"Why? Are you afraid of it?" enquired an ironical Zelda.

"No... well... it was rather fast... I didn't know that..." but Link was interrupted "That's what you get for mocking me," reprimanded the princess "those spiders are the well-known Walltulas, common in grottos and caverns around Hyrule but I believe that their habitat extends further away. They are believed to have migrated from the kokiris woods, due to a frost, many years ago and are incredibly swift. If you stand still, they wrap you around to eat you alive together with their offspring," she explained "Besides, you were lucky that it wasn't interested in stinging you. Their poison tends to numb you, while the silk acts as an anesthetic," she then summed up.

"Anesthetic?" asked Link.

The princess laughed "Some things never change. You're still oblivious to the subject you hated most, you still don't know anything about chemistry!" and once the laughter subsided, she went on with her explanation "To anesthetize is kind of putting to sleep, and while you're asleep, the Walltulas can eat you without you feeling any pain. Because of that you don't die fast either, so they can feed from you longer, without risking your decomposition,".

"Ok, I guess that does it, I don't want to know anything more about it," said Link, while removing the spider-web that was covering him, "at least I don't care about how they can kill me slowly... But I would like to know how I can kill them faster,".

"Light is usually rather useful. They have an incredible sight, given the fact that they have many eyes, but since they live in dark caves they are used to darkness," explained the princess while holding the sphere in her hand, "it suffices with lighting up the area to blind them completely and you can take advantage of that distraction, as we did," she summed up as she resumed her journey through the cave.

"Well then, I guess we have found another great use for your... By the way, what the heck is that thing?" asked Link, wondering about the shiny sphere.

"It's basically a mix of substances, enclosed in this glass sphere, which turns out to be quite sturdy. It has the same chemical compound that allows the fireflies shine, mixed with a rather special oil and a catalyzer that reacts when heavily shaken," explained the princess in a nonchalant way, as it was something that should be obvious to everyone.

"Cata... what was that?" asked a bewildered Link.

The princess once again bursted to laughter "Catalyzer! It's a chemical that works as an activator," she tried to resume in terms the young man could understand, "during the day it charges up, absorbing sun light and, when you shake it, it releases the stored luminal energy,".

Right then, the sound of moving wings was heard deep within the cave. Link sensed it first, since Zelda was going on with her explanation.

"Shhh... did you hear that?" asked the man.

Zelda paid close attention and quickly tried to pull something from her belt.

"Oh, no... no, no, no... where did i put it?" she said to herself while she was feeling her waist and pockets.

"What is it? What's wrong?" asked a now troubled Link.

"BATS!!" Shouted Zelda, still going through every pocket she had.

"But... those aren't such a big problem, princess," said a now relieved Link.

143

"To the ground!" Zelda ordered, while she took out of one of her pouches the thing she was looking for and kneeled.

Link didn't react fast enough. A bat, the size of both his hands put together, wide open, grabbed his shoulder and, given the speed he had, thrown him to the ground. Zelda blew inside another sphere. This one was hollow and with some holes on it. It didn't seem to do any noise at all, nevertheless, the bats that arrived after started to crash with the walls and flew erratically, passing by the young couple, fleeing as fast as they could. The bat that Link had, strapped to his shoulder, seemed to have gone mad.

Link, who, taking into account the number of strange things that were going on, never sheathed his dagger, stabbed it, killing it instantly.

"What... the... hell," asked Link, while taking the furry animal from his shoulder and checking the wound made to it.

He had two small punctures, near his collar bone, three centimeters away one from another.

"Is everything in this cave bigger than normal and inclined to kill us?" asked the young man.

"But bats aren't such a big problem, Link," answered Zelda, making a funny face, before offering a helping hand, "you know what, Link? If you hadn't killed him fast enough, it's likely that, by now, you'd be fainted on the ground. You see... these aren't the average cave bats; these are the infamous Keeses and they have the ability to drain half a liter of blood in a minute. At least the ones of that size. So, think about this, Link... If you have about five liters of blood in you, and ten of those keeses decide to take it from you, how long do you think they would take?" asked the princess.

Link didn't answer, he was just reflexing on the subject.

"not even half a minute until you pass out," said the girl, "Luckily, they aren't smart enough. Although they do have some rather well-developed senses; Smell, allows them to bite straight where the highest blood flow is and Hearing, which helps them navigate through eco-location. So, if we scramble the frequency at which they hear, we can scare them off," explained Zelda, as she showed the hollow sphere with holes that she was holding in her hand, "I mean, who, in his right mind, wouldn't get scared at the loss of the sense of location?".

Link took a moment before saying anything.

"Are you sure that I came to this cave alone... Even once?" he asked in disbelief.

"I don't know if you did. At least I didn't... not before your memory incident," she answered.

They both went on their way, deeper still into the cave. Link went closer to Zelda now, and wielded his dagger, paying close attention to his surroundings. Then, as if Zelda couldn't react in any other way, she screamed "AHHH!!".

"AHH!!" Link also screamed, as if he was a mirror for the girl.

"Oh no... no, no, no!" she claimed, looking at a giant slug.

Link moved her aside and jumped over the slimy bug, grunting at it. The slug, literally, exploded after he landed on it.

"There, this one is dealt with," he affirmed still catching his breath, "What was with this one? Some deadly poison? Corrosive acid?" he asked, still on edge.

"No, that kind of slug is harmless... but by the gods, they are disgusting! And to think that I almost step on it... Disgusting!" the princess answered.

Link couldn't believe what he just heard. He was speechless.

"Ok, let's move on, shall we?" said the carefree princess.

"I want you to know that, right now, I feel a bit of guilt," said Link as he cleaned himself, "It's not that I mind attacking beasts and critters in self-defense, but this slug wasn't, precisely, a menace,".

"If it makes you feel better, it couldn't have been, since it was already dead. That's why it was so swollen and exploded just as soon as you touched it," she clarified.

Link thought to himself "Why on Hyrule did Zelda get so alarmed with a dead bug?" but instead of asking that, he just smiled "Well... to be honest? It does, kind of... By the way, how far away are we?" said Link, in an attempt to change subjects.

"Not much further, actually. We just need to climb that wall and reach that ledge," answered Zelda, pointing to the stone that was coming out of the wall in front of them, about ten meters high.

"Doesn't seem that hard. Are you sure that we just need to climb? Or is there any other weird critter from this cave that can come try to kill us?" asked Link, half joking, half worried.

"Don't fret. Just a climb," Said Zelda, "Be sure to grab onto the firm stones and not from the loose ones, otherwise… Well, I don't think you'll actually die, but you'd hit yourself really hard,".

Link started to analyze the wall, assessing the best route to follow. Zelda looked at the lad cautiously, but didn't start to climb, she just stood there, and Link, caught up in his thoughts, didn't notice that. The young man was strafing left and right, looking at some rocks closer than others. His eyes moved side to side and calculated distances, with the help of his fingers. About a minute later, Link smiled as if he finally was satisfied with his choices. He turned around to tell Zelda what he discovered but, once he found her staring at him, he swiftly changed the subject.

"What is it? Why do you look at me like that?" he asked.

"Like that… how?" she asked back.

"Like… if you were watching me as some kind of animal," answered Link jokingly.

"I looked at… more like remembered the first time we did this climb. You did exactly the same thing," Zelda replied, "it's instinctive in you. While you don't like to study, per se, you tend to study your surroundings quickly and come to, usually, the right conclusion. You've got an admirable gift for situational analysis, Link,".

Link took a deep breath and puffed his chest at this compliment "Well… since you've said it… I think I found the best route to move forward," he said, proudly.

"Let me guess. We start with the rock at your right; then, we go up through the same line towards those other two over there, since we would be able to stick our feet on those cracks; we then pass to that one on the left and we go up through that V shaped

146

spot is, putting our backs on the side to give us some safety," said Zelda, while signaling the way with her hand, "Finally, we take advantage of that ledge there as a checkpoint to decide what we'll do with the final three meters since, from here, we can't see a clear route for that last part,".

Link took a couple of seconds to be able to recover from his dismay and articulate proper words.

"How did you?... that's precisely what I was going to suggest!" he said.

"Well... it's exactly the same route you suggested the first time we came here," answered Zelda, smiling at him, and walking towards the wall, she added "come on Link, I know the way like the back of my hand," and then jumped onto the first stone. Link shrugged in resignation and followed her.

Soon enough, they've reached the checkpoint ledge and stood on it "Do you want to plan the way forward or should I just tell you what you did before?" asked Zelda.

Link peaked at her, sideways, "second option, thank you,".

"Very well then, follow me," Said the princess, while jumping to another stone, leading the way, and Link followed.

After climbing the remaining meters, Link set foot in solid ground. There was a kind of narrow hall and, on its end, a wooden chest, about fifty centimeters wide and thirty centimeters deep. It was rather old; the wood showed some cracks and the metallic edges had many rusty spots. The princess stood near the chest and the lad came close to it. He looked at the princess and then put his hands over the chest and tried to open it, but it was locked. Since it wouldn't open, he decided to try and lift it to see if taking it with him would be an option, but the chest was stuck to the ground. It seemed as if its lower end was melt within the stone of the cave.

"I guess that... after a few hard kicks, I could maybe rip it and take it with us..." Link said.

"Or... since I brought you all the way here, you could ask me if, by chance, I have the key..." chimed the princess "I mean, so we can avoid recurring to violence as our first solutions, like Neanderthals,".

"Nean... what?" asked Link, trying to make sense of the never before heard word.

"You're so cute when you're oblivious of certain subjects," replied Zelda, "Neanderthal is the name used to refer to the cave-men,".

"Well, it's ironic, but we're in one. So, I don't see why I can't act like one of those," joked Link.

Zelda let out a subtle laugh; she grabbed one of the fabric pouches that hanged from her belt and, from it, took out a small key with the letter L chiseled onto it. "here, it's yours,".

Link took the key "Well... this does make things easier,".

Link put the key into the lock and turned it. The sound of the mechanism unlocking was heard throughout the cave. He put both his hands on the sides of the lid and lifted it. Into the chest, there was something with the shape of the letter V, wrapped and tied with a cord. Link untied it and removed the cloth to unveil an orange boomerang with four green perpendicular lines on its wings, two on each. On its elbow there was a light but beautiful etching, containing a piece of a red rupee; The tips of its wings were reinforced with a sheet of very light steel. Link grabbed the boomerang with both hands and suddenly, another memory came to him.

His hands held the boomerang, just as he did now, but they were smaller, younger... quite younger. He could smell wet grass. It was sunrise, he could feel the adrenaline rush, like a child who escaped home to go play. But also, something was amiss. He looked up and saw a goat, just like the ones at Ordon's farm, coming at him at full speed. Filled with a crippling fear he watched as it came nearer and nearer for a few seconds, which seemed like years to him and let him take in every detail. The hooves, splashing mud; the horns, leaning forwards to tackle him; the eyes, shining with a rabid fury; the snout, wet and letting off steam. The impact was imminent and Link could see the animal's face so close that he could observe every facial muscle in tension, producing and aggressive expression. Three meters... two... one...

Suddenly! Something on his side shakes him. He's rolling on the floor, together with whatever hit him. Everything happened so fast and now he's watching the grass from above… Higher than usual… Someone is carrying him. He felt someone's shoulder under his belly and, since he was still breathing and was still conscious, he felt he owed this person his life.

"Are you ok, Link?" he heard amidst the confusion. Could this person know his name?

"Link… do you hear me? Are you all right?" Said Zelda, pulling Link out of his memory.

"Eh? Yes… Yes, I just had another memory," he answered, closing his eyes and shaking his head, trying, with no success, to grab a hold of some other memory, "I think this cave was really useful," said the boy, "In all these years, I barely remembered anything and today I already recovered two memories from before my accident. This last one I had already dreamt about… but never so close, so… real,".

"I'm so happy to hear that!" said a smiling Zelda.

"Yeah, me too!" answered Link, joking with her.

Link kept his sight at the boomerang and felt a kind of awkward silence taking hold of the moment. He could have kept it, but decided to address the elephant in the room with a question that, probably, made the moment even more awkward.

"Zelda… What were we?" he started asking. The princess blushed and lowered her head as he went on "were we siblings of any kind?".

"NO!" she rushed to answer, "luckily we're not," she whispered, and went on "You see, I've known you for as long as I can remember. We were really young; we were practically brought up together. I mean, you had your friends and I had mine and stuff," Zelda made a pause and started her way back to the entrance, as Link put the boomerang in his belt and followed her "Then, as time went by, we grew apart. But in the later years of school we became close again," she added while they climbed down through the wall.

"And why did we become close again?" Link asked.

"Mutual convenience… I guess?" she answered hesitatingly, "I needed some help with some hard subjects and you definitely needed my help with the soft ones," she added cheerfully.

"Seems logical," Link said, not fully understanding what she meant.

"I think so… Well, in later time, before you lost your memory, something may have brought us even closer," the princess said, once again hesitatingly, now standing on the ground.

"Oh, really?" Said Link, trying to hide the feeling of an adrenaline rush streaming through his blood, "you mean…" he started to say as he came close to the thing he was most interested to know, but suddenly, a tremor shook the ground, concluding whatever idea he could have been working towards.

"What the hell was that?!" Link asked.

Their eyes met, both of them surprised and speechless. Zelda was the first one to talk "The settlement!".

She started to rush to the exit of the cave and Link followed. Soon they reached the part of the cave that needed to be swam through. Without hesitation, the princess unsheathed her dagger and dived into the water-filled tunnel.

She was going full speed, ignored the first air pocket and Link followed her. In the second one, she barely emerged to take a deep breath and went back into the water, but Link had some spare air into him so he overtook her. Zelda was impressed, if the Link she remembered was fairly athletic, the new version exceeded all expectations.

They both emerged and swam hastily through the last part of the tunnel, up to the shore and then rushed towards the exit of the cave. As they came close to the waterfall, Link could hear the sound that metal does when clashing with itself. The chirping sound of steel when scratched was growing louder and louder and then, as Link took a leap outside the cave, he could see it.

CHAPTER 11

CHAOS

Link didn't know where he was at. This time, adrenaline rushed through his veins. Time stood still for a moment in front of him, letting the terrible sight sink in, as it was an infernal painting of sorts. On the background, smoke coming from the settlement's tents could be seen and two soldiers fought back against an enraged demon who dripped drool from his mouth and steam from his nose. It had incredibly small pupils and his blood shot eyes were almost as red as his irises. It was bald and his head shown several deep cuts. The demon was fighting fiercely, dressed in light clothes, which allowed him a wide range of movement, but no defense whatsoever. The soldiers seemed to be related to each other, most likely father and son. They parried the demon's attacks as best as they could. Behind them, a woman and two kids were fleeing while she covered the little one's heads, trying, in vain, to offer protection. A few meters away, a soldier was laying on the floor with two lances, still on demon's hands, piercing his body while one of them stood over him and the other was looking for further victims. Link could observe how archers were shooting arrows from a vigilance post nearby. Many demons were falling, still, more of them were still coming. Some had already managed to reach the improvised wooden tower and started to climb it. Amidst the chaos, the young lad saw his uncle, bashing his shield against two possessed ones and rising his sword, giving them death. It was less than a second that it took him to get a hold of this disaster. It was as long as he had, before Hood got him into the scene.

"LINK!" screamed the old man as he threw a sword at him.

The young lad grabbed it midflight, just in time to repel the attack of a demon closing in at great speed. A clash of swords, another and another one. Link broke the putrid subject's defense and sunk his blade in its chest. Zelda, who was arriving just behind the young lad, overtook him. She jumped and grabbed the demon's sword before it touched the ground. Now the young lady was wielding a dagger in one hand and a sword in the other. She seemed like a wildcat defending its turf. Her eyes sharp, gritted teeth and crouched stance.

Three demons came running, the first one didn't even get to put his guard up.

If Link was hesitant about the princess's fighting capabilities up to now, it was over now. She run her blade through the possessed guy's throat and didn't flinch in the slightest when its blood splashed over her face. It didn't take Zelda more than a second to pull her sharp blade from her enemy's throat and use it to repel the attack of the second demon arriving. Far from overpowering the princess, the demon fell back, leaving his belly unguarded. The princess didn't hesitate. Her dagger was now fixed between the sixth and seventh rib of his enemy. Even though it was a demon, he was hurting and threw another attack at the princess. The sword swung and the princess, who had ducked, felt the sharp breeze over her head. The rotten being's luck didn't change for the better. The lady, who, as she was ducking, had unstuck the dagger from the demon's side, took advantage of its turning while swinging and pierced it's back, sinking her dagger right above the lumbar vertebrae. It growled, but Zelda didn't remove the dagger, but moved her sword over his shoulder and stopped right at his neck. She knew that demons aren't afraid of dying, but are in no rush to return to their realm either, so she used it as a hostage of sorts. The last one in arriving had no interest in his companion's well-being at all. There's no love, friendship nor respect amongst demons. That's why, without hesitation, it stabbed the other demon in the chest, trying to reach Zelda, standing behind him. She took a leap back, avoiding the thrust and, with a kick, pushed the impaled demon forward. It fell on the ground on top of the other one and the princess then did what the latter failed to, only that she did succeed at stabbing both of the demons through their chests. Link didn't make it in time to help her, never mind though, she didn't need him to.

"Link! I need to reach my tent!" The princess screamed.

The young man started walking towards her and grabbed the shield from the soldier that was lying on the floor. "understood. I'm right behind you," he answered.

The princess, started running, both weapons in hand. The lad followed closely. As they went by, Link could see his uncle fighting alongside Hood. They didn't seem to be in immediate danger. Still, he was hoping that nothing bad happened to them. Suddenly, two demons came running from inside the woods. Link and Zelda split as they both chose their respective targets. Link's target jumped, the lad ducked and rose his shield above his head and bashed his enemy, who fell to the ground. This time, Link didn't hesitate and stabbed his enemy through the heart.

The princess's rival had no chance to react. Zelda threw her dagger and it landed right between his eyes. Link watched as the lady recovered it from the demon's corpse and couldn't hide the awed expression on his face.

"No time to do the noble thing and go for the heart, Link," said the princess as she saw the lad's face, "we're at war and these aren't even human," she added as they both went on their way.

"The humans trapped in there… don't they feel anything?" asked Link, worried as he saw the demons sporting hylian clothing.

"Regretfully, they do," answered heavily the princess, "but it doesn't hurt anymore than having the demon inside their bodies," she then paused to catch her breath, "the best we can do is free them from their suffering… And something else, if you damage the body too much, it's possible that the demon leaves the body and the person is left dying… I assure you; they always thank you with their last words for saving them from certain doom,".

Soon, they were at the watchtower and helped the archers to finish off every possessed soldier.

"I need a bow and a quiver!" Link shouted to the guards above as he sheathed his sword.

"Sir, yes sir!" answered one of them while throwing what was requested.

After how Link had helped them, no-one would have dared to deny him, even less, knowing that the princess was with him. But Link wasn't thinking about it. His mind was somewhere else. His sight showed this and the princess knew it.

"Spill it, Link. What is it? What's the plan?" she asked.

"Over there. That horse. We can use it," he answered as he headed towards it, "We ride. You lead. I Shoot," he said once they reach the animal.

They both got on the horse. Zelda spurred it and they went on their way. Link grabbed an arrow and put it on the bow. It wasn't long before he set it loose.

One by one, demons fell. Some of them by Link's arrows, others cut by Zelda's blade as they passed near the horse. The tent was a few meters away. Zelda could see her bodyguards, fighting against a handful of demons.

"Keep going until we reach them, fast!" ordered Link and the princess complied.

It was no more than twenty meters and they were heading at full speed when Link put his bow on his back and stood on his toe tips on the horses back. He unsheathed his sword and, as they passed near the guards, he jumped over a demon, ending his life.

Another enemy was coming from behind him, with a great sledgehammer on his hands. Link saw him, ducked, dodging his attack and rolled back on his back.

"Sir! Behind you!" warned a soldier as he saw that another minion was trying to take advantage of Link's unprotected position and lunged at him with a spear.

Link jumped to a side and saw that the carriage that Astor rode up to the settlement was less than five meters away from him. He got up, pulled his dagger out and threw it at the hammer wielding demon. The dagger sunk on the demon's chest though it only slowed him down. The Lad didn't need anything more, since he seized his chance and swept by his side while he was staggered and avoided any damage. As he got close enough to the carriage, he jumped into it through the back side, grabbed his shield and quickly got out through the front "It's showtime…" he whispered to himself.

The hammer wielding demon, dagger still stuck into him, headed towards the back of the carriage, in pursuit of Link. Luckily, he didn't see when the lad sunk his sword on his back.

"right, now for the one with the axe…" whispered this time.

He started to run faster, put his shield in front of him and rammed the demon, who dropped his spear. But the young man couldn't afford to be courteous and wait for his enemy to grab his weapon. At least, that is what he was telling himself. He tried to convince himself that what he was doing was the right thing. That what he was doing was the best for the poor soul, who was suffering inside that body, forced to act against his will and that, if the demon got back up, it could kill him. Not only him, Zelda too.

"Dead Zelda…" he thought, "NEVER!!" he screamed and his sword fell at a swift speed against his enemy's heart. After finishing it off, Link hasted to offer his help to the guards that were protecting Zelda's tent.

Meanwhile, Zelda had gotten off the horse and was heading into the tent hastily. As she passed by, with dagger and sword in hand, she took care of three demons along her way. Link and Zelda arrived at the same time at the tent, and both could see another horde of rotten soldiers getting near through the main road at full speed.

"Miss, are you OK?" asked the guard, the same one that previously warned Link.

"Yes, Cooker, I'm ok. Link arrived just in time to lend a hand," she answered without taking her gaze away from the horde. None of them did, "I'm going in to get the staff, I need you to hold them off as long as you can,".

Coocker nodded and the other guard spoke, "Of course, my princess. We'll do all we can to give you all the time you need,".

After hearing the voice, Link noticed that it wasn't a man inside the armor, but a woman. He wouldn't have imagined it, since she was fighting with incredible fierceness. Though it wasn't so weird, after seeing Zelda fight.

155

The woman spoke again, "If I don't get another chance. Thanks for your help, Mister Link," and taking a fighting stance she then added "I hope we can acquire victory tonight,".

After hearing this, Link remembered that, when he jumped off the horse, she was in a complicated situation, roughly fighting back the attacks from the minion who he killed with a slash from his sword.

"I'm sure we will, my lady," he answered, and also took a fighting stance.

A few meters away from the main tent, the battleground kept Link's uncle rather busy.

"Astor, to your left!" roared Hood.

Astor, who moved gracefully despite his size, stopped a demon's attack with a sword he found. The enemy tried to attack him again, he was carrying a two-handed axe, but Astor, still fought back with his sword in one of his hands. Once he repelled a third attack, he punched the demon right in his jaw, knocking it down. Hood, who had disposed of his rival, headed towards Astor, killing off another minion on the way. Astor, not paying much attention to the old man, leaned down and picked up the gigantic axe.

"This is more my style," he said as he grabbed the axe, using only one hand.

"I would like it too… if I could grab it so easily," answered back Hood and caused Astor to laugh.

"It's all about eating properly," joked Link's uncle.

Both men seemed to enjoy the battle in some sort of way. The protected each other and joked around when time allowed, to ease some pressure. Soon, a pile of dead bodies had formed around them. It was incredible to be capable of joking in such a situation. It was as crazy as the war itself, nevertheless there they were, both fighting, side by side.

"If I die here and you don't, I want my grave to say here lies Astor, who died saving an ordinary elderly" he boasted, as he grabbed the bow and quiver of a fallen soldier.

A few demons came close through a veil of smoke that had formed from a tent that had caught on fire. The first one fell

156

immediately, with an arrow in between his eyes; the second one could take three steps away from the smoke before receiving an arrow through his heart. Two more were getting closer and also got arrows of their own. The last one headed towards Hood. He reached to his quiver, but his hand couldn't feel any feather.

"Astor?" said the old man.

"Get down!" shouted the stocky man. And Hood managed to duck just in time to let Astor swing his huge axe from behind him and part the demon's chest in half.

"Thank you," said a smiling Hood.

"Don't worry. I'll make sure that your grave says Here lies the best bowman in Hyrule, pity he run out of arrows" answered Astor, amidst laughs.

"You're right, we ought to get more. Help me check the bodies, maybe we can recover a few ones" said Hood, while walking around, checking the fallen.

After restocking with a few, usable enough, arrows, Astor headed towards the old man, "we should hurry back and rejoin the others, they might need help," he said.

"Of course, with this many arrows should be enough," the old man replied and both of them started jogging towards the main tent.

"We'll need to get a horse," said a breathless Astor, "I'm fat… and you're old… we'll get there once the party is over,".

"True… maybe behind that tent…" Hood answered. They both leaned through the side of the tent an there it was. "How did you know?" asked Astor. "I didn't. I saw it when we passed by the first time and I guessed that, since everything happened so fast, it might still be there" Hood replied.

"I'm glad that your memory and luck are on our side then. Now, I only hope that this poor little horse can withstand the weight of both of us," added the stocky man.

They both got up. The horse was big and powerful. Hood was on the back and carried a loaded bow. Astor held the reins in his shield hand and the axe in the other. Hood guessed the path that Zelda took by the arrows that Link left behind and soon they both saw, above the shelters, the roof of the main tent.

Zelda went hastily into the main tent, begging that in her absence nothing bad happened to the guards nor Link. There wasn't much time, so, she headed to the back of the tent and moved away a rug, unveiling a wooden trapdoor. The lady took a key from one of the pouches that hanged from her belt, unlocked it and headed down through a narrow wooden ladder. She was now underneath the base of the stage where the tent was built. The place resembled a secret stash. There was enough food and room for a person to live for about three months. From the walls hanged a handful of swords, war hammers, halbards, bows, crossbows and shields. The lass avoided a few wooden boxes that were in her way and went to the corner further away from the ladder. Once she arrived, she removed a plank from the wall. While the whole place was covered in planks like this one, the one she took out was a rather special one. It covered a weird and convex hole with a semi-spherical shape. She then took the sphere that she used to produce light in the cave and put her in this hole. It started shining and beneath it, the contour of three triangles appeared. One above the other two, forming the shape of a bigger triangle and in the center of it, a fourth one, but upside down. This last one moved to the inside and rose, leaving exposed a cavity of about fifteen centimeters on each side. Zelda put her hand in and pulled out a piece of stone and, without hesitation, put it in one of the pouches in her belt. After that, she took the sphere from the wall and everything went back to the way it originally was.

After that, she ran to another corner and moved aside a box, exposing a loose plank on the floor. She removed it and took a staff that was underneath. Without delay, she ran towards the stair, she climbed up and went to the entrance of the tent and exited to the battlefield.

Outside the chaos reigned supreme and, in less than a few seconds, Zelda could see many sequences that were happening at the same time.

On one side, a demon had shield bashed the princess's body-guard, hitting her head and denting her helm.

"Gracielle! Nooo!!!!" shouted Coocker as he saw this and went to her aid.

He managed to kill the demon, but in return, it took his right arm, since the man with the halbard had now a deep cut in his biceps. Another demon came rushing. The guard took off her helm and used it to knock the demon down with one lucky blow. Coocker rose the halbard with his left arm and used it to end the life of the demon lying in front of him.

Near them, Astor was handing out axe swings. Shield in hand, the stocky man knocked his enemies down and cut them in halves, no quarter given. He was outnumbered, but Astor didn't seem to be the one that was possessed a short time back. He had regained his bravery, and with it, his skill and style. Once upon a time he used to be a skillful swordsman and very proficient in hand to hand combat. In fact, before picking up blacksmithing, he taught at a school, precisely fencing. Zelda knew this, she was her best student. Not because she was the best at fighting, but because she was the one that put the most effort into learning.

Finally, by the squint of her eye, the princess saw Link and Hood. They seemed to be one person. Their movements were synchronized at such a level that it seemed as if they had fought together throughout their whole lives. It was an epic and beautiful to behold sequence. Link let an arrow loose, stopping a demon who was throwing a spear in its tracks; Hood stopped it with his shield and threw an axe he found at his feet; Link let another arrow loose and fell another demon, this one was heading towards the old man, with a curved sword that got stuck in the ground; Hood took advantage of this sword, grabbed it and quickly defended from another attack. They both were attacking and defending as if they were two persons with the same brain.

Zelda knew there was no time to lose and stood in the middle of it all. She grabbed the staff and stuck it on the ground with one hand. With the other, she squeezed the little stone she got from the wall and her body began to shake.

The five others came close to Zelda. Each one fighting their own battle. The floor started to vibrate, the princess and everyone else could feel it.

The lass was in the middle, eyes close, moving her lips but producing no sound at all. Suddenly, she opened her eyes and a light, similar to the one produced by the sphere she had, came from inside her. The sandy ground rose, producing a sandstorm, denser in some places rather than others. A demon run towards Coocker in the middle of the grainy cloud, it rose his sword and, when it seemed that Coocker, who was too hurt to defend himself, was about to be struck down, a cloud of sand, even denser than the rest, hit the minion as if it was a huge fist of stone.

As the demon hit the ground, the fist dissolved only to reform near other two thugs that were attacking Astor, who could hardly hold his own for such a long time. The sand hit them both and sent them flying far away from the stocky man.

Soon, the five defenders of Zelda realized that the sand was doing the job for them and closed ranks even closer to the princess, surrounding her completely.

Then, Link could see that the sand surrounding the princess started to spin into a whirlwind that made her levitate. The young bowman was about a meter away from her and could feel the bast amount of energy, flowing from the staff wielder.

The five of them formed a protecting pentagon. All of them had their shields in hand, "What is she doing?!" asked Link amidst the swirling sand.

"She's increasing her energy to eliminate the demons!" answered Gracielle, who was at his left.

"How… how does she do that?" ask the lad.

"I'm afraid that it's a secret…! Once she wakes up, you can ask her yourself!" answered a bruised Coocker.

"Once she wakes up?!" repeated Link.

"Yes!" Gracielle interrupted, "I'm afraid that, after this, she'll be quite exhausted,".

As the seconds went by, the sandstorm got denser and denser.

No one could see anything half a meter away from themselves. Then, Zelda shouted and her voice resounded in the area. Sand tornados were rising all together and disintegrated all the demons, leaving the healthy soldiers unscathed. Everything was surrounded by some sort of rocky veil that was eroding their enemies in a split second.

The princess ceased her shouting and the light that came from inside her stopped. The sand storm that was enveloping her dispersed, setting her, softly, on the ground. In the same fashion, the rest of the storm ceased and clarity reigned supreme in the area. The ground was sadly filled with fallen warriors. Zelda was watching with squinted eyes, as someone who just wakes up would. Link headed towards her, to ask her how she felt, but she rolled her eyes back and fainted. The young lad was barely one step away from her and, noticing the impending fall, caught her before she could hit the ground.

"We need to take her to her tent," said Gracielle.

"Ok, let's go," answered Link, as he held her on his arms.

"We should do some recon. We must find and tend to the survivors,". Coocker suggested to Hood and Astor, while he applied some bandages to his injured arm.

"You're right," said Hood, "Once we're back, I'm going to stitch that arm of yours," added Astor.

"Lucky me…" replied the evidently disgusted soldier, "I hate needles,".

"You're a crybaby," teased Gabrielle, and then waved to Link "Right this way to the tent,".

The three of them reached the tent and Link laid Zelda on a bed.

"Will she be ok?" He asked.

Gracielle answered "I guess so. She barely has a few scratches. All in all, she looks…".

"Perfect… right?" Link finished the sentence, without noticing how it sounded.

"I was thinking more along the lines of unharmed, but if she seems perfect to you, I have no objections about it," said Gracielle, while a little smile draw upon her face.

161

"I mean... Of course. Intact, healthy, soft..." tried to rectify the lad, who was just sinking deeper and deeper.

"Soft?" the lady bursted to laughter, "Soft and beautiful, nice depictions,".

"I mean she has no injuries or anything to worry about," a blushed Link answered.

"Awww... Link, you're so cute! You're worried about the soft and pretty princess," Gracielle replied, twisting the lad's words.

"No! I mean, yeah... what I'm trying to say is..." Link stopped and took a deep breath. He realized that it was pointless, whatever he said was only going to make the case worse. So, the blushed lad turned around to face Gracielle, turning his back to Zelda, "Ok. Never mind the fact that I was trying to say that she seemed to be enjoying of good health. It may be true that she might be attractive to me, but, as I'm telling you this, I also ask of you that you keep this to yourself and don't tell her anything," Link summed up, accepting defeat.

"Or I might just hear it directly from you...." Whispered Zelda, who had just regained consciousness.

Without turning around to look at her, Link opened his eyes wide and his face got a bright red tone, but the princess went on.

"Regardless, what or how you feel about me... or the other way around, is not urgent now. The pressing matter is to gather the clans,".

"And we will, but once you had recovered your strength, princess," said Gracielle, "For the time being, you should focus on resting,".

"Gra, I've told you a thousand times that you don't need to be formal with me, I consider you a great friend of mi... mine..." but Zelda fell asleep once again.

On top of his blushed face, inside his head, his brain recorded a few line of words that he wouldn't forget... Gather the clans.

CHAPTER 12

CLANS, RACES AND WISE MEN

The day after the chaos was a sunny one. It made winter seem not so cold. Link was charged with mounting guard, protecting Zelda. But, given the extreme effort that everyone had to make the day prior, he had fallen asleep with his sword leaned on the bed where the princess slept. Their heads not even thirty centimeters away one from another. He was sleeping on the floor, sat down with one stretched leg and the other one flexed. Over his knee, his right arm was hanging with his hand still hanging onto his sword. His other arm, thrown onto the ground, beside his shield, sported a few scratches on the outside.

The sun was starting to shine into the room through the small rips on the fabric of the sturdy tent. Sometimes, the light was interrupted by the silhouette of people, passing by outside the tent. People that Hood, Astor and Coocker found by the end of the previous day. Survivors of the attack of the demon horde that, a few hours before, had fallen, relentlessly over the most important settlement of Hyrule.

While Hyrule was divided in many settlements, this was the biggest one and, until yesterday, it had over fifty thousand habitants, from which, at least five thousand were soldiers.

Sadly, today the numbers had dwindled by more than the half of them. Some fled due to fear, others simply died in the battle.

Zelda's eyes opened. She saw the roof of the tent and then she remembered what happened the day before. Automatically, she felt her pocket and found the stone. Breathing out calmly, she looked around, searching for the staff of sands which so effectively had expelled the evil monsters from the settlement.

After a short while she found it over her right shoulder, resting on top of the back of her bed. Finally, she moved her head

163

to the left side and saw Link's, bent forward. After all this, she got up, sitting onto the bed, gazing at her protector and tried to stand up, without waking him up, but to no avail. Link had felt the movement of the bed and had already risen his head and opened his eyes.

"Sorry! I must have fallen asleep when the sun rose and I felt that people outside the tent was starting to come out…" said the lad as soon as he realized that Zelda was awake.

"Don't worry Link, you can lay on my bed and rest for a while longer," replied the smiling princess, patting on her bed.

Link, feeling at fault for falling asleep, hurried to answer "there's no need. I can stay awake,".

"Link… I'm wondering… Do you consider yourself a proper hylian?" asked the princess.

"Yes, of course," answered Link at once.

"then you surely are aware that, if your king, or any member of the royal family, gives you an order… you have to obey. Right?" went on the princess.

"Well… yeah… I guess so," hesitantly answered the lad.

"Excellent! Then Link, lay in my bed and get some more rest. That's an order," concluded the smiling princess.

Link stood up as best as he could and sat on the bed, his face filled with uncertainty. He felt like in a crossroads of sorts… Was the right thing to do to stay awake… or obey the command? But tiredness got the better of him, he chose to obey and dismayed onto the bed.

Zelda smiled, she took advantage of the fact that she was now alone in the tent and went back down into the hideout beneath the tent and stashed both the stone and the staff. Then she came back up, passed by Link, covered him a bit better, got a coat and exited the tent.

Outside, many settlers saw her coming out and kneeled.

"There's no need," said the young lady. She didn't like the formalities of royalty.

Hood passed by, with a few logs under his arm.

164

"Hello Hood," she said as she noticed him, "I see that you don't bow... Don't I represent a powerful figure to you?" asked the lass.

"Of course, you do Zelda. It's just that I've heard you say many times that you hated formalities and I wouldn't want to do something that would disgust you," answered the old man.

"Curious, I don't remember having said it many times in front of you, anyway, you're right. I don't think that you have to reduce yourself to show respect. It feels wrong," explained the princess.

"You're a noble person, princess. I don't mean your title, I mean in your heart,". Replied Hood.

"Hood, can I join you and talk for a bit?" asked the princess.

"Of course, right this way," said the veteran, pointing towards the watchtower, "I was gathering these logs for the men who are repairing the tower. If it's all the same to you, we could head that way while we talk,".

"Oh yes, of course," answered the princess.

They were both heading towards the tower and the princess engaged in conversation.

"I don't really know who you are, but a long time ago, someone really close to me told me I could trust you with anything I needed. That's why I would appreciate your advice" she said.

"Anything you need, Zelda," the old man answered.

"Well... it's just... I feel I'm losing the backing of some hylians. The attacks are becoming more frequent and more and more settlers flee... Sincerely, I'm a bit worried about the future," the princess explained.

In light of her worries, the old man rushed to answer, "Zelda, you're a young princess. You're filled with dreams and spunk. But asking them not to bow before you, as avoiding all the other gestures of authority, weakens your image as a leader,".

Hood had left the princess frozen with his cold hard truth.

"I don't believe that what you do is wrong, of course, but you need to find the way to make those who still remain here feel hopeful at your side. They must appreciate your wisdom and feel your power… You need to find the way to toughen up without the need to humiliate or hurt anyone. You're the maximum figure of authority here and you must show that… I think you should speak to your people. After all, you're the only one who can do that," explained the old man to the still shocked lass.

Hood kept on walking, but Zelda was standing like a stone in her place. The old man took a couple extra steps further before noticing this, and once he did, he turned around to look at her, "Are you ok?" he asked. But the princess didn't answer. She turned around and started running towards the main watch tower. With a small hop, she climbed to the third step and kept climbing.

"Hylians!" She shouted, "Gather 'round!".

Hood, who was near the tower where he was taking the logs, saw that the men in charge of fixing it were climbing down and joining their leader. So, he laid the logs on the ground and decided to join them. People was coming from all the settlement and in less than five minutes, thousands of them where gathered at the main tower.

"How many?" asked the princess, "How many more need to die?" no one answered, "Don't you see? Why do you think I don't like the bows?" she asked to the audience, without waiting for an answer, "I'll tell you why. The bow is a sign of submission. And if you think that, being docile, you're going to defeat Ganondorf and his demons, then you've got another thing coming,". People started to look at each other, "You see… Things are going to get worse with that attitude in mind. Maybe I was misunderstood. I expect to be respected for what I am and not by the fear I can instill in you. You are survivors, act like it!" claimed the princess as she looked many of them in the eye before speaking directly to some of them, "Shad, I saw you fight off five demons with your daggers only!" the multitude directed their gazes to a skinny man with torn clothes and a nerdy look that contrasted with the tale of the princess, "And you, Ele. You managed to make three demons fall in a sand trap using only a couple of ropes…" this time, everyone turned to see a short girl who seemed rather agile.

166

"Mark, you dirty butcher," said Zelda with a smirk, "I saw how you used a demon as a shield while you finished another two off with your sword to protect Ruddy, who was also doing his part," claimed the princess, to make everyone notice the bulky man with the apron and the young boy at his side.

"What can I say?" said the man, waving his butcher knife around, "I'm not going to sit around, doing nothing, while watching how my family gets killed,".

"Good job Mark!" someone in the crowd shouted, "Of course it was a good job!" repeated Zelda, "That's what we are! A big family! And that's how we're going to remain, fighting side by side! Starting today, no-one bows to me. I want you to wave your fist, bash a shield or raise a sword. No more signs of defeat!". The crowd was roaring, "Starting today, only signs of victory, only then I'll know you're with me. Only then, I'll know that Hyrule is in good hands!". People started raising their hands and scream in excitement, "I say enough is enough. I'm going to lead you, and together, we're going to take back Hyrule's castle, which was brutally and unfairly taken from us!" claimed the princess as she watched her people and a fire burn in their eyes.

Gathering them and getting their respect was taken care of, now she needed to give the hope. So, she rose her hands, asking them to calm down.

"As you all know, yesterday, new blood joined our settlement. One of them, my prior fencing teacher," said Zelda, referring to Astor, who held a sword he found on top of the main tower, "Other, with skills which are hard to believe," this time talking about Hood.

People was looking to the newcomers with awe and the fact that they were still alive and didn't flee backed Zelda's leadership.

"Lastly, someone who I've known since I can remember. Someone who you all have heard of, through unbelievable stories and, I can assure you, you haven't heard them all. Someone who, right this moment, planning the recapturing of the castle and the liberation of many innocents. Someone who assured out victory the moment he set foot on the settlement... Yes, dear hylians, our hero of previous years has returned. Link is back to recover Hyrule's splendor! And I say that those who are here, all of us, we can help him!" claimed Zelda, and people bursted into euphoric screams.

Zelda didn't waste the chance, "For Hyrule!" she screamed.

"For Hyrule!" some replied, "Hurray Link!" others shouted, "Long live Zelda!" was the chant of others.

"Now, let's go back to our chores, we're rebuilding this settlement! If you know of someone who fled, look for him, tell them the village of hope has relit its torch with the fire of heroism!" and as she finished her speech, she started to climb down.

As soon as she reached the ground, Zelda started to walk towards Hood. As she passed by, people didn't bow anymore, they waved their fists and showed their tough joy on their faces. The lass reached the old man, he smiled and whispered to her ear "He's sleeping, right?".

"Of course he is," answered Zelda, "But for now, people has hope and respect is still standing. And everything was possible because I remembered a book I've read a long time ago, about kings and queens of old,".

"Oh, young Zelda, if I had your age, I would marry you. You have that easiness to resolve problems, elegantly, that can seduce anyone," said Hood, which made the princess blush a little.

"Well, Respect and hope have been dealt with. What now?" asked the lass.

"I see you want to be done with this as soon as possible… Now you only need a plan," answered Hood, "let's help around the camp for a bit, that way we'll give Link a little more time to rest,".

"Good idea! I'll try to gather as many usable weapons as I can find and take them to Astor, so when he has a moment, he can sharpen them back," said the princess "As I understand it, he's rather proficient with blacksmithing,".

A few hours went by and the sun that had risen was now above their heads. The princess's speech seemed to have a rather positive effect of everyone. While it's true that fear was still

168

around, hopeful phrases such as "if I'm still alive, I'm clearly hard to kill" or "unspeakable? Who? Ganondorf? No. Unspeakable is what I would do to those who've hurt us!" were now more frequent amongst the hylians. And not only that, words like "Hero", "Chosen one", "Leader" and "Link" were also heard around.

Unwillingly, Zelda had piled the pressure in the figure of the young lad, but he was still sleeping soundly... at least until his nose caught certain smell...

"What is that?" asked the lad, eyes still closed.

"I think a good morning is in order... or rather a good afternoon," said Zelda, who was sitting at the end of the bed.

The lad opened his eyes, subtly, and tried to stand up as fast as possible, but got entangled with the sheets that the princess had put over him, and fell, face first, on the floor.

"Do you always wake up like this?" asked the lass to Hood, who was leaning against one of the pillars of the main tent.

"No, sometimes he uses his feet. Though that takes a lot of mental effort for him," answered the old man, mocking him.

Astor and Zelda laughed as Link got up with his face entirely red.

For a moment, no one said anything, then, Zelda felt that Link was ashamed. Maybe it was because she knew who he felt about her, or maybe it was only her rank. That was why she was the first one to speak.

"Link, I want to clarify something," she said.

The lad looked at her with a look of bewilderment on his face.

"I'm the princess, the highest figure of authority for hylians... from that door onwards," Zelda explained, pointing to the entrance of the tent.

Link looked, but found no door. Then, he looked back at Zelda, with an eye still halfway closed and an awkward expression on his face.

Zelda noticed it and added "It's figurate speech, Link... What I mean is, outside this tent you have to treat me as your leader. But in here, when it's only us, you can treat me as you did when we were kids..." she added.

Link was getting ready to speak, but the princess interrupted him, "I know you don't remember what happened then. But we used to be really close and I'd like you to treat me that way, since you're the only thing, from my past, that's till alive," she could hardly finish the sentence and her eyes seemed to be all watery.

"Anyway, inside this tent, I'm just Zelda to you. The same goes for you Astor, who I love as an uncle of my own; And you Hood, whom, while I didn't know that much, I swore to a dear person to me, I would treat as a member of the family," she summed up.

After a brief pause, Link started to speak.

"You see, princ- Zelda," said the lad, as he realized that he was using her title yet again, "for as long as I remember, which is not much, mi uncle taught me to show a fair amount of respect to the royal family. The things he told me were amazing and, sincerely, it's not easy for me to suddenly become a part of such a majestic way of life... But I guess there's no time for an ease in into the lifestyle, since we need to hurry and stop Ganondorf's advance,".

The princess turned to Astor and Hood and, pointing at Link, she told them "That's why I like his style,".

Astor and Hood looked at each other, smiling. Hood rose an eyebrow, "well... think this is a nice talking subject for dessert. Dinner should be ready. Shall we?".

After a wholesome lentil stew, the whole party had eaten their fair share.

"How's Coocker?" asked Hood.

"He's fine," answered Astor as he finished chewing, "the wound seemed deeper than it really was," he sipped his wine and added, "Eight stitches were enough. In a couple of weeks, he'll be as good as new," and looking towards Zelda, he said "I heard you let Gracielle take the day off. That's nice of you,".

"It was the least I could do. Although, I didn't give her a day off... I ordered it. That woman is stubborn beyond belief. And even more loyal than stubborn," said the princess.

"And what about you, Zel," asked Hood, "how are you, after what happened yesterday?".

170

"Zel? I like the sound of it, it's been a while since someone called me that way. Anyway, I'm fine. While it's true that I used a large amount of energy, it did me no harm. I just need to rest. Probably, I won't be able to use it for a few days, but with some meditation, good sleep and some healthy food, like those Astor prepare, I esteem that I'll be ready in no time," said the princess, smiling, "still, I don't think we're going to need to use the staff in a long while. An attack like yesterday's require a lot of demons. Something tells me that it's going to be a few months until Ganondorf tries to stomp us again,".

"And, about that energy… I mean, after using it, you fainted… you don't remember anything after projecting all that energy, do you?" asked Link, a bit timid, speaking for the first time about it.

"Well, as a matter of fact, I do. For starters, I remember that I owe you for holding me and bringing me to my bed. And also, I can remember some debate about the beauty of my skin," said the princess, teasing the lad, "and lastly, I remember that I told you that it was important to gather the clans," summed up Zelda, now speaking seriously.

Link, face red like a tomato, dodged the first two subjects "What do you mean with that clan thing?" he asked.

Zelda let Link's omission of those subjects slide and explained "I assume, Link, that you know that, in this world, there are different species, not only animals, but also humans. That is, of course, due to evolution depending the surroundings. This split has been deeply studied by historians in Hyrule. That's why, depending who tells the story, things may vary a little. Still, after comparing quite a few of them, in my opinion, those of hylian historians, are the ones that convince me the most," after saying this, she leaned forwards, moved everything that was onto the table to a side and went on, "There are many races, but we only consider as Clans to those which show a significant cognitive evolution," she looked at Link and, as she saw his bewildered face, she added "Cognitive… as in knowledge. Like they had the chance to mentally mature enough to be able to reason. Those races, are the ones that have a Sage amongst them. The Sage is the one that's going to defend the points of view of their clan in the council of the seven sages, so he's expected to have rather good mental skills or leadership traits. It's thanks to this council that the clans can coexist in harmony,".

"So, there are many races, but only a few have a sage, and those are the ones called clans," Link summed up to himself.

"Correct. There are six clans, to be precise. They split almost by the same time as you lost your memory. Back then, a battle of tremendous scale was fought. Since this battle is considered to have been won, it's known as The battle of the bitter victory," explained the princess, who could see how Link was completely focused on what she was saying, "So, as I was saying, each clan has a sage. The Goron's sage was Darunia, but after some tragic events, people believe them to be extinct; The Gerudo's sage, the clan of which Ganondorf comes from, is Nabooru, who left the clan a long time ago; The Kokiri's sage is Saria; The Sheikah's is Impa…" after saying her name, the princess stopped, it seemed to hurt her to remember her, and looked to the rug that covered the trap door where the staff was hidden, after a moment, she went on, "And we, Hylians have… or well, had, Rauru… Truth be told, I don't know what's happened to him. Some believe he died a long ago in the battle of the bitter victory, others, say that they saw him after it. I really don't know what to believe. I went once or twice to the temple of light, but with no luck… That place gives me the creeps. More than a temple of light it seems of darkness… and that owl, gods it's creepy," a shiver run through the princess "I don't want to think about it,".

Link was counting sages with his hands "If it's the council of the seven sages… why are there only six?" asked the lad.

"In the council, each sage is joined by a person who would succeed them, should something happen to them. Also, the six of them can choose one of the sages to be a leader of sorts, in that way, his successor would take his place as a sage," explained the princess.

"So, there's a clan that has two sages… Which is the clan that has two sages right now?" asked Link, making some deductions.

"Regretfully, right now the council is disbanded. I mean, it is unknown if every clan has one sage, let alone two..." said Zelda.

Link wasn't satisfied with the answer and Zelda noticed this.

"Now, if you'd ask how was the council composition last time they gathered, I could tell you that, when the Sage leader died, of natural causes, Rauru was elected as the new leader and my father was chosen to be the Hylian sage, leaving me as his successor. So, it was Hyrule who had two sages," Zelda told the lad.

"Unbelievable... So, not only you were my friend and the princess of Hyrule, but also you're the daughter and successor of a sage!" said an amazed Link.

"And there's still more, lad," said Astor, leaning back in his chair and crossing his arms.

"Still more?" asked the lad.

Astor looked at Zelda, letting her go on, she smiled and did so, "Until before the death of the King Gustaf of Hyrule, leader of the sages and... my grandfather, the council was formed by Him, obviously; Rauru and his successor, my father Daltus, representing Hyrule; King Zora and his successor queen Rutela, representing the Zoras; Impa, who succeeded her uncle Sherok, the sage of the Sheikahs; Darmani and his successor Darunia, representing the gorons; Kuden the hermit and his daughter Saria, successor of the Kokiri clan and lastly Ganonfort, the king and his successor, the young prince Ganondorf, representing the Gerudos... Although he was older than Saria, they were the youngest successors,".

Link couldn't believe what he was hearing, but there was even more to come, Zelda's tale went on "When my grandfather died, the sages reunited and decided to name Rauru as their leader, but this wasn't the most pressing matter in the meeting. The passing of my grandfather was predictable and the sages already had an idea of how the election was going to turn out. Curiously, the focus of the assembly was the succession of the gerudo sage," Zelda made a brief pause, to recall what her father, close friend of Rauru, told her, "It seems that some information had leaked about Ganondorf, the prince, was trying to get the sage status to be able to manipulate everyone to make them help him to gather the tri-force once again… In the beginning, Ganonfort was outraged. Imagine how hard must it be for a father to receive such an accusation against your own son. But Ganonfort wasn't a bad sage and, after that long meeting, he decided to switch his son for a young thief, incredibly cunning, who, at a young age, had stolen from the royal family and Ganonfort, instead of sending her to jail, decided to adopted as her daughter and welcomed her into his family and trained her as a member of his army's intelligence corps… As you see, Ganonfort had a very objective view of life. And that is why he was such a respected sage. I guess this is what unchained the ill events that came, from the hand of the young prince Ganondorf,".

The princess once again paused to take a sip from her glass of water and went on, "Moving on, I don't know if you were aware, Link, but being a sage isn't like being a king. When you're a king, your title doesn't die with you, it passes along to your first born. But a sage can abdicate his position if he believes that there's someone better suited to take the place or if you feel like your capabilities are not the same as once were. Following this logic, shortly after my grandfather died, many sages decided to pass the title to their successors, and they now had to look for successors of their own, in case something happened to them. In short, the council was now formed by the new sages, who were the prior successors. They were Nabooru, Saria, Impa, Darunia, Rutela and my father, and they were led by Rauru, whose whereabouts are unknown,".

Link thought for a second and realized something, "But… if your father, the sage, is now incapacitated… it means that you're the sage of Hyrule!".

"I don't think it matters now, since the council is disbanded," explained Zelda, with a hint of sadness in her voice.

"I'm sorry to contradict you Zelda," interrupted Link, "but we only need six sages to name the seventh if the actual one is missing. The way I see it, we have one right here, we only need five more… It's just a matter of visiting the other clans' settle-

174

ments to join forces and fight the tyrant Ganondorf,".

Link stood up and hit the table with both his hands palms, "So, tell me, Zel. Which clan should we visit first?".

CHAPTER 13

THE STRATEGY

Astor stood up and started to gather the cutlery used for lunch. Hood headed towards his luggage, which was leaning against one of the supports of the tent. Zelda remained seated and, with a movement of her hand, signaled Link to also remain there with her. The lad, who had already stood up, sat back down, watching how everyone moved in synchro, as if a signal had made everyone but him aware of something. Hood came back with a couple of stones, some pieces of parchment, a compass and some charcoal. Astor finished gathering what was left on the table and shook some crumbs with a table cloth. Hood then unfolded one of the pieces of parchment, which turned to be a map, seemingly of the lands near them, and put the stones in the corners to hold it still.

Zelda sipped from her glass of water, grabbed a bag filled with colored stones and, put one on the map "We live in a large world, made of a big main land and surrounding islands. Some people consider this island to be another continent altogether," said Zelda, pointing an island located at the northern part of the map, called Wasteland, "but in reality, the study of our planet, to this day, is to my belief, incomplete. Hyrule's castle is located, practically, in the middle of it all," explained the lass as she put her hand over the first stone she laid on the map, "To the southeast, about twenty days on horseback, is the settlement where we are right now, passing a big branch of the great Zora river, " she marked the map, with another stone, "further south, are the Ordon plains, which, if I'm not mistaken, is where you come from," Zelda paused, grabbed more stones and went on, "Simply put, the divisions amongst countries is made with the rivers that split the land, leaving the gerudo tribe at the northwest, beyond the forest with the same name; the sheikahs to the southwest; the gorons to the northeast and the zoras to the eastern corner. In the eastern seaside, and closer but still east-side, are the kokiris, heading southwest from the big Deku tree," Zelda had set all the stones she held on her hand onto the map, to signal each location.

Link took a brief moment to study the map, "Right, strategically, I believe that going northwest would be the furthest away and, knowing that Ganondorf is a gerudo, I don't believe that whoever is in charge will be interested in collaborating with us, unless we can prove that we have enough strength to make a difference,".

Zelda was amazed by Link's attention to detail, "Excellent Link! I see that you're rather proficient with strategy planning. Of course, the gerudos are, the way I see it, our last target. The Sheikah non the less, are not that far away, but for reasons that I will explain later, will come right before the gerudos. Finally, we have the kokiris, zoras and... gorons maybe..." said Zelda as she twitched her mouth, "If there are any left at all...".

"I'm sure that there must be some of them remaining, Zel," said Hood, with a hint of optimism in his voice.

"So, this would be the prototype of our journey. First, we find the kokiris, then we head towards the zoras and gorons, right?" asked Link.

"I'm afraid not, Link," answered Zelda, "Zoras and gorons were really close to each other as races, but, after the tragic Darunia mishap, the zoras have blocked their entrances... Few can enter their cities nowadays and, those that can, tell all sorts of stories of their expansion to open seas... Which could be interpreted as moving away from the territories conquered by Ganondorf. If it was up to me, I'd say the zoras are our third option,".

Link was trying to put the puzzle back together, "I see... Then, taking into account that, finding an alternate route to the goron city, without help, would be rather hard, our only choice is to start with the kokiris. Am I right?".

"Without a doubt, the kokiris are our most viable choice to begin with, but there's something about them..." said Zelda.

Link sighed, in resignation "Oh come on... What's wrong

with them?"

"Well, they are tightly tied to nature, being this their mother and main authority. So, in order to reach them, you have to earn the forest's trust," answered Zelda.

"Oh! Right… Sure, that's not a problem at all," replied Link, waving his hands on the air, "So, basically, all I have to do is go into the forest, head straight to the nearest tree I can find and tell it: Hello there, Mr. Tree, my name is Link and I would like to, humbly, request an audience with the sage that represents thee. So, that's pretty straightforward,". The lad looked at Hood, in search of complicity with his joke.

"Well… yeah, as a matter of fact, you've got to do something like that," answered Zelda.

Link looked shocked; he stared the princess in the eyes "WHAT?! You're expecting me to go to the forest and start talking to the trees?".

"Come on, Link! That's nonsense! Only one tree, Deku," replied the princess.

Link could not believe what he was hearing "When you previously mentioned the Great Deku Tree, I thought it was some landmark tree of sorts. I would have never believed that I would have to, actually, parlay with a chunk of wood,".

Astor threw a harsh look at Link "Respect, Link,". He looked at his uncle and froze in the spot. It had been a while since Astor treated him like a little kid and this made him rethink his words, "I'm sorry," muttered the lad.

"What did I teach you about others beliefs?" asked Astor.

"You're right, uncle, it was a poor choice of words," answered Link, "it's just that… I can't believe that I'll have to talk to a tree,".

"Don't fret over it. You took it back and I know it wasn't your intention to mock the kokiri's beliefs. But be careful, in order to reach them, you'll need to be more open minded. Nature won't let you in if, first, you don't let it in," Zelda cut in, "You won't be able to see a single kokiri until Deku doesn't accept you or they decide to show themselves. But don't worry, this isn't something you couldn't accomplish in the past,".

179

Link opened his eyes wide, but said nothing. He looked at Hood and then Astor, as if he was looking for some data in their expressions, but there was nothing to gather, at least not referring to what the princess said.

"Well... then it's settled. We have our game plan and we can now set course. Let's head to the forest," Said Link as he nodded with his head.

The rest of the day went by as the group prepared themselves for the trip. Astor sharpened the weapons; Hood readied many arrows; Zelda marked some heavily detailed maps and Link inspected his clothing and weaponry. A nice positive energy flowed at the settlement.

At nightfall, Zelda, Astor, Hood and Link gathered into the main tent to have supper. Link's uncle had prepared an exquisite potato and egg salad, to garnish a roasted cucco that looked incredible. Link helped Zelda, who was setting the table and then they all sat down. As they started to eat, no one was speaking, Link seemed to be caught up in thoughts.

"So... are you coming with us, Zel?" Link asked.

Everyone stopped eating and looked at each other. The princess then answered "No, Link, I won't be joining the two of you,".

"The two of us?" Link asked.

"I hope you don't mind, but I'm going to stay here, Link," said Astor, "I've taught you as best as I could, my nephew. Now, your journey doesn't continue with me, but with your mentor," he went on, as he looked at Hood, "I believe I'll be more useful here, since there's no blacksmith to tend to the weapons, and it's more likely for the settlement to be attacked, rather than you two,".

Link looked at his uncle "Well that's a shame! I'm really going to miss the good food!".

"Don't worry about that. Aside from sharpening your blades, I also taught Hood a good recipe or two," answered the stocky man.

"So... Hood... Only the two of us! Two brave young... Well, a young man and an old, bitter, man, starting the adventure of their lifetime, right?" joked the lad.

"Well, Link, don't take this the wrong way, but you haven't lived even half the adventures I did," replied Hood, ignoring the fact that Link called him old, "and as for brave... You still haven't proved much really. You just risked your life... What? Once, maybe? In yesterday's little skirmish? You have no idea of how many battles you've got ahead of you, champ," fired Hood, right back at the lad. They all laughed at the comeback, even Link.

After finishing with the meal, they all collaborated with the clean up and went to sleep. Zelda in her bed and the other three on the ground, on top of some soft, padded, bags.

As they all laid down and were ready to sleep, Hood had some final words for the day "Tomorrow we leave at sunrise, Link. Luckily, it'll take us a month until we reach the Great Deku Tree. So, rest well, we have a long journey ahead of us. Good night everyone!".

"Good night!" was the general answer and they all fell asleep.

"Ko, Koko, Kokooooo!" crowed the male cucco of the band, waking the whole settlement up.

Astor was the first one to get on his feet and started to prepare breakfast. Zelda followed and helped him by making some toasts. Link and Hood followed, a few minutes later, almost at the same time. The four of them had breakfast and happily talked about anything but the journey to come.

Once they were done, Hood stood up "I'm going to get the horses and equipment ready,".

Then, Astor also got up, started to clean up the table and went outside the tent to wash the cutlery in a cauldron with water that was sitting out there. Zelda headed towards her bed, which was no more than two meters away and sat on it.

Link, noticed that she had watery eyes. He got up and headed towards the princess.

"Zelda... What is it? Why are you crying?" asked the lad.

"I'm not crying... well, maybe just a little," she answered, "Link, I've missed you so much... I wanted to see you so badly... and these few days just flew by,".

"Don't be sad, Zel... While I don't have the same memories that you do, I also feel like this time was rather short. And, add to that, the fact that you spent half of that time fainted and I slept through the other half..." Link was joking to lighten up the situation "Don't think that the idea of staying isn't tempting. Just stroll around, chat and whatnot... but if I stay, we could only endure a few more attacks. And then, what?".

"I know... This journey is paramount to turn this story around," Zelda unwillingly accepted, "Still, I'd like not to be the princess and be able to join you," she added, as she held Link's hand, who was now sitting by her side.

"Zel, I promise you'll be there with me every step of the way. I'll find you allies in no time, so I can come back as soon as possible... After all, I think that, between us, there's still something left unspoken," said the lad, remembering what happened at the cave.

"There's no doubt about that," answered the princess, "but it's not the first time it happens to us,". She let go of his hand and hugged him, leaning her head on his shoulder, "come back soon, please,".

The lad was caught by surprise and didn't know where to put his hands. He decided that, hug her back wasn't a bad idea.

"Don't worry, I'll be back in no time," he answered, which made Zelda hug him even harder.

The lass, still leaning on his shoulder, turned her face and kissed Link on his cheek, so close to his mouth that he couldn't avoid being surprised, something that the princess missed, since she had her eyes closed.

Zelda stood up, wiped her tears and walked Link to the entrance of the tent.

"I'll fetch the maps for you to take, see you in a while," she said.

"Ok, I'm not going anywhere without saying goodbye," answered Link.

He went outside and met his companion. Hood had two horses equipped with two well loaded saddlebags. Link pet the one he was going to ride, he remembered Epona and smiled. Whispers started running through the curious hylian crowd, who were gathering around. Suddenly, from said crowd, a little boy, about eight years old, came out running.

"Mr. Link, Mr. Link!" he was screaming.

Link turned around and saw this little kid, with a quite sturdy wooden sword. He smiled as he thought about how noble the kid was, trying to help bringing him a sword, even if it was going to be quite useless. Or at least that's what he thought, until...

"My parents told me that you might be going to the forest of the great tree... I know it, and I know that he's not bad, but he doesn't like its family to be abused," said the kid, "Nevertheless, if you defend yourself with this sword, the tree won't see you as someone who's trying to hurt him. I know, because Mr. Deku tree himself gave the wood to my father so he could make this sword,".

Link couldn't believe what he was hearing. Eyes fixed on the sword, he looked at hood to see his expression. The old man answered back with a smile.

"Well, this is lucky. If I were you, I would seize this chance, it really is a nice sword. Actually, I'm carrying my own," and moving his robe aside, he showed a sword identical to the one the kid had, but with some weird symbols carved out.

"Ivan!! Ivan!!!" came screaming a woman from amidst the crowd, "Ivan! Don't bother Mr. Link," she scolded the little boy, "Sorry sir, my kid can be rather enthusiastic sometimes,".

"Don't worry, it's not a problem," Link answered.

"Mom, I'm just giving him the sword dad made with the deku wood," the kid explained.

"And does your father know of this?" his mother replied.

"He now does," said a man who was coming closer, smiling. He carried some wooden boxes on his hands, which looked to contain food. The man was about fifteen centimeters taller than Link, fair skinned, like his son. His face blonde and eyes brown. His ears were not pointy, like those of hylians originally from Hyrule, but more rounded like those from Ordon plains.

As Link saw them, he remembered the owner of the goats, which he used to train, his neighbor Braulio. The man looked really energetic, but still had some bruises from the day before.

"Dad!" joyfully claimed the boy, "Hello, Ivan; Juli, my dear. How are you?" answered the man and, as he turned around, he stretched his open hand at Link "My name is Moy, pleased to meet you, sir,".

Link shook his hand, "the pleasure is all mine," he answered, "your kid is really kind, but I can't accept such a lovely piece of handwork,".

"Oh, don't worry about it, I have many of those at home. You should keep that one, it'd be an honor for me,". He took the sword from the kid and put it on Link's hands, "I know you must think that a wooden sword is useless if you have a steel one, but it turns out to be quite handy, if you don't want to seriously harm your opponent,".

"I don't know what to say, thank you very much... I have nothing to give you in return though," said Link, but he was cut short.

"You don't have to give me nothing, sir. You've done plenty for Hyrule already... in the past," said Juli.

Zelda came out of the tent with the promised maps. Juli smiled at her and lowered her head and so did the kid, while Moy showed a clenched fist, showing his support for the princess's cause.

"Hello, Moy, I see you've met Link," said the lass, "Moy is a good citizen, with strong convictions. Maybe you've met him before, his family comes from Ordon,".

Link tried to remember them, looking at Moy and Juli, "... no, I can't remember, but anyway I can sense your enthusiasm and I'm glad that you're here. It takes people like you to beat Ganondorf," said Link as he got on his horse and, after checking that Hood got onto his, he said "Well, I think it's time to leave, we can't linger on if we hope to be back soon,".

As he jumped on his horse, a man in the crowd screamed

"Long live Link!" and shortly after, others joined "Good luck, Link!"; "Long live the resistance!"; "Long live Zelda!"; "Hurray Link!"; "We're counting on you!". Link looked at the crowd, excited. Two days ago, he was arriving at the settlement, no knowing anyone and, while he didn't know many still, they all put their hopes on his journey.

"Long live Hyrule!" Zelda shouted.

Link looked at her, her face filled with satisfaction and answered back "Long live Hyrule!".

The crowd went wild and the brave heroes started riding. Some kids run a few meters, following the horses. Many adults, including Zelda herself, waved the raiders goodbye and, after a few moments, they had vanished amidst the foliage.

For about a week and a half, Link and Hood rode non-stop. While on daylight, they only stopped to eat and feed their horses. At night, they looked for the nearest creek to reload their water supply, fish, light a fire and mount a small encampment. Usually, they chatted and Hood gave the lad some good advice about how to sheathe a sword or grab an arrow from a quiver, all to better Link's technique, should a fight come along. All in all, they had a rather fair weather, the first week of travel was a bit cloudy for a couple of hours in the afternoon, but far from being something bad, it helped them to avoid overheating while riding. Luckily, winter gave them a truce for a couple of days and, while the forest was southeast of Hyrule's castle, it was northwest from the settlement, so winter wasn't as harsh as it was on the southerner lands.

Well into their thirteenth day of ride, Hood suggested a brief rest.

"Link, do you see that clear field up ahead?" he asked, as he slowed down.

"Yes, I do. And a creek, right?" Link replied.

"Yes, and, if I'm not wrong, we won't find one like it for a few days. How about we try fishing before moving on? Besides, my horse seems rather tired. We've been riding at quite a fast pace," said the old man.

"Well... It's a good idea... And, while I know that fishing isn't science, could you give me some advice? Since we left it's been you who had caught all the fish," the lad requested to the old man as they reached the creek's shore.

"Of course, what I'm about to teach you, is something you've already been taught before. It's just that you've forgotten it, because of your accident," said the old man.

"Look, Hood, either we stop talking about my past or we talk about it, without you saying something along the lines of I can't tell you that, or anything like that. Your choice," the lad replied.

"All right, don't get mad. I won't talk about your past," said the old man as he pulled a thin string and some kind of oval piece of metal, twisted into the shape of a little fish, with a hook clasped to it, from his saddlebag.

He walked up to a little tree, "Link, can you hold this for a brief moment?" he said as he handed the lad the string with the little fish and the hook. He unsheathed his sword and cut a branch from the tree. Then, he pulled his dagger and used it to shape the branch into a rod.

"It's not quite like my rod, which, by the way, I left at the settlement, so we could travel lighter. But the wood from this tree is quite pliable, so it'll do," the old man claimed, "Here, you should tie the string to little teaspoon, to the branch I gave you, follow me," and he started heading towards the creek.

"The little teaspoon?" asked the lad.

"Yes, teaspoon," the old man insisted, "You see, there are different ways to fish, but since we don't have bait, we're going to take advantage of this little contraption, which is known as teaspoon, because of its shape,".

"Oh, I see... And how are we going to get the fishes to bite without bait?" Link couldn't understand how this scheme was going to be successful.

"Well, I admit this is not the best way to do it," accepted the old man, "but, if you pay attention to stuff like the weather or the way the creek runs, you can guess that, in these waters, we might probably find trout, salmons or maybe something along that line, which tend to swim against the stream. Knowing this, and since we have no bait, all we have left is using that little guy to attract some fish," explained Hood, "the teaspoon mimics the movements of a fish every time you pull from the string. This would be better with the appropriate equipment, but we'll have to make do with the current of the creek to simulate the movement of a little fish,".

"Wow! I can't believe it! You're quite wise!! How is it you never tried to represent Hyrule?" said Link, flattering the old man, "I mean, it's not like this make you the smartest man on earth, but I noticed that, all you say and do has some interesting reasoning behind it, and it doesn't seem to be chance,".

"Thank you for the compliment, but in my family, there's someone wiser than me," said Hood, and without leaving space for Link to say anything he went on, "aim for that place, over the backwater," he said as he showed Link a spot on the creek, "meanwhile, I'll feed the horses,".

Link started fishing and stood there, thinking.

A few minutes went by and the lad had accommodated himself on a stone that was nearby. He had the makeshift rod stuck to the ground beside him. In the quite of the afternoon, he started to contemplate the landscape, taking in the beauty of it. Suddenly, he stopped at a plant he didn't recognize. It was at the other side of the creek, so it was hard to get a clear picture of it. Link focused all his attention on that weird bush. He couldn't see its roots, but he could see its main branch. It was quite wide for such a short plant. The tiny top, of about fifty centimeters of diameter was dense, rather rounded and the leaves had a clear green shade, which stood out from the dark green foliage around it. The main branch had three holes, one seemed to be a snout of sorts and was located a bit beneath the other two which were symmetrical one another. They seemed to have something shining inside of them, like two eyes, made of sap, which had a very peculiar amber color. The lad couldn't stop thinking about the strange bush, he felt like it was glaring at him. Suddenly...

"Link! The rod!" Hood screamed at the lad, making him notice that something had bitten.

Link rushed to un-stuck the rod from the ground. He took it with both hands and started to struggle with the fish.

"It seems to be a big one," said Hood observing how much Link had to fight with it, "When you feel it easing a bit, give it a little tug to the side and pull it out,".

Link felt the fish giving up and he took his chance. The fish was big enough for both men to eat from it.

"Nice catch, Link!" praised the old man, "You got us dinner!".

Link smiled at the old man and then took his sight to the other side of the creek. He couldn't believe his eyes when he couldn't find the bush he was staring at.

"What is it, champ? Aren't you happy to have caught such a piece?" asked the old man.

"Yeah... I am... it's just that, I thought I've seen something over there... I could swear a bush on that side of the creek was giving me the stink eye before the fish bit," the lad told Hood.

"Really? That's odd... Well, it's probably nothing. We should move along. We can ride for another two hours and light a fire so we can roast the fish before it goes bad," said Hood, paying no attention to the lad's tale, "By then it will probably be nightfall and we'll be able to get a full night sleep and recover our strength for tomorrow,".

Link obeyed, but had a strange feeling, like if Hood was keeping something from him. Anyway, it didn't seem like much and decided to gather his stuff and get on his way.

Once they were ready, Hood started to ride and Link followed. Before leaving, Link looked once again to the other side of the creek, but this time, two weird bushes were there, standing still. Now, it was four bright amber spots haunting the lad.

"Link! It's getting late!" screamed the old man from afar.

"It's two of them now..." and as he turned around to look for them, Link saw the bushes were nowhere to be found.

CHAPTER 14

SARIA

They both rode, going deeper into the woods, which had a vast amount of diversity in its flora. It was so incredible that Link couldn't help but try to see every tree there was. Green reigned supreme in all its kinds. Despite of what little light the sunset let the riders enjoy; the lad could gaze upon different fruits with as many colors as the rainbow itself. Fireflies joined in, to sparkle some magic into the picture and the forest had a new sense of night life. Sunshine finally left them completely, but the moon took over to provide just enough light for them to move on.

"How about here, Link?" asked Hood, "That tree seems like it was struck by a lightning and is rather dry. We can use some branches to light a fire and also, should a storm start, it's not likely for another lightning to strike here… you know how the saying goes: Lightning never strikes twice," joked the old man, which made the lad laugh.

"I guess you're right, although I doubt it's going to rain. The sky is rather clear," the lad said, while he stopped his horse beside a tree, "and I agree with you. This dry wood is going to burn quite fast,".

Both unmounted and tied their horses to the nearest tree. The animals started to eat and drink from the grass and little puddles around them. Link and Hood chose a dry branch from the lightning-stricken tree and took it down. Hood unsheathed his sword and made a few chops on it. Then, both of them leaned it against the tree and, with a swift kick, snaped it into three big chunks. Once again, Hood used his sword to pluck the tiny little branches that came from the chunks and use them to start the fire. The lad headed towards the old man's horse and, from its saddlebag, took out a lamp and a little shovel.

"How about here?" asked Link, as he chose a spot on the ground.

189

"Yeah, that should be fine. Can you dig the hole while I find a twig to stick the fish?" the old man replied.

"Of course, no problem," the lad answered, then, he took the little shovel and dug a hole, about thirty centimeters deep and forty centimeters wide.

Soon, Hood returned, twig in hand, "Did you remember to make the breathing holes?" he asked.

"Yes, matter of fact, I made three of them," Answered the lad.

On their first night on the road, Hood taught him many ways to light a fire. One of them was digging a hole on the ground, it should be small, with a few holes nearby, which should lead to the deeper part of the hole, so that fresh air could pass through and keep the fire burning.

"Excellent work. Did I tell you why is it better to make a fireplace like this?" asked Hood.

"You did. This way we can control the heat so that it only goes upward. Also, this way is the one that produces the least amount of light and helps avoid prying eyes," answered Link.

"Well… I see that you learnt your lesson," said the satisfied old man.

"Who taught you so many useful things about living out in the wild?" asked the lad.

"The same person who taught you, one of the teachers from Hyrule school," replied the old man.

"I didn't know you also went to school!" said Link.

"Well yes. I was lucky enough to assist when I was young. Help me out with these logs," Hood answered as he was carrying the wood for the fire.

Together, they made a kind of huge brochette with the fish and put it on top of the logs that Link set at the sides of the hole. Hood poured some oil from the lamp over the wigs and, with a little stone and his sword, the old man made a few sparkles fly over them and the fire started burning. From his backpack, Link pulled a few thin rods of iron, some cord and a big, thick piece of fabric.

"I'll help you in a minute," said the old man.

"Take your time, I'm going to start stretching the tent," answered the lad with the fabric on his hand.

Hood made sure the fire was steady and able to cook the fish. Then, he went near Link and helped him put up the tent. A couple of minutes later, they were both sitting in front of the fireplace, with the tent behind them.

"I believe we have a few tomatoes left in the side pocket of the little rucksack," said Link.

Two days ago, they've found a tree filled with ripped tomatoes and had taken a few.

"Let me check…" said the old man, as he headed to his horse, "You're right, my young friend!". Hood pulled a little plank and his dagger, "Check the fish while I chop these, will you?".

About an hour later, they had eaten and were sitting beside the fire, contemplating it. They remained sitting, in silence, for a couple of minutes until they decided to get into the tent and get some rest.

Once inside, Link immediately fell asleep. Spending the whole day riding had left him spent and closing his eyes was something that came easy to him. The white noise outside was really relaxing. The wind blew calmly and stopped once in a while, which left them listen to the owl's hoot. The crickets could be heard from time to time. About seven or eight ours went by when Link got woken up by a sound outside the tent. It was still night time, and many minutes were left until sunrise. The lad thought about going back to sleep, but he heard the same noise again. It was similar to a toad's croaking, but it had some tune to it, which made it seem like a way of communication. It was then that the lad decided to go out and check where this noise came from, but as soon as he popped his head out of the tent, he once again saw the bush with amber eyes, staring at him, not even five meters away and froze in the spot.

Moving as slowly as he could, Link got his head back into the tent.

"Pssst… Hood… wake up," he whispered, "I think there's something watching us outside the tent,".

191

"What the heck are you talking about?" grumped the old man, still half asleep.

"I think there's someone watching us," the lad repeated.

"How many eyes can you see..." asked the old man, still laying on his side and without even opening his eyes.

Link shyly peeped through the tent's door, but it wasn't only two by now, but more like twenty glistering amber lights, looking directly at them were all around the place, all in pairs of two, and the ones that used to be five meters away, were now about three meters from the tent. The lad turned around and looked at Hood, without knowing what to do.

"They used to be two, but now there's like twenty little lights... they look like bushes, but I think they're moving," the lad said.

Hood heard him and got up immediately, "Your wooden sword. Where is it?" he asked.

"it's on your horse, why?" asked a now worried Link.

"Well... Do you remember that sword that could be used for practice or repelling your opponent, without harming him?" Hood asked the lad.

"I do. Why do you ask?" the lad was fearing the answer that was coming.

"Because we're now surrounded by enemies which we can't harm, if we expect to get the Deku tree's respect," the old man bitterly answered.

Link knew this was coming, "What? What do you mean with..." he tried to ask, but Hood interrupted him "I'll explain later. Right now, we must loosen the tent and move it from the inside. We'll use it to reach the horses, like if we were some kind of giant monster. I guess we can escape unscathed if we take advantage of the surprise factor," said the old man, who was thinking out loud.

"What? Escape unscathed? Hood... How much damage can we receive tonight?" asked the lad, who was getting a little nervous by now.

"Not much, I hope. But we might get a bruise or two," Hood answered, "Now, help me with the tent. Ready? We move on three. One… Two… NOW!" the old man said.

With a strong tug, the tent got unstuck from the ground and they both headed towards the horses. Hood screamed and made all sorts of weird noises inside the tent. Link didn't understand why, but he thought it'd be wise to mimic him and soon enough they reached the horses and gather their weapons.

"Only the wooden sword and your shield, Link. The rest we pick up later," said the old man.

They got their hands out from under the thick fabric and picked up their weapons. Hood threw the tent aside and they were out in the open.

Just like if the had multiplied about twenty bushes, all with different sizes, were surrounding them. Suddenly, one of them swell up, like if it was breathing in through its central hole. It closed its amber eyes and shot from its snout something that Link couldn't quite identify. The lad, instinctively covered with his shield and, whatever it was that the bush had shot, hit it, making it vibrate as it landed.

"Wow! What was that?!" asked the lad.

"Deku nuts, Link," answered Hood, "Be careful, a direct hit can cost you an eye,".

"Well, that's reassuring. What now?!" wondered Link.

"Now we strike back!" replied the old man as he stroke the nearest bush with his wooden sword.

Link followed him and targeted another bush, but it was faster and dodged the lad's swing with a swift hp backwards while it got swollen. This time, Link didn't rise his shield in time and the nut the bush spitted landed square on his shoulder.

"Ouch! Damnit, it hurts!!" complained the lad.

"I told you to be careful. A few more hits and you'll be done for. Take a defensive approach and only attack when you're sure it will hit," instructed the old man, while covering from another shot.

The lad took cover and, again, his shield took the hit. "TOC; TOC; TOC;" Three more hits against his shield. This time, Link managed to get nearer and the bush wasn't so lucky now. Once certain hit was all it took for the lad to leave it laying on the ground.

"What the heck are these things, Hood?" asked Link, who was now back to back with Hood.

"They're known as Deku Bushes," answered the old man, as he fell another one, "not all of them are aggressive. This kind is known as Mad Bush. They are quite... clingy to their territory and they attack as soon as they consider an invasion is on the go,".

"I know they're forcing us, but it doesn't feel right to knock them down like this... they seem rather weak," said Link, as he dodged another attack, "It makes me feel like we're the ones on the wrong here,".

"Yeah, I know, don't worry about it. You'll get your chance to apologize later... Right now, this is what we need to do,". Answered Hood, as he bashed another bush with his shield, "you won't hurt them too much, Link. They pass out rather easily, but they're sturdy. Tomorrow, they'll be as good as new,".

The lad felt a sudden relief and counter-attacked. From time to time, some Deku nuts hit them, but they weren't making too much damage and, in time, one by one, the bushes fell.

"It's hard to use a sword against them," noticed Link, "they're really short ranged and it's not effective against these long-ranged enemies,".

"I know, but I gave one of my blowpipes to my son and Astor kept the other one. That's why I don't have any non-lethal, long range, weapon right now," Hood replied, without making a big fuss out of it.

Link took notice of Hood's words "I didn't know you had a son,".

"Did I say son? I meant... Link, watch out!" Hood managed to cover a flank attack headed towards Link, "We better focus on this fight right now, shall we?".

There were only a few more bushes still standing, when, from

194

amidst the darkness, the shining edge of a steel sword made its way from amongst the weeds.

"You're mine!" said a crackling voice.

A demon was running towards a bush.

"NO!" screamed Hood, while running to tackle him before he could reach his target.

The old man managed to barely intercept the demon, before it could run the bush through with his sword.

Hood's shield made a loud noise as the demon's sword landed against it. The bush fixated its two amber eyes in the demon's eyes and noticed that Hood wasn't his enemy, but the possessed one. It all happened in an instant. The demon had let his guard down; the bush swell and hit the demon with a nut, right between his eyes; Hood took advantage of this and bashed him with his shield while releasing his wooden sword; he punched him in the face three times before the demon could hit the ground. The demon, laying on the ground, let go of his sword. Hood broke three of his ribs with a fourth blow and took the sword from the ground.

"You're free..." Hood said, as he run the sword through the possessed one's heart.

The bushes, those that were still conscious, watch everything unfold, as did Link, and ceased their attack. Five more demons appeared.

Three of them headed towards Hood and the remaining two towards Link. The lad could only repel their attacks with his shield, since he wielded a wooden sword and he knew it wasn't going to withstand a single clash against a steel one. Hood, on the other hand, fought back using his shield and the sword he took from the fallen demon.

Both hylians were getting close one another, step by step, repelling attacks. The lad noticed that, one of his enemies, was having a hard time controlling his body. His attacks were erratic and didn't have a pace. Link suspected he wasn't even using all of his strength to attack and the blows he threw were rather weak. Meanwhile, the other one didn't seem to mind about anything more than watching Link die painfully.

195

"Hood! I really wouldn't mind a hand here!" Link screamed.

"Hold on, Link! Use your shield!" replied the old man.

Link received yet another blow to his shield, "Well, that's all I'm doing right now!".

Hood managed to push two of the demons back with his shield and surprised the third one, sticking his sword through his neck.

"Rest in peace," the old man said, as he removed the sword, "one less, Link!" he claimed while nearing the lad. The bushes seemed confused, but, after what seemed to be a brief discussion in a weird language, they started shooting their nuts to the possessed beings who attacked Link.

The lad heard the buzzing sound the nuts made as they passed by him. All of the nuts hit the more aggressive of his enemies, like if they were purposefully avoiding hitting the other one.

The wounded demon screamed, as he filled with rage; his mouth filled with foam. He pushed Link aside, using his hand to move his shield aside and run off towards the Mad Bushes. The lad tripped and fell backwards. The shield got loose and, while waiting for the inevitable attack of the other demon, he watched as he came closer to him. He seemed to be the same age as Link. His skin still had some color on it and his eyes were blue, with some red splashes. He wore some rustic clothes; had a green vest and same color, worn out, pair of trousers. He sported some wounds that hadn't healed yet and other wounds were badly infected.

As the demon reached Link, his sword inevitably fell upon Link and got stuck.

The lad was shocked. The demon stood still in front of him and the sword was buried in the ground, mere centimeters away from his left ear. Link, still in disbelief, opened his mouth to say something, but the demon beat him to the punch.

"He- Help the... bushes," he begged.

Link noticed that one of the demon's hands was trying to grab back the sword, but the other one was not allowing this, firmly grasping his wrist, like if the owner of the body was trying to fight back the demon possessing him.

"Link! Quickly! Now it's your chance, flee! Do as he say!" shouted Hood, who was checking on the lad from afar.

Link stood up, grabbed the steel sword from the floor and his shield. He started running, heading to where the bushes had fled to, "There's something weird with this demon!" he warned to Hood, "I'm not sure he wanted to attack me!".

"I know. Go now!" was the only reply he got from Hood.

Link was running full speed through the woods. He jumped over a huge root and sensed it was starting to dawn. While on the chase, he found the demon's footprints and followed them. Meanwhile, one of Hood's enemies decided to abandon his fight and follow into the lad's path, also dodging or moving aside the branches and roots that crossed his way.

Avoiding obstacles in any way he could, the lad made way through the overgrown forest, still following the footprints. Suddenly, he found a cave of sorts, although, he never realized when was it exactly that he found it.

The lad felt a sharp pain on his ankle, something bit him and threw him to the ground, "Ouch! What the heck?!". There was some sort of weird, rather big, plant grabbing him. He tried to escape, but it was going to be impossible to do so without using his sword. He couldn't hesitate, "I hope the great Deku doesn't mind about this..." he said to himself. With a single, swift slash, he separated the tiny top of the plant from its own stem.

The lad released his foot from the piece of plant that was grabbing him and, still a bit sore, he got up on his feet. He headed into the cave at once, and realized that the darkness barely let him see the way. It wasn't a problem though, since the footprints soon ended, letting him see his enemy's feet.

The lad could see how the demon had the bushes cornered against what seemed to be a dead end; a big stone wall, covered with moss, that signaled the bottom of that cave.

"Hey! You!" Link shouted, "You were fighting me, tough guy. Remember?"

The demon groaned while he turned around, "Then, first, I'm going to deal with you and I'll finish off this bothersome salad later,".

197

A few meters away from there, Hood was fighting the remaining demons.

"Well... it seems that one of you is already down and two more left and that one can't even help you," Hood told the only enemy he had left, "I think that your luck has run out,".

"I wouldn't be so sure about that, old man. Age-wise, numbers are against you," the demon mocked Hood.

"You got it all wrong, my age helps me plenty," said the old man, letting his shield fall on the ground, just in the place where the fire they made the prior night used to burn. "Precisely, it was due to my age that I learnt that it's always better to know the battlefield you're at," the old man told the demon, and right after, he kicked the edge of the shield with his heel, which sent flying a handful of still burning embers, straight into the demon's face.

"AHRG!" screamed the demon, "you damn cheating old man!".

In a swift move, Hood wielded his sword and run it from side to side through the demon's chest.

"Coming from one of Ganondorf's minions, I'll take it as a compliment," the old man said, "Oh! Something else, through the years I also learnt something else, aside from battlefield reconnaissance. I never get tired of this, but the surprise factor always puts you in an advantageous position and, many times, even wins you the battle,". Hood could see the demon smile at him, weakly, as he died "Enjoy your freedom," the old man told him.

In a turn of events, the remaining minion started moving, as the demon probably won the fight against his host and headed towards Hood, letting out a raged scream.

Hood saw it coming and, without overthinking it, he punched him with a right cross in the middle of his face, knocking him down.

"I have something special for you," said the old man and, grabbing him from his vest, he dragged him up to his horse.

"Let's see... what do we have here?" said Hood as he searched through one of his saddlebags, "let me see... Let me see...

Yes! Here you are!". From one of the pockets, he had pulled out the sharp dagger that Astor had sharpened a few days ago.

The old man looked at the possessed boy laying on the ground, "If I'm not mistaken, you were left-handed, so I better stick this here,". He turned him around and stuck the dagger in the back of his right arm. The boy's body twitched, his arm got swollen and the cerulean gemstone in the middle of the dagger started to darken. A few seconds after, it was completely black. The old man pulled the dagger from the boy's arm and, searching through the same saddlebag, he pulled a stone, some water, a few herbs, some string and a needle.

The fainted boy's skin started to gain more and more of its natural color while Hood cleaned and stitched his arm. Only a couple more stitches remained when…

"Ouch! Who are you and what are you doing!?" said the waking boy, as he tried to stand back up.

"I'm the one who just saved your life. And what I'm doing is trying to avoid that you bleed out. If you're man enough to take two more stitches I can finish up," replied the old man.

The boy looked at Hood, then checked his arm and tried to remember how did he end up in that situation but his sight clouded and he fell on his knees. His eyes were heavy and not being able to remain awake, he fainted and fell backwards once again.

"Pfff… weakling," said Hood, as he headed towards the fallen boy. The old man finished stitching his arm and rubbed some herbs on it, leaving some sap on the wound. Then he firmly bandaged it. Lastly, he grabbed him and put him on Link's horse.

In a hurry, Hood tided up everything they've used the night before and what he used to heal the boy. He grabbed the dagger and stuck it into a half-burned log, located into the fireplace. The demon left the dagger and was entrapped into the log. Hood, kicked it to the bottom of the hole and covered it with dirt.

"Have a nice one…" said the old man and climbed onto his horse and, while holding both the reins of his horse and Link's, he followed the footprints of the bushes, Link and the demons.

Meanwhile, at the cave, Link was fighting the remaining demon. This one seemed skillful. His clothing was the one of a hylian soldier, so Link assumed the demon was takin advantage of the skillset of the host body.

"You thought it would be easier, didn't you?" mocked the demon.

"For an underling, you're really talky… Don't you think?" fired back the lad, which only enraged the demon even further. "AHHRRG!! YOU DAMN RAT!" the demon threw three reckless sword slashes.

Link defended with his shield and, while he did feel the heavy blows on his forearm, he seized his chance to strike back with his sword.

The sharp blade cut through the air and landed square into the demon's knee, which fell down, kneeling in pain.

"We're roughly the same height now, right?" said the lad once he was face to face with the demon who was around thirty centimeters taller than him.

"If not me, another one of us will kill you in my stead… There's a lot of us, little cockroach," the demon threatened Link.

"Well, then I'll try to save an arrow for each one of you," he answered and with the bash of his shield straight to his head he finished the fight. He then let go of his shield and headed towards the bushes.

"I hope that, after all this, you won't be inclined to attack me," he told them, not knowing if he was being understood, "you're safe now,".

The bushes shook. Link turned around and was confronted by the last demon of the whole party. The one that abandoned his fight with Hood to follow him.

"No shield, nor sword. It must be my lucky day!" said the demon, realizing that Link was now defenseless. And just as he was preparing to attack the lad, the demon stopped moving, rolled his eyes backwards and fell on his knees and then sideways to the ground.

As he fell, Link could see a bunch of darts nailed to the demon's back. He looked over the demon, to where the light was shining through into the cave and managed to witness a female shape getting closer. Shortly after, he recognized that the silhouette belonged to a young woman; dressed in green, she wore a brown belt with leather pouches on it, a few daggers and two blowpipes. She had fair and rather shiny skin, green eyes and blonde, greenish, hair. She seemed to have some camouflage-like paint on her face, obviously, also of a dark green tone.

"I see that you've saved a few bushes which, undoubtably, must have attacked you before," said the young girl, "The forest thanks you for that. Is there anything else I can help you with?".

"Well… actually, there is," Link answered while picking his shield from the ground and removing his sword from the demon's leg and sheathing it back, "I'm looking for the Great Deku Tree. I need to ask it for its help to find the wood's sage… If I'm not wrong, her name is Saria,".

"Interesting," she replied, "you are actually correct, her name is Saria, but you won't need to ask Deku about her,".

Link was confused, "Why? Do you know where can I find her?" he asked.

The lady looked at him, smiled and answered, "Of course I do. Right now, she's right in front of you,".

CHAPTER 15

THE KOKIRI VILLAGE

The lad was astounded. He was standing in front of the very person he came looking for.

"It can't be that easy…" he told himself. Nevertheless, it was.

"If you don't mind me asking," the forest sage broke the silence, "do we know each other?".

"We… might. I had this inconvenient some time ago. I'm not sure how, but I lost my memory," the lad explained, "anyways, my name is Link, pleased to meet you,".

"Link? Link from Hyrule?" said Saria, in disbelief of what she just heard.

"Yes, as far as I know, the only one. Do we know each other?" He asked. He still had his hand outstretched, Saria dodged his hand, headed straight to his chest and hugged him tight, "Link! I can't believe it! You're back!" the girl was overflowing with joy.

Link didn't understand what was going on, but he was getting used to this kind of things happening to him. She then let go of the hug.

"Look at you, all grown up… Well, not much in height dough, but, that morning beard looks good on you," the sage teased the lad, "And what happened with your hair? You used to grow it out. I see you're sporting a shorter cut now," she said as she played with the lad's hair.

"So… it seems we do know each other… Three weeks ago, I was nobody and today I'm close friend with two of the seven sages," Link teased out loud.

"You've met another sage?" asked Saria.

"Yeah, well actually one that became a sage, since her father isn't capable of assuming the role. I believe you know each other, her name is Zelda," Link answered.

"Ah… I've already seen Zelda then," replied Saria, unenthusiastically.

Link noticed the lack of joy in the sage's answer, "Yes... It was her that showed me how to reach you,".

"Things must be really bad for her to lead you to me..." said Saira, "and... You two... Are you a thing? I mean, is there something going on between you two... romantically speaking?" the sage asked, nonchalantly.

Link wasn't that dumb, he made ends meet and realized that for some reason, which he felt, was at least partially related to himself, Saria was jealous of Zelda, "I'm not sure. She's a nice girl, but I think that what we've got going is not more than a close friendship," he answered, though inside he knew it was a bit of a white lie.

"I see..." Saria doubted the truth in Link's reply, "I thought you'd come with someone,". Link then remembered he left Hood behind and quickly started running back to where he left him.

He thought that, if two demons went after him, then only two remained; and one of them seemed to refuse to fight, so it wouldn't be to hard for the old man to win that fight unharmed.

But all of that didn't matter. As he exited the cave, he saw the old man, the two horses and four people. One of them was on top of his horse, the other three were the demons that Hood defeated and were tied by their feet, with a rope to the back of his saddle. The old man was dragging them along.

"You took your time, didn't you?" the old man greeted Link.

"I'm sorry," relieved, the lad answered, "This is Saria, the sage of the forest," he added, as she exited the cave.

"I know. Hello, Saria," the old man replied, unsurprised.

Link wasn't surprised about this kind of things anymore, "Ok. Saria, this is...".

"I know. Hello, Hood," she interrupted while greeting the old man.

The lad was now standing between them, "Oh, great. Thank the gods this isn't an awkward moment!".

"On the contrary, Link," answered Saria, "I've been waiting for you for over seven years,".

The girl looked at Hood and then directed her sight towards the man on the horse, "Is... Is that Mido!?".

"Yes, it is, my lady," replied Hood

Link recognized the man who, while possessed, fought against him, "That's the demon that attacked me a while ago!" Link said while reaching for his sword.

"Was, Link. Was," the old man interceded.

"Is he dead?" both youngsters asked at once.

"No, he's just fainted, and no longer possessed," Hood said, "If you can, bring back the two demons that are inside this cave and tie them to the horse. I want to take them far from this sacred place,".

Link Hurried in "I'll get them,".

"Thank you, Link," said the sage, "once you return, we'll head to the village to left Mido at his place and talk about your quest,".

Link nodded and went to fetch the demons. It took him less than a minute to reach the place where the bodies were and less than five to head back out of the cave with both of them. As he headed out, he saw the old man and Saria chatting amicably. Then, Hood noticed Link's arrival, "Can you tie them over there with the others?".

"Sure, no problem," answered the lad.

Once the demons were tied, the group walked through the woods, towards the kokiri village. Hood was holding the reins of both horses in his hand. Saria was in the middle of the group, talking with both hylians at her sides.

"We won't take much longer, it's not more than a kilometer north of here," the sage let the other two know. They both nodded and followed her.

About fifteen minutes later, Link saw that, right in front of them, a lush wall of trees was standing. They were tightly close to each other and it seemed like, the deeper they went, the closer together the trees seemed.

"This is one thick forest," said the lad.

"It's a distraction method," explained Saria, "Anyone wondering around would simply look for an alternative route, something that would allow an easy way back. This way, we keep possible enemies away from our settlement. Nevertheless, if you follow the path, getting though the trees, you'll reach a wall of timber built by the first kokiris and maintained by us,".

After the explanation, the lad couldn't hide his amazement at their dedication "I see you've hidden yourself really well!".

"That's actually the point, Link. We kokiris are… or at least everyone else say we are the most peaceful race of the bunch. We'll always prefer running rather than fighting… at least most of us. Although, there are a few exceptions, which are becoming more frequent lately, like the one you carry over your horse," she said, referring to Mido, "In any way, kokiris best weapon is camouflage. Most of us can mimic over fifty wild animals, which comes really helpful in tight situations,".

"Incredible… What a clever idea," praised Link.

"Let's keep going. Right this way," led Saria. The three of them passed through some trees, Link, noticed that Saria seemed to be using some markings etched on them, like inscriptions, as guidelines. They all had different symbols on their crusts, nevertheless, the sage seemed to be able to follow the right path easily. After a little while, they faced a tall wooden wall. Saria knocked and, from the other side, a little bird-like whistling was heard. The lass answered with a whistle of her own. The wood cracked and got open, as if it was a narrow, double-decked, door.

Once inside the village, a few curious kokiris came near. Saria neared Hood, and whispered "make the horses dragging the bodies go through the back of those wooden planks over there,". The old man obeyed and hid the horse, making it take an alternative route to the stables.

Saria waved, summoning three kokiris.

"You two help him. Cover the bodies with a blanket, so the kids can't see them," she ordered to the skinnier ones, "You, help me get Mido home," she then ordered to the stockier one.

"Yes, my lady," they answered coordinately.

"Link, I'll get some food and water for your horses in a second, for now, I'd like you to come along with me," requested Saria to the lad, who obliged.

The sage walked a few meters until she reached a stage of sorts and climbed the steps.

"Kokiris of the forest!" she called out, "I'm afraid I have to tell you that war has reached our doorstep," the crowd was listening closely to the lass, "We knew this would happen sooner or later. Yesterday, six demons attacked a few bushes, less than a kilometer from here... One of the possessed was no other than Mido," a few of them started to murmur, concern was growing amidst the lot, "But we are lucky, since we're receiving support from the other races, "Saria said, while introducing Link first and then Hood, who was arriving from the stables and passing through the crowd, "Two hylians defeated all the demons; saved the bushes and, miraculously, rescued Mido, ripping the demon from inside him," the crowd started an uproar, "The great Hood and his pupil, whom you might already know, the young Link, were the ones responsible for such a tremendous task!".

The mass of people was getting really loud by now and Link's name could be easily heard amongst their sayings, "Is that Link?"; "Is Link truly back?"; "I thought that Link was dead!"; "Where was he all this time?" were some of the lines that could be heard from the mob.

Saria kept on rallying the kokiris, "I know that we are a peaceful race, but one of us almost died at the hands of the demons, and hylians want us to join them in their fight... I say, maybe it's time for the us to teach Ganondorf that the forest... Nature!... Was; Is and will be sacred!".

The crowd went crazy, it seemed like quite a few of them was harboring the idea of fighting against Ganondorf.

The lass calm everyone down before going on, "I know some of you will be scared, but I can assure you, this is the right thing to do... You also need to know, that this is not going to happen right away. We'll have time to prepare. And we won't be attacking on our own, our goron and zora friends will be there to join us," explained the sage, to ease the worries of many, "I will be letting you know how we're going to handle ourselves though this ordeal. For now, go along with your daily routines and don't get discouraged. The Great Deku Tree has our backs,".

207

The crowd fused in a round of applause and chanted the sage's name. She descended from the stage and headed towards Hood.

"Did you like my speech? Was it what you were hoping for?" wondered the sage, with a hint of satisfaction on her face.

"Excellent! Just as I requested on the way over," replied the old man "I know you... decorated the truth a bit and made a few omissions... and, well, you did take for granted some stuff that you don't know will come true. But I can assure you, for our next big engagement with Ganondorf, at least four of the six races will be joined in the army against him,".

"I hope you're right," answered Saria, "This town is my life. I don't know what I'd do if something happened to it,".

Link closely watch the whole conversation unfold. He was admiring the way in which Hood was making the whole resistance army come together, like a chess match. Sometimes a bit haphazardly and hopeful at best, but he was incredibly sure about the decisions he made.

"I'd like to visit Mido, before burying the fallen ones," requested the lass and both men agreed with her.

The three of them headed to the boy's house. Along the way, Saria asked one of the kokiris to bring food and water to the horses. Also, she asked for the saddles to be removed and put all the raider's equipment on the guest house.

Once they arrived at Mido's house, Saria went in without knocking on the door. The boy was lying on the bed where the stocky kokiri left him.

As he sensed someone approaching, the boy opened his eyes, "Saria? How did I get here?".

"These two saved your life, Mido," said Saria, pointing at Hood and Link.

"You're Link, right?" the boy asked, directing his sight towards the lad, who nodded, "Incredible, I was saved by my old friend and rival,".

Link wasn't amazed at the fact that the boy knew him, but the other part caught his attention. "Rival you say?" wondered the lad.

"It's something silly, don't pay attention to him," Saria cut in, "Tell us about this mess you got yourself into. Do you remember something?" she asked the boy.

"Very little. I don't really remember how long ago it was..." answered the boy, who was trying to recall the way things happened, "I went outside, to patrol the forest and I crossed five demons. At first, I only saw four of them, since on of them was clever enough to hide. He was wearing a hylian guard suit and was rather stronger than the rest. He was the one who held me while another put a flask with some black smoke in my mouth... After that, things get blurry,".

"A flask?" Link was confused.

"Obviously it was an entrapped demon," said Saria, "But, why would they carry him that way so that it could possess you?".

"I guess it wasn't precisely Mido they were looking for, but any kokiri at random," assumed Hood.

All of them were shocked as they heard him and awaited some more in-depth explanation from the old man, who elaborated.

"Demons, once they get to oppress their vessel's soul, gain complete control of it's functions, such as speech, skills and even memory. I think they hoped to reduce Mido and learn the way to access into kokiri territory," further explained Hood.

The kokiris inside the house looked at each other, worried. Mido felt guilty and Saria responsible for the current situation. But then, Hood spoke again.

"At any rate, there's nothing to worry about. Mido was never fully controlled... and if you say that there were only five demons and a sixth one in the flask, that means that all the demons from the group have been eliminated," the old man explained. The forest-dwellers where now relieved.

Putting a hand on Link's shoulder, the old man spoke to the boy, "What we'd like to know, Mido, is... How long were you possessed?".

The boy tried to remember, but it was hard for him, "Well... I can't really..." but Saria interrupted, "Three days. He headed to the forest three days ago. It's been three days since I've been looking for him throughout the forest,".

Mido realized that, while talking, Saria's eyes got all watery, which left him perplexed. He didn't know that the lass was so worried about him being missing.

"So... three days, eh?" pondered Hood, "Well, Link, it seems that your rival is rather resilient," the old man encouraged the kokiri boy who was lying on the bed.

Link remained silent, since he didn't understand the importance of that number. The old man realized it and, before someone else could say anything, he added, "To think that, some folks can't even hold for a few hours... and the most strong-willed ones, hold for about two days at most... This one is a tough bone to chew on,".

Mido puffed his chest, proudly and Saria's amazement was hard to hide.

"Well... we have a job to do, right?" said the lass, leading the hylians to the door.

"Hold on, I'm joining you..." said the young kokiri boy.

"No. You're going to stay and rest," ordered the sage, "Maybe, once you've fully recovered, we'll talk about it again,".

The three of them left Mido's house and headed towards the stable where they've left the horses. The hylians checked on their steeds and, since they were being cared for perfectly, they left to the guest house to grab some of their stuff.

As they reached and enter the house, the men discovered that some cheese, a few toasts and three jars filled with fruit juice had been left over the table for them. Hood looked at Saria and smiled at her. She reciprocated the gesture.

"After the long morning you've had, or rather we've had, and knowing that it's going to be a long day before we can return to the village, I recommend we have a good breakfast before leaving," the lass suggested to the hylians.

Link looked upon the old man, awaiting his approval, "Of course. I believe our job will wait for us, should we be a little late," joked Hood.

The three of them had breakfast, while they were chatting.

"And what about the fairies?" wondered Hood, which took Link by surprise, as he sipped from his cup of juice.

"Well… it's a bit early. They usually leave at midnight and don't return to the village until a bit before sunset," the sage responded.

The old man lamented that, "Ahh! I imagined so… Although, some of them do stay in from time to time, right?".

"They do, I guess Tael is going to want to spend the night here, once he knows Mido is recovering," confirmed Saria, "Since he's been missing, Tael did nothing but worry about him and blame himself for not joining him on the patrol,".

"And why didn't him join Mido?" asked Hood.

"A while back, the fairy king asked all of them to return every day to the kingdom. I believe that he does this to have a better population control. Minishes and fairies probably already know that the world is in turmoil right now," the sage conjectured.

Link was bouncing his glare between Hood and Saria, not understanding a single word he listened. Suddenly he found a perfect moment and asked away "Excuse me… fairies?".

The other two looked at him, "You know that kokiris keep tight bonds with fairies and minishes, right?" assumed Saria.

"Minishes…?" Link was out of his depth.

"Ahh…. You don't remember anything at all from before the battle of the bitter victory, do you?" remembered the sage and the lad confirmed her thoughts, "Ok then, we'll talk about this on the road, I wouldn't want to engage in such an extensive chat right now," the lass told him.

As they were talking, a young lady came through the door. She was agitated, "Saria! You're back! Did you find anything?" she asked while trying to catch her breath.

"Yes, Fado. Mido's been found, he's all right. Right now, he's at his home, resting," explained the sage.

As the young lady calmed down, Saria introduced her "Hood, Link, she's Fado, Mido's sister. Fado, these are Hood and Link, they're the ones who saved your brother,".

"Link? From Hyrule?" Fado asked.

Hood got up and, while the other two exchanged pleasantries, he headed to his backpack "I was checking if I didn't leave anything back at our encampment," the old man told the sage.

"Well, Link, thank you so much... we're lucky to have you back," said Fado, as she excused herself from the guest house.

"I'm sorry, by any chance are you going to your brother's house?" the old man asked the girl.

She nodded and, before she could rush out, the old man handed her a loaf of bread and a slice of cheese, "Here, take this to him... Oh, and this too," he said while grabbing a glass full of juice, "it's really good and, since he's been possessed for so long, he's probably famished,".

The girl didn't know how to react, so the sage interceded, "Do as he says. This man has my utmost trust and he seems to know quite a lot about this subject,".

"Thank you, mister, you're really kind," thanked Fado. She then grabbed a plater from the shelf nearby to put the items handed to her and left towards her brother's house.

The group finished up with their breakfast and, before heading out, Hood gave Link a few pointers, "Grab your sword and shield, the boomerang... And the bow and a few arrows,".

The lad did as what was ordered and only got those items. Once they reached the stables, they realized the demon's bodies where wrapped around a blanket and left on top of a small carriage, small enough to be dragged through the narrow main door of the village.

"It looks like you've got it all covered," the old man told Saria.

"What can I say? My people know me. I do like to be expeditious," accepted the lass.

The old man looked at the lad, "Link, would you take the reins, please?" he asked him, to which the lad agreed, with no problem.

Once they were outside the village, the men followed Saria on foot.

"The graveyard is a bit far from here, it'll take us… let's say two hours to reach it. But that will give me time to tell you a couple of things, Link," explained the lass.

"Really? What do you have to tell me?" the lad asked.

After a brief silence, Saria responded, "Well, for starters, what happened to Navi… your fairy companion,".

214

CHAPTER 16

UNEARTHING TOOLS

"A long time ago, the minish and fairies were considered like sibling races. Maybe because both species lived-off from nature, or maybe because they shared their small stature. After all, there are no known intelligent life-form, apart from them, whose height is less than an inch. Minishes excel in technological crafting, mainly mechanical machines and levers. Also, they have extensive knowledge in the field of chemistry. Many grant the discovery of gerudo gunpowder to a minish group that lived amongst them. On the other hand, fairies share a tight relation with flora and wild-life if this world. Their magic is based on their communication with their ecosystem. Should you harm the environment, the fairies will know about it. Still, they do understand that every race needs nature to survive. They can tell apart someone who hunts or fishes for need from someone who does it for fun or simply to harm. In this fashion, they can tell when you cut down a tree to make a house, shelter or maybe a bonfire and they can differentiate it from someone who just harms a flower for mere fun.

If you want to earn the trust of a fairy, you must prove your love for nature. And that, is something that kokiris know how to do well. At any rate, not long ago, a young boy, son of a she-minish and a fairy, left his family to join Ganondorf. As I understand it, the young halfling used to say over and over again that minish and fairies weren't slaves from anyone. Although, really, while both races lived in a symbiotic relation with other races, no-one forced them to do anything. Nevertheless, this boy kept affirming that he was the descendant from two of the oldest lineages on the planet and, because of this, he was superior from the rest.

The boy had high intellectual skills, inherited from his mother, and a wide knowledge of nature, inherited from his father. Using this skillset, he created a potion, using the blood of a hylian, which allowed him to increase his height. This potion allowed Vaati, the halfling boy, to look like a slightly taller and really thin, hylian.

It's believed that, initially, he joined Ganondorf in order to get close enough to kill him. But after his plan failed, he ended up working for the tyrant, as his assistant. The mighty gerudo king, in a sly maneuver, granted Vaati a fragment of the Tri-force of knowledge, which made him his most powerful ally.

After this, the minish and fairy leaders from each region gathered to discuss this turn of events. Far from reaching a consensus, they ended up arguing and drifting away one from the other. This caused a separation in the eldest species in the planet which still last to this day.

The minish decided to cut their ties with every race and hide away. That's why any kid younger than around six years old, probably, never saw a living one. Fairies on the other hand, abandoned all races, except from kokiris. We, backed by the Great Deku Tree, are a trustworthy bunch and this convinced fairies to remain amongst us in our main village throughout the day. That's the reason for them leaving at sunset and coming at sunrise. The glow they cast is hard to find at those timeframes since it blends with the environment. I guess that tonight, with some luck, you'll be able to see Navi, the lovely fairy that joined you when you were a kid, Link," elaborated Saria. The long explanation left her breathless and the lad was looking at her, silent, trying to soak in all that new information, or rather old... but forgotten.

"How is it that I had a fairy? I'm not a kokiri..." wondered Link.

"For starters, how are you so sure that there's no kokiri blood in your family?" answered Saria, "As far as I know, both our races are quite similar... I'd say that, were it not for the facial hair, which is a rare thing amongst kokiri folks, there is no physical difference between us and hylians,".

The sage's words caught the lad unguarded, "I never thought about it...". Link, caught up in his thoughts, looked upwards and noticed that the treetops were getting thicker. The further into the forest, the less sunlight shone through. Also, it was a cloudy day and it was getting cloudier by the minute.

"Always the same story. I can't take a quick walk to the graveyard without the sun leaving me!" kidded Saria, "Nature seems to like pulling my leg this way. She knows how much I despise this kind of places," the sage's joke lightened up the mood and they were able to laugh for a while, as they kept going.

After a few minutes, they've reached a sort of wall, made of fixed stones, about two meters high, which went on and on, throughout the forest.

"Well... We've reached the graveyard," claimed the lass, "if I'm not mistaken, the entrance is a few meters away to our left,".

After a few steps, Link saw an iron, double-decked, door. Saria opened it and headed in. Hood and Link followed her. Link observed the inside of the graveyard wall and found some weird etchings on it. The place was divided in sectors and they had entered to the main one. On the base of the wall, beneath the drawings Link found, there were some black candles, which let out a dim blue fire. The main hall, were the lot was right now, was about twenty meters wide and thirty meters deep. To each side of the corridor, six mausoleums, with different inscriptions each, could be found and, even if he tried his best, Link couldn't decipher what those inscriptions meant. Once they reached the center of the room, Hood read a plaque, which was written in a language the lad didn't know.

"Graveyard of the lost forest. Place of peace for every clan," translated out loud the old man.

Link, in awe, looked back and deducted that the six crypts they passed belonged to each clan.

"What brings you here, Saria," said a deep mysterious voice.

"Dampe! I've told you a thousand times not to show up like that out of thin air! You're going to give me a heart attack," answered the lass.

"That wouldn't be so bad… We could spend more time together…" joked the voice.

Link looked at the man who popped out of the shadows. He was wearing a dark brown overall, torn at its base. He seemed to be covered in moss and his skin looked shineless and pale.

"This is one ugly man," Link whispered to Hood as he saw the man's face. His mouth was huge, with few teeth left, his skin wrinkled and heavy eyelids. The man looked as if he had just woken up and lacking a good night's sleep. He also seemed to be rather dirty.

"You've brought friends with you," said Dampe.

Link tried to introduce himself, "Hello, mister, my name is…" but was interrupted, "Not you, dumb kid. I'm talking about the cartwheel," said the murky man, referring to the carriage with the dead bodies, "Anyways, I know who you are, Link, I haven't been away from the world for that long yet,".

A shiver run down the lad's spine. The murky man moved to a side and focused his attention on Hood.

"Hmp… this is curious," he said, while sniffing like an old dog.

"What? You're telling me that your nose still works?" asked the old man, which made Dampe laugh.

"Look who's here… Have you been playing with the ocarina?" nonchalantly wondered Dampe.

Link and Saria looked at each other, intrigued as how could the pair know each other.

"Everything is possible, undertaker," said the old man, "By the way, we're here to bury these poor fallen ones in the forest. Do you have something for us?".

"You can use my old friend. It's right over there," he answered, pointing to a shovel, which was leaning over a dusty grave, about ten meters away from where they were standing, "The one with its T shaped handle wrapped in some yellow cloth,".

218

"Good… And, where shall we bury them?" Hood asked.

"In the next sector, there's a rather large spot unoccupied," advised the murky man, "also, be sure to return the shovel once you're done. It's not a gift, but a loan,".

"Thank you, Dampe. Oh, I almost forget… Do you have any information about the hook-bracelet?" the old man enquired.

The question surprised the murky man, "You came to fetch that to?" and, without waiting for his answer he directed him "It's two sectors ahead, after the forbidden zone, inside the last crypt… I believe you know the forbidden zone is filled with poes, right?".

"Nothing to worry about, my friend," Hood claimed, "Thanks again," and, grabbing the reins of his horse, he started walking. Without much hesitation, the two younger ones decided it was smart to follow him.

"Hood… What is a poe?" Link asked.

"It's a spirit, my boy," answered the old man, "A soul that, for some reason, couldn't leave this world,".

The group reached the free spot and prepared to bury the bodies. Luckily, there was another shovel lying around there, a bit more rustic than Dampe's but still useful. Hood grabbed this beaten-up shovel and both men started digging.

"I have a question, mister, I've never been to the forbidden zone and I'd like to know if these poes are dangerous," said the lass with a shying tone on her voice.

"They try to be, but, honestly… none of them pose much of a threat," replied the old man, dismissing her worries, though Saria wasn't wholeheartedly convinced with this answer.

"But… Can they, maybe, hurt us?" the fearful sage asked.

"Where is the brave Saria from a while back?" teased Hood.

The lass frowned and blushed. She was a bit embarrassed and a bit annoyed by the old man's jab.

"Don't worry, we won't leave you here," the old man said, talking about the graveyard.

For a long while, they dug non-stop. After about four hours, the hole was finished and it was deep enough to earth all the dead men. Non the less, Hood didn't want the demons repossessing those bodies, so he told Link they should burn them before burying them.

"Hood, there's something I still don't quite get," said the lad, "If we killed those demons, and for that reason they were forced to leave those bodies... Why is it that they can reclaim them once they are dead? I mean... Isn't the dying thing the main reason why they left them?" wondered the lad, remembering how possession was explained to him by the old man.

"You're right on track, but it's not as simple as that," said the old man while pouring some oil on the wrapped bodies, "At first, they can possess a body inhabited by a weak soul. It's the easiest for them, since this way, they can choose anyone, provided they're weak enough, but if that body dies, the spirit of the person is freed. That soul, which has been imprisoned by the demon, gathers such a strength in its final moments, that is able to break the hold the demon had and regain control of the body, expelling the demon from it.

Once the person dies, his spirit leaves and moves on. But that body can only be occupied once again by a spirit that has previously been inside it. Which, in this case, means the demon. Still, this is a handful for them," the old man pulled his sword and, with a stone, produced some sparks that he let fall over the clothes drenched in oil, "It's hard enough to return to the world of the living, add up that they need to find the very same body they occupied, it becomes an almost impossible task... But, there's still a chance. So, if we first reduce that body to ashes, well, no chance at all,".

"Oh! I see, so, cremation is the best choice, though not the only one," summed up the lad.

"What do you mean by that?" asked the old man.

"Well... if we cut their heads off, even if they did return, they couldn't do much," the lad answered.

The old man comprehended the logic on Link's train of thought, "Emm... yes, that's true. But out of a sense of honoring the person they once were, I'd rather do this by fire than by steel.

Of course, if they were a lot of them and we were out of time, we probably would do as you suggested... but right now, there is no-one hurrying us,".

Saria was closely listening to the old man explanation, "So, shouldn't we wait for the bodies to fully burn, before throwing dirt over them?".

"Actually, yes. That's why we're leaving the horse here and we'll keep going on foot," said the old man, as he left his shovel, "Link, bring Dampe's shovel, just in case,".

The old man nodded and the three of them headed towards the forbidden zone of the graveyard.

"Hold on! Wait for me!" a voice screamed from afar.

"Mido? What are you doing here? I told you to rest," said the sage.

"And so, I did. Fado came and left breakfast beside my bed, while I was resting. I must have slept for a few hours and then I ate what she brought me, though a bit on the late side, for my preference. I must admit, though, that it was the best glass of juice of my life. Evidently, it had been a while since I ate anything, because that juice brought my strength back," replied Mido.

That last bit Mido said stuck with Link. He kept re-running the events of that morning in his head. He was speaking with Fado, when Hood got up and left the table, then he returned and offered the breakfast to Fado... "Did the old man have anything to do with Mido's current state?" he thought. Slowly, he turned and look at Hood, trying to get some answer from him. He only looked back at him and brought his index finger to his lips and gave him a wink. The lad remembered that blue stuff that Hood gave him the first time they met and was now certain that he was responsible of Mido's current health.

"Oh, come on, Saria, let the kid stay," the old man insisted, "Evidently, he wants to protect you,".

Both kokiris blushed a little and avoided eye contact with each other, "Besides, I would never reject some backup... He looks capable. The way he resisted possession and the way he recovered so quickly, at least to me, it suggests he's a tough one," Hood flattered the kokiri boy.

221

"Alright, but, as soon as he feels ill, even a tiny bit, we all get out of here," dictaminated the lass.

"If you want, you can head back to the village, Saria. I feel indebted to these two," said Mido.

Saria looked at Mido with mixed emotions. On one hand, she was a bit angry that he low-key called her coward. On the other hand, she thought that he had such a noble gesture at coming that she couldn't be mad at him. For an instant, she saw in Mido what she liked about Link, that heroism, the solidarity and the will to help others. All of that made Saria feel some weird attraction for the kokiri lad. After all, he was quite handsome. The only difference was that she always considered him as a family member. "Well... shall we?" Hood ended the romantic scene.

The four of them went along for a while through the cemetery. The puddles of water and the cold of the gravestones rose a musky fog, which thickened the further into the graveyard they went. After a few minutes, they reached a wall, similar to the one that enclosed the whole place. This time, there was no door, but an empty archway, with two stone pillars, one at each side of it. On top of this entrance a warning was clearly readable: Do not pass. Forbidden Zone. Both side walls had an inscription, written in another language.

ᚱᚾᛖᚼᚹᚱᚙ ᛏᚼᚼᚼᛝᛏ

"I think I'm more afraid of not knowing what those walls say than from the inscription above," joked Link, trying to ease the tension.

"Nothing to worry about," said Hood, who knew what was written, but chose to omit that, "Once inside, you might see quite a few poes. They usually avoid the living, but, sometimes, some of them get unsettled and attack using what seem to be a ghostly scythe,". The group wasn't happy with the news, "Just, do as I do. Walk behind me, by no reason can anyone run or scream. Don't be afraid and we'll make it, safe and sound, to the door of the crypt," the old man said.

The three of them had no other choice but to obey Hood. Saria went right behind him, grabbing his robe with a hand. Mido was just by his side, while Link was covering their backs.

"There are two of them to the left, be silent," whispered Hood.

The younglings saw two ghostly figures, fading away. They could see their frightening, fluorescent, shape in a light blue, almost white, color. Only their face and neck were visible. Beneath them, they wore a robe, torn on the bottom. The most peculiar and outstanding thing was a kind of lantern that each of them held in one of their hands and it was its light that let their contour shine.

As they moved forward, they passed by another group to their right, marauding over a mausoleum nearby. They were only five more meters or so away from the gate of the last crypt when a poe crossed their way.

"Don't look at it. Don't flinch. Don't scream nor do any sudden move. We're going to pass through him," claimed Hood.

The old man went a bit ahead of the rest of the group, to prove it was safe and passed through the ghost as if it wasn't there. The poe flew around Hood, examining him, but the old man paid him no attention and just kept on walking. The younglings looked at the old man in awe and followed him a few steps behind. Hood passed through the entrance archway into the crypt.

As if he was no longer interested, the poe turned around and softly glided towards the kokiri lass. She paralyzed, opened her eyes wide and felt the gelid ghostly presence caressing her. The old man turned to her and, from where he was, he gestured her to remain calm. Saria felt Mido's hand grabbing hers tightly. She looked at him and his calm and confident expression was enough to make her gather what courage she needed to take a long, calm, step and pass through the poe. The two young men did just the same and, soon, the whole group was at the other side of the archway.

As he passed by the old man, Link looked at the old man and sighed. "Well done, champ," said Hood as he patted his back, "we're safe here. After passing those pillars, this area is free from spiritual presences," he explained as he led the group to the entrance of the fourth sector, which had a similar inscription.

ᚨᚺᚻᛁᛁᛃᚨ ᚨᚾᚨᚺᚲᛏᛁᚺᚾᚠᛖ

"I saw some scribbles just like those ones in the las entrance," signaled Link, talking about the etchings on the entrance.

"No, Link. They were not just like these," corrected the old man, "They were similar, but they fulfilled another task. Each sector has a reason and different scripts. In the script of the first sector, the entrance, the perimeter is marked to make every spiritual presence to acquire a physical form and also to block the exit of any non-living being. It's an old charm that allows a safer interaction between those who are still alive and those who haven't yet moved on to the beyond, even if the cases of this happening are rare,".

The old man stopped his explanation so that the younglings could appreciate the place where they were right now. That crypt was different from the others Link saw. The main difference was that, this one, didn't have a roof. The comfortable space was about four meters wide by three meters deep. It possessed three rectangular, stone-made, coffins which displayed many etchings on their surface.

The old man started walking amongst the coffins, "After the first sector, we arrive at the freed graveyard. That one has no charms and it's were we buried the bodies of the possessed ones,".

"I'm really glad that I'm not amongst them," said Mido, as he remembered that, for a few days, he was also part of that group.

The old man smiled at him, "I too would be glad in your stead… After that, the forbidden zone follows. The inscription on it's walls works as a powerful magnet, luring in those spirits trapped in this world and leaving them stuck in this place… Which doesn't mean that there aren't any poes outside, roaming free, but, at least, those who get here, can't leave," Hood went on, as he hit the side of the lid of one of the coffins, "And, at last, we arrive… Here," the old man completely removed the stones that worked as the lids of the three coffins.

The younglings looked in awe into the big coffin. They found that there was no body in it, but a narrow ladder made of stone which descended through a dark corridor. Hood lit his lantern and started the descent through it. The younglings looked at each other and, in resignation, conceded that, the best plan, was to follow the old man.

After descending about five meters through the steep ladder, the group reached a room with three archways. Hood caressed the wall of one of the three pathways. He smiled, "By the gods, do I love my lantern," he said.

The younglings didn't understand why the old man said that. But they looked at how Hood used his crimson lantern to enlighten a closed area and, instantly, they saw how one of the walls started to shine in some places, as if it was pointing a road to follow. "Right this way," led the old man.

They all started walking until, suddenly, Saria stepped on a loose stone and a metallic noise was heard, as if some kind of machinery started working.

"Oh… crap," cursed the old man, "I always forget this kind of stuff,".

A loud noise sounded from where the group came and, from a big hole on the ceiling, a cylinder, covered with pointy stones, fell. It took the whole width of the passage and, slowly, started spinning towards the four of them.

"Don't be afraid, but, right now, you'll need to follow my lead quickly. Do exactly as I do. You got it?" said Hood, who received a unanimous nod of approval.

The old man started trotting through the passage, checking the walls. The younglings followed him closely. Link noticed that the cylinder was gathering speed, "I think we should be hurrying," he claimed, a bit worried.

"I know, I know!" answered Hood as he hurried up.

The lot was picking up the pace, and so did the cylinder. The passage led them to a series of splits in the road and, guided

225

by his lantern, Hood chose one of the roads, then another and once again another. Everything was moving faster. From time to time, the splits were not into two ways but three. Their pace was incredible and Hood was leading the way wit shouts, "Left! Right! Right! Left! Right! Center! Left!... Duck!!" he screamed as he slid beneath a hole into what seemed like a dead end. In a moment's notice, they found themselves in a slide made of stone. They descended for about a minute until, abruptly, the slide disappeared and the four were free-falling, for about three meters, until they submerged in a pond of crystal-clear water.

Link was the first one to pop his head out of the water, "Where are we? I can't see a thing... Hood?".

"Over here!" the old man's voice was heard in the darkness, "My lantern went off. I have to reach solid ground to light it,".

"Mido!! Mido?! Where are you?!" wept Saria

"I'm right over here, Saria, don't worry. I'm ok," he said closing in amidst the absolute darkness. Once they reached each other, the kokiris gathered in a hug.

"Hood, we won't be able to keep this up for long. With the shovel, my shield and sword, it's becoming quite hard to keep myself afloat," said Link as he spit the water that he was trying to avoid swallowing.

"If you're finding it hard, imagine how much I, with my over twenty years more than you, am enjoying this," complained the old man.

Then, without notice, another loud noise was heard. It seemed that the cylinder had completed its route. Little fires started to lit on tiny pipes on the wall. Little by little, the room was illuminated and everyone could see the way to go. Once outside the water, Link contemplated the room where they were found.

In the middle of the room, there was a kind of round swimming-pool, five meters wide and two and a half meters deep on its deepest point. It seemed like half a sphere, filled with water. The fire from the pipes burned about two meters above them and the ceiling could not be seen. Because of this, the lad guessed that the room should be well over five meters high. The group

226

squeezed the water out of their clothes. Hood sat down and tried to see if the lantern was still useful.

"Link, while I fix this, would you check the room? See if you can find the hook-bracelet," said the old man.

Although he didn't know what Hood was talking about, he nodded and started to check the walls. The two kokiris decided to lend the lad a hand.

"Hey! Link! Check this out!" called Mido, looking at the floor near where he stood, "The ground here looks different,".

"Maybe there's something buried beneath," Saria esteemed.

Link grabbed Dampe's shovel and dug for just two minutes, until the shovel hit something.

All of them kneeled and kept on digging with their hands, uncovering a small chest. The younglings lifted it and begun to examine it. The lock was inexpugnable and the chest was way to heavy to carry it all the way back... once they could find out how to return.

"Look at the back, there's an inscription here," noted Saria, "My T friend might have been useful; My T friend might be useful once again; Still, you'll never know unTil you check," recited the lass.

Link thought about it, but couldn't get any ideas, he looked at Saria and Mido, expecting some help, but they had the same clueless look on their faces as he had.

"I wonder why those T letters are so heavily emphasized," Saria said.

"Maybe the key is hidden in something with that shape... or that resembles one, maybe?" occurred to Mido.

They were completely lost. Saria looked over and over at the chest. Link's mind wondered, trying to find some sort of solution and Mido paced around, scratching his head.

"Why don't we ask the old man? Maybe he knows something," suggested the kokiri lad.

Link had an epiphany. He opened his eyes wide, "That won't be necessary," he said as he grabbed Dampe's shovel.

"I doubt you'll be able to smash it open with that shovel, Link, the frame looks really sturdy," said the kokiri lass.

"I won't break the chest," Answered Link as he removed the bandage from the handle of the shovel, "When Hood told Dampe that he needed to bury the dead bodies, he told the old man he could use his friend,".

"Who's Dampe?" Mido wondered.

"The man at the entrance," replied Saria

"I didn't meet anyone when I got to the graveyard..." commented Mido.

Link went on with his explanation, paying no attention to their chat, "... then, this riddle says that this T friend helped... I believe it means the handle. And finally, the riddle says that it can still help, so I guess the solution is in the shovel... but where?".

Link finished removing the cloth that covered the handle, which was hollow. The other two came closer and Link checked into the hole in the shovel. He smiled and reached with two outstretched fingers into it.

"I thought that so many Ts should mean the T-shaped handle of the shovel," he summarized while pulling a little key from the hole.

The three of them looked at each other, expectantly, then, Link put the key into the chest's keylock. It went in easily and the lad turned it, making it sound as he did. Then, the chest opened up.

CAPÍTULO 17

SHARP

—¡Hood! Look what we've got!" screamed Link, showing off the brand newly acquired tool. The lad took a hard look at the contraption. It looked as a long glove, made of leather, with its fingers cut off. Link tried it on and tightened the bucklers, to get a tight fit. Close to the part where the wrist was located, the glove had a kind of roller and, wrapped around it, a chain made of incredibly tiny links, built with a very hard metal. Finally, at the end of that chain, there were three tiny hooks, in the shape of a claw. Behind the roller, there was a tiny box from which hanged three metallic cords with rings at their ends. Link assumed that this was the mechanism that made the roller work.

"What is that?" Mido wondered at the sight of the three cords.

"I'm not sure…" answered Link.

"With that you control the hook-bracelet," Hood intervened, "You put those on your fingers, as if they were rings… Obviously, the largest one goes on your thumb,".

The lad put the rings on, as instructed, "Now what?".

"Show me the palm of your hand," said Hood. Link complied and as he did, he could see that, on it, there was a tiny hook, "If you pull from that, the claw will get fired away. Then, if you close your three ringed fingers, the claw will copy that and close, trapping inside it whatever its holding grabbing tighter whatever it hit when shot," explained the old man, "Finally. Can you see that little lever on the side of the roller?" The lad checked and then nodded, "Well… that's the safety pin. It keeps the hook to get fired at random. When you want to use it, you need to lower that little lever to free the mechanism,".

The lad examined the tool and its mechanisms, "What would happen if I shot it at the middle of the roof?" the lad asked, "The chain is probably ten meters long. It should be more than enough to find out how high is the ceiling,".

Hood thought about it, "It's actually a good idea. Here, take the lantern, I've already fixed it,".

Link held it on one hand and aiming with the other to what he believed to be the center of the room, he pulled the trigger on his palm. The hook was sent flying at high speed and the next thing they knew, it had landed on something. With his arm stretched upwards and the chain hanging from the darkness, he look at his three companions.

"Look, Link, on the side of the roller you can see how many meters of the chain have been unrolled," Said Hood, pointing the lad's attention to the little gauge which had stopped, showing a number six and half of a number five, "According to this, I'd say that, from your hand to the ceiling, it's five and a half meters, give or take. A word of caution, remember that when you close your fingers it will take you up to the roof. The harder you close, the faster you'll climb. Also, if you stretch the fingers, the claw will open. Keep that in mind, you'll be about seven meters high from the ground and, while it's true that there's a pool beneath you, it still wouldn't be a comfortable fall," warned the old man.

The lad took a mental note of the received information and slowly closed his fingers. Instantly, he flew up in the air. "Ease up a little!" screamed the old man. Link barely loosed his fingers and his speed decreased. He kept climbing upwards until he was about ten centimeters from the claw and heard a clicking noise.

"Don't worry, the bracelet possesses a safety system which makes you come to a full stop before you crash against your target!" the old man shouted from beneath.

Link looked like a human chandelier, hanging from the roof, emitting light from the lantern. The room was left completely enlightened and, still, Link could only see two little openings on the wall, half a meter one from another. From one of them, the stone-slide from where they arrived was popping out. From the other, nothing did. As a matter of fact, the lad observed that this hole had a plain ground in which they could walk.

"I think I've found a way out!" the lad informed to the group.

"Excellent! Do you think you can swing yourself to it?" suggested the old man.

The lad guessed it was possible. He loosened his fingers a little further and descended about three meters and swung back and forwards to try to reach the hole.

"Careful, Link!" Saria warned. "Yeah mate, try not to fall!" Mido added.

The lad scrapped with his feet the edge of the hole, waging the best time to let go. He took a few more swings and, mustering all his courage, he fully extended his fingers. The claw did the same and let go of the ceiling. The lad was sent flying and passed through the hole.

"Link! Are you Ok?" Saria Shouted. "Link! Are you still there?" Mido did so, even louder.

"I'm Here! I'm fine!" Link's voice was heard coming from the now enlightened hole on the wall.

"Look around, see if you can find a place to stick the claw and come down to fetch us," said Hood.

The lad searched the place around him and chose to shot his claw against a sturdy looking stone. Afterwards, slowly descended to the ground, where his friends were.

"I'd suggest we climb up one by one," the old man claimed. An idea which Link fully supported.

"Ladies first?" asked Saria.

"No way," answered Mido, "I'll go first, then Saria and finally Hood. That way she'll always be accompanied. Down here with Hood, on the way up with Link and up there with me," he elaborated.

"Sounds like a solid plan!" congratulated Link. He outstretched his hand to the kokiri, "Ready when you are,".

The kokiri grabbed Link's hand and he softly clenched his fingers, which made them climb up. After a few seconds, they were already on the top.

Without releasing the claw, the lad descended once again and, after a little while, the four were up in the room. They all walked slowly until they reached the center of it. There, a little pedestal rose about sixty centimeters from the ground and a handle could be found in the middle of it, with a plaque underneath.

ᕮᕼᕪᒋᕼᒉᎩᕮ.
ᕼᎩ ᕿᕼᕼ ᒉᕪ ᕿᒉᕼᒉᕮᕼᒋᕪ ᚒᕒᕒᕼ ᕮᒉᕿᒉᚒᚒᕼᕮᕼ.

"To move forward, wits and courage are needed," translated the old man.

Link and the kokiris were a bit confounded.

"It means that something unpleasant is safekeeping the exit," said Hood, leading their attention to an opening, blocked with some iron bars which came from the roof and floor, "Mido, I see you're armed with a sword and a blowgun. How good are you at using them?".

Link, who already knew how the old man handled himself, pulled out his sword and shield and readied himself.

"Saria, we're going to need you to pull that lever. We're probably going to fight against something," claimed Hood.

Saria was concerned with the old man words, still, she grabbed the lever. The old man and Mido unsheathed their swords. The three men positioned themselves as to get the whole room covered. Afterwards, the lass pulled the lever and the bars started to go up and down, slowly, freeing the exit.

"This will take a while," sighed Mido.

"Get ready, here it comes…" said the old man.

Suddenly, a sharp noise could be heard. It sounded as if a lot of chirpings came from everywhere. About then metallic lids opened from all around the room and many bats started to come out of them.

"Bats?!" claimed Mido.

"Not bats! Keeses!" said Hood, "They're worse! Link…" but the lad interrupted him, "I know, Hood! Ten of them can drain your blood in a minute. Mido! Don't let them touch you!" he ordered the kokiri lad.

The room was filled with keeses, flying around. "I have an idea! Hood, follow my lead," ordered Link. The lad started bashing his sword against his shield and slid it around it, which produced a rather bothersome noise.

"Good idea, Link!" said Hood, noticing that the keeses loathed the noise and started to bump one another, "This is it, Mido!" the old man shouted to the kokiri, hinting him to start dealing with the troublesome beasts.

"I hope Deku doesn't take this badly," Mido said as he landed blow after blow on the keeses.

One by one, they fell. There were only three left, when another kind of noise was heard. Hood and Link stopped producing sounds with their shields and they finished off the remaining keeses.

"I think something else is coming…" noted Saria, "But the door isn't still fully opened,".

Again, another set of metallic lids opened, but this time, they were located at the base of the room's walls and the sound of hundreds of tiny steps could be heard.

"I guess that, if at first it was keeses, these must be walltulas!" said Mido.

"Most likely. Link, do you know about those?" asked Hood.

"Yeah, I do. Their poison is a powerful sedative and you've got to be careful with their strings," answered the lad, "actually, I have a plan for these too. Everyone, get close to Saria!" he then grabbed the lantern and put it off.

"What are you doing?" a warned Saria whispered.

"As soon as I turn this on, we must kill as many as we can," he ordered to the other two.

"Nice plan, as you blind them, we'll get a few seconds of advantage to strike first," claimed Mido.

"On my mark. Don't look straight to the lantern or you too will be blinded," warned Link.

The four of them could hear the footsteps getting closer and closer. They waited for as long as they could until Link felt one of the walltulas climb onto his foot, "Now!" he turned the lantern on and its light stunned the bugs.

The arachnids were being dealt with swiftly. The men run them through with their swords before they could react. A few of them recovered their sight, but it was too late. Soon they were all finished.

"The exit is almost clear!" said Saria, as she saw that most of the bars had retracted.

The three men waited patiently, without lowering their guard, but once the exit was fully cleared, some monsters came in, walking like zombies.

"Ok… these I don't recognize," said Link.

"These are Redeads" replied Mido.

"And what are those? Asked Link.

"They're zombies, Link," Hood answered, "Un-dead beings that feed from the soul of the living. Don't let them get near you. Their bite drains your energy, leaving you incredibly tired to fight back and making you an easy prey. That's if you're lucky. Worst case scenario, they suck so much energy that, if you aren't strong enough, you can die. Besides, their screams are rather stunning. One more thing, be aware, they don't feel pain. Don't expect them to flinch from your attacks,".

The weird human-like beings entered the room. Link noted that many of them had some bandages, similar to the ones found on mummies from the gerudo dessert, something he read about in books. Their faces, on the other hand, were covered by masks, which seemed to be made of wood. They didn't have eyes, but two dark empty sockets.

The lad wielded his shield and ram against one of them as it entered. He slashed it three times, but the redead seemed to be intended on getting up again. Without notice, another one came from behind the lad. Hood took it down with a hard blow from his foot. The men were fighting hard and the reded kept coming.

"Chop their heads off!" said Mido. In less than a minute, over ten enemies could be found around them. Hood cut the head of one of them and so did Mido with another. Link lured three of them towards his location and delivered a blow to their knees. The redeads fell and laid on the floor. Still, the monsters kept on going, dragging themselves if needed, apparently, without feeling anything. The lad then, took advantage of his position and got close to one and took his head off.

"Clever, Link! Let's split up!" said the old man.

The three of them scattered, splitting the redeads amongst them and slowly took them down. Soon, every enemy was dead on the floor, beheaded. Every one of them, except for one.

"Help me!" the lass scream was heard throughout the room.

The three men were far away from the lass. It was impossible for them to reach her, on foot, before the redead, which had both of its hands over her already, could take a bite.

The adrenaline rush made Mido able to see it all happen as if it was in slow-motion. He realized he wasn't going to reach her on time, "Noooo!!" he screamed as he ran towards her and, incapable of doing anything, he watched as the monster sank its sharp teeth on the lass's shoulder.

Link shot the claw from his bracelet and it hit the head of the redead. As he stood, sword in hand and chain and claw hooked to the monster, he closed his fingers, pulled the zombie to him and cut its head.

"I came all this way to get the sage's help to save the world from Ganondorf... Not one being on this earth is going to stop me from completing my task," said the lad, face splashed in redead blood.

Mido made it just in time to catch Saria before she hit the ground. The young kokiri carried the fainted lass on his arms.

"We must go, the bars are starting to cover the exit once again!" screamed Hood.

As he headed towards the exit, Link passed by the kokiri and picked up the sword he dropped when he caught the lass.

"GO! GO! GO!" said Link as he passed by the kokiri lad.

It was as they were crossing, that Hood realized they were missing something, "The lantern!" the old man shouted.

Cleverly, Link pointed his hand at it and shot his hook. The claw entangled itself on the lantern's handle, gripping it tightly. Link closed his hand which made the Lantern head swiftly towards them and hood caught it mere centimeters away from the lad, "Nice one, Link, you can let it go now," congratulated the old man.

Now, they were all at the other side of the exit, "Which way now?" asked the kokiri lad.

The old man used his lantern to light the path, "This way, follow me," he claimed and started trotting. The young men followed him. Once again, they were running through alleyways and bifurcations while the old man led the way.

Finally, the alleyways were over and the group arrived at a small room with two more archways, just like the one they've left behind. In the middle of it, there was a narrow stair that went up for some good few meters.

"We're here!" Link claimed, "I can recognize this stair, we climbed down through here,".

"You're right, Link, Let's head up," agreed the old man.

The three of them swiftly climbed up the stairs, the lass did so, in the arms of her kokiri companion.

"Will she be ok?" asked Mido.

"I sure hope so," answered Hood.

As they exited the same coffin the went into before, Hood wasted no time, "Link, please put the coffin's lid back on," the lad did as requested, then he headed towards the kokiri lad, "Mido, when I say so, you'll run towards the next sector of the graveyard. In her current state, Saria's going to work as a magnet for those poes. Her soul is weakened and they're going to want to enter her to get out of here. Link and I will cover you, just in case, but remember… Do not stop until you're out of this sector filled with poes,".

Link finished re-lidding the coffing and removed the dust to see who did he have to thank for hiding the bracelet, "Farewell, beloved… Dampe?!" he read on the top end of the grave. In disbelief, he checked once and again to make sure he didn't misread, "Here lies Dampe, respected hylian from the kakariko village," a cold shiver run down the lad's spine.

"Link! Come on! There's no time to lose!" hurried the old man, "You brought the boomerang, as I told you. Rigth?".

The lad confirmed it, still, he wondered how a wooden boomerang was going to be helpful in this situation. Link just used it for fun on spare time while he improved his running and jumping skills, while also boosted his trajectory reading capabilities.

"Excellent! I want you to throw it. The rupee piece on its center will lure the poes in and will give Mido a few seconds advantage," explained the old man, without going into further detail, "Are we all ready?" he asked.

The youngsters nodded and Hood gave the go signal.

Mido started running, full speed, into the poe sector. Link threw his boomerang and, once it returned, he started running alongside Hood. After that, the poes forgot about the boomerang and noticed the presence of the dismayed lass and flew towards her.

One of them almost reached her, "Aaaahrg!!" Hood jumped and ram the ghostly being with his shield, but this time he didn't pass through, he actually did hit him. "Link! Aim for their lanterns!".

The lad saw another poe, closing in fast. He jumped in and attacked, aiming straight to its lantern, which made the poe flee in a hurry. Fighting them back didn't seem as complicated as he thought it would be. Then, Link saw that Mido, ahead of themselves, was getting near to the exit and himself and Hood, while twice as far as the kokiri lad, where getting there too.

"No-one escapes my graveyard!" growled a ghostly voice.

A poe, far more terrifying than the rest, had emerged on the middle of the running group. Mido made a long jump and managed to exit the perimeter which enclosed the poes. Hood and Link were still inside, with the exit blocked by this new foe.

The specter was covered in reddish robes and on his face shone bright two white eyes which illuminated a bushy moustache beneath its nose. The ghost still retained some of the shape it had while alive. Link deduced that it should have been a short man, rather stocky. It wore a helmet which, actually, resembled a turban, like the one a Gerudo sheikh would wear. On it, a reddish gem was on display, resembling a sun and small pieces of the same jewel imitated the rays of light from it.

This ghost had a lantern, just like any other poe, but on the other hand, instead of a scythe, it carried a baton, just like the orchestra directors do, although this one seemed to have quite a sharp edge.

"Hood… We just have to avoid it and get the heck out of here," whispered the lad.

"I can't Link. I've been wanting to do something for a long time… I must face him. You can leave, Link," replied the old man.

The lad stood still while looking at the Hood, "Well… getting rid of the annoying voice of an old, grumpy, man does really sound tempting… But I would also lose the chance to learn from a great mentor… It seems that this ghost is going to know the sharp blade of my sword one way or another,".

"This is no place for someone as alive as you. Or is your intention to join the dead?" the ghost claimed. Link run towards it, took a leap and… BAM! The ghost hit him with his lantern, sending the lad rolling into a group of nearby tombstones. Then, the spirit attacked Hood, who repelled its attacks with his shield and riposted, but the ghost blocked with his baton. Through the side of his white eye, the ghost saw Link approach at full speed. He grinned and vanished as he rose in the air.

The ghost took this chance to mock the two of them, "Do you believe you can harm me? If I so desire, I can rise up and you won't be able to reach me,".

The old man sheathed his sword and took his lantern. He poured as little oil as it had left in it on a bowl-shaped tombstone nearby.

"Link, light it up," he told the lad and he used his sword to make a few sparks and set the oil on fire.

The old man grabbed the arrows from his quiver and set them into the flames. The arrowheads were now drenched in flaming oil.

"Use your bow, Link," instructed Hood.

"What… What are you doing?" wondered the ghost.

Hood loaded his bow and set loose an arrow before the spirit could finish his sentence.

"Do you truly believe that some useless arrows can do somethi…?" but the ghost wasn't able to finish his sentence since one of the arrows pierced through his robe, "Argh! What is this?!" the angered spirit was astonished.

"That oil is a gift from the gorons!" Hood shouted at the ghost, "You're not so smart now, are you?".

The spirit's flight was becoming erratic. With a swing of his baton, he commanded a handful of poes to join the fray. Link was caught with his guard down and realized that the incoming slash from a scythe was unavoidable. So, as it descended Link braced for impact, but a sword got in the way.

"Mido! What are you doing here?" asked the surprised lad.

"Saria is safe on the other sector and you need me here," mido answered while he kicked the lantern of the attacking poe.

"Yes, but she will die if none of us left this place alive to take her to a healer," Hood interceded, "Guys, you two hold this position! I'll deal with their leader," the old man ordered.

The two youngsters fought back the smaller poes, covering Hood, while the old man fired his incendiary arrows to his target. As he was running out of arrows, Hood's latest shot hit the ghost square on its chest. The ghost replied and threw his baton at the old man, hitting him on his arm. Both screamed in pain and the nearing poes took this chance to swarm the position and attack Hood, throwing him to the ground. The specter's leader saw the old man with the injured arm lying on the ground, overwhelmed by four poes, defending himself only with his shield.

Taking advantage of this window, the ghost-leader turned his attention to the fiery tombstone and saw that there were no more arrows, which was odd, since he was sure that there was at least one left. "You were looking for this?" Link asked the floating spirit. As it heard him, it slowly turned around and, to his shock, observed the lad, whit the last arrow loaded on his bow, readying himself to set it loose.

The lad released his projectile and the fiery arrow landed on the lantern-holding hand of the ghost. The hit made him release the lantern which fell to the ground and its light vanished.

The weakened spirit felt over a grave. The rest of the lesser poes fled the area, leaving the three men exhausted, but alive.

Mido lent a helping hand to the old man and assisted him as he got up from the gorund. Hood removed the baton stuck in his arm and, grabbing a bandage from his belt, tended to his wound. Then, the men approached the fallen ghost.

The old man blew on some dirt which covered the tombstone over the grave in which the spirit was now lying and a little, round and deep hole on it was now visible.

"Link, use your hook on that hole, please," the old man requested the lad. The ghost could do nothing but observe what the group was doing.

The lad found the requisition odd, but obliged. He aimed at the little hole and shot his hook. It went through what seemed to be a piping of sorts by the noise it made as the hook passed by and after going for about ten meters, it stopped.

"I think I've got something," said the lad.

"Pull back a little," replied the old man.

The lad squeezed his fingers and the locked hook made a metallic noise and pull Link's arm into the hole. The lad fought back, "It's stuck," he said.

"Never mind, I've got what I wanted," the old man claimed as he took a square, stone-made, lid besides the tombstone, "You've unlocked this old sturdy box, which is ideal to hide stuff into…" he added while taking it out of the newly discovered space, "You can let go now, Link,".

The lad called back the hook and the old man opened the package he recovered. He untied the cord that was wrapped around a piece of fabric which covered a little instrument.

Link's eyes opened up wide, "Is that the Ocarina of time?".

But the old man had already started to play a tune. Link was rather proficient in music, so he was able to recognize the first notes of the song: d; F; D…

Hood kept playing the lovely, rather sad, song. Link felt how the wind rose and the heavens rumbled. Suddenly, a weird rain started to fall, out of nowhere. The young men looked at Hood in awe. Link felt that the old man was the one responsible for that storm. Each note echoed on the weather, which seemed to sing along with its wind and rain.

Hood finished his song and, when he hit the last "C", it seemed to reverberate throughout the whole graveyard. The clouds vanished and the rain stopped.

The old mand looked at the ghost, "I have a message for you, composer. The thousand raindrops, called upon by my song, are my tears. The thunder that beats the ground my fury. Calm will come at last, with my pardon. You're free, Sharp, your brother knows you're sorry,".

The spirit's evil grin vanished. Now his face showed calm and serenity.

"Thank you, good man," it said and, looking upwards, he then added "I'm sorry, Flat," and he faded away.

242

CHAPTER 18

THE POWER OF THE FAIRIES

—¿What was that about?" asked Link, still in disbelief about what he just saw.

"That, was mercy," answered the old man as he wrapped the ocarina on its fabric and once again tied it up with the cord, "something I wanted to do for a while now,".

The old man put the ocarina back on the stone box and closed it. As he did, the metallic pipe sounded and then the old man put a stone into the hole on the gravestone to cover it up.

"Why did you do that? Now we'll have to open it back," said Link.

"We'll do so later on. Now, we have to go back... before it's too late," replied the old man who was already heading towards the sector where Saria was.

"She's over here," led the young Kokiri lad once they were out of the poe sector.

The three of them arrived at the lass's side and Mido picked her up and carried her. Link noticed that her clothes were dry and confirmed that the rain from before came from the song played by the ocarina.

"I arrived here at horseback," said Mido.

"Excellent! Mido, Link is going to take your horse and I will carry you and Saria on the carriage where we brought the bodies. Hope you don't mind, but it's our best option," explained the old man.

Link then remembered that they needed to cover up the bodies that they've left behind to burn, "We still have to finish our work with those bodies," the lad told the old man.

"I don't think so..." answered Hood, who then showed the lad that someone covered them up for them.

"What? How? Who else was here...? And why did he finish our work?" a bemused Link asked.

"Don't worry, Link. I've told you, I'm over two decades older than you… Obviously, I'm a bit ahead," said Hood while he grabbed the shovel that he had left behind and putting it back into the carriage.

"You knew about this?" Link asked.

"As many other things I can't tell you about. But we've talked about this and I know you trust me," replied the old man, who then grabbed the reins of the horse and started the way back.

The lad nodded and, together, they went back until they reached the entrance hall. As they approached the exit, a voice reached them from amidst the graves.

"The shovel, please," Dampe popped out from behind a mausoleum.

Link was shocked. He remembered that tombstone with the man's name on the other sector.

"What's wrong, boy? You just got out from a place filled with ghosts… At least I have a body," said the ragged man, assuming the lad had seen his grave.

Link unhooked the shovel from his belt, "The… The key is inside," he blabbed as he handed it to him.

"Thank you, but I cannot hold it. Would you lean it against that grave over there?" requested Dampe.

The frightened lad agreed. Dampe, after seeing how afraid Link was, couldn't help to look at Hood and smile.

"I wonder… When was it that you stopped being afraid of me?" He jokingly asked the old man.

"It was a long time ago, Dampe, long before leaving… Any news for me? I take that everything is going well, right?" asked Hood.

"All according to your plan. Actually, they're already inside," Dampe answered.

The young men looked at each other, not understanding what was going on, but the older men didn't seem to care about that.

"Excellent. Then, we're heading off, Dampe. See you soon," the old man bid goodbye to the ragged man.

"I certainly hope not, old friend," the ragged man replied and, as he saw them off, waving his hand, he got lost amidst the darkness.

The old man passed by Link's side, "In time, you'll understand," he said to him, after seeing the expression on his face.

Link shrugged his shoulders and followed him. The old man headed outside the graveyard leading the carriage which still had the shovel Hood took.

"Shouldn't we give that back too?" asked Link.

"No need. Dampe only cares about his friend. This one, we can keep," replied the old man.

Hood got onto the horse which pulled from the carriage. Mido handed the lass to Link, got onto the carriage and readied himself to receive the lass back.

After passing the fainted Saria to the kokiri lad, Link asked him where did he tie his horse, to which Mido showed him the spot and Link went to fetch it.

The hylian lad got onto Mido's horse and got it moving. The old man did the same with the carriage. The raiders let the horses lead the way, since they knew the way back home. From in between the trees, some light started to shine through and Link noted that they've left the graveyard's grounds.

"There's a big difference between the Kokiri's village lands and the Kakariko's village ones, right?" Mido said to Link as he saw the last looking up to the sky.

"The Kakariko village?" Link wondered.

"Yes... You don't know anything about it, right?" Mido asked back and Link confirmed his theory.

"A long time ago, when things got dangerous, many folks left towards the Kakariko village, a young town, filled with hard-working people. Most of its inhabitants were hylians, but there were many kokiris and gorons too, since their lands were close by. As it turned out, the village quickly populated and grew until one day, as it was to be expected, Ganondorf set his sight on it. The folks moved once again... At least those who managed to escape," said Mido, disheartened with his memories.

"So... it's a ghost town now?" asked the hylian lad.

"I'd say so, yes. From time to time, someone camps on the abandoned houses, and some people head over there in search of certain potions, led by the belief that somebody on the town is well versed in witchcraft… Although I believe they're all lies," explained the kokiri lad.

"And the graveyard… it belongs to the village?" asked Link

"Yes, graveyards are a hylian and sheikah tradition. Gerudos have some similar rites, as I understand… But gorons, kokiris and zoras don't," explained Mido.

"I didn't know about that…," said Link.

Time went by and the brave travelers were nearing their destination.

"It's all about following the markings on the trees," said the young kokiri as he saw they were getting close to the village.

"I know, Mido," replied the old man.

The young men were surprised to see Hood follow a specific road amongst the trees. Soon, he stopped, climbed down from his horse and headed towards the big door made of logs. He knocked thrice. Someone, over the other side of it, whistled and Hood answered back with a similar whistling. Both seemed like two birds singing, still, that was enough to make them open the gate.

Once the gate was opened, the guard was surprised by Hood, "Saria is injured! She needs medical attention, a redead bit her,".

The worried guard made way to the group. Hood hurried back to his horse and headed in and Link went right after. Many kokiris gathered around once they saw Mido running while holding Saria on his arms. The lad headed straight to a hut with its walls painted white and its roof red.

"You join him, Link. I'll go fetch something," claimed the old man. Link agreed and went after Mido.

Inside the medical hut, there were two kokiris. An old and slouching man who held a cane and a young blonde kokiri lass, with white skin and big, sky blue, eyes who wore a green head-band and tank-top and, on top of it, a long, white, robe. The old man was surprised when the group entered the hut.

"Mido? What's wrong?" asked a bemused Fado.

"Fado... it's Saria, she's hurt... a redead..." said the lad, gasping for air.

"Calm down, follow me," said the lass, appeasing Mido, as she headed towards a clean room with a well-tended bed with white sheets, "Put her on that bed,".

The kokiri lass began her check on Saria. The lads were standing right beside her, a few steps away from the bed.

Mido noticed that Link was worried, "Mi sister is the best kokiri doctor, if someone can tell us what to do, its her," he claimed in an attempt to calm him down.

Right then, Hood entered running through the door and gave Fado the little flask with a bit of blue liquid remaining.

"Here, this will earn us some time," claimed the old man.

Fado grabbed the flask and examined it, "Is this what I think it is?" she asked.

"Yes, it's Bloodspirit potion. Also known as "The blue potion" or "The draught of life and energy"," answered the old man.

"Who... When... How did you get this?!" asked the lass.

"It's a long story, one for which we don't have time right now," the old man replied.

Fado nodded and gave the drug to Saria. She opened her eyes and tried to speak, "M- Mido... thank you. If only I had known sooner... who I had besides me..." but she couldn't finish her sentence before passing out again.

"We need something as strong as the blue potion but in larger amounts," sentenced Fado.

Then Mido remembered something, "The only thing as strong is...".

"Fairy dew," interrupted the old man.

"Yeah... That's even stronger... right?" asked Mido.

"Well, yes, quite more. One tear from the Great Fairy has the strength of a full vial of blue potion," Fado explained.

As she finished her sentence, a tiny light swiftly passed by the window.

"Speak of the devil..." said Fado.

Link looked through the window and noticed that it was getting darker. His gut grumbled, remembering him that he hadn't eaten anything since breakfast.

"I believe we should eat something before leaving. We're in for a long night," said Hood, who seemed to have read the lad's mind.

"Before leaving? Where are we going?" wondered the lads.

"Link and I will go get a tear from the Great Fairy from the forest," said the old man as he exited the room. Everyone exited after him.

"But mister, I doubt you'll be able to do that," claimed Fado.

"Right! To begin with, you don't even have a fairy," added Mido.

"You're right, but a long time ago I did and so did Link," replied the old man without turning around.

Still glancing through the window, Link could see how many fairies were arriving form all over the place and headed to long wooden posts, about two meters high, that were displayed all over the village. On their highest point, these posts had a big bowl made of glass and, inside those bowls, a little table, no bigger than a hand, and many little chairs could be found. Seemingly, the fairies ate there and, while they stayed in them, provided the village with artificial lighting.

"Those things… That's a very clever contraption," noted Link.

"Right? It was a great idea to use the light, produced by the fairies, to illuminate the village, while they're eating and relaxing," said Fado.

"It was Saria's idea," added Mido.

"That's why the fairies will understand why we need their help," claimed the old man.

Then, A blue flash of light arrived at the room, "Liiink!!!" a fairy had thrown itself to the chest of the lad, arms wide open, as if it was trying to hug him. The lad felt a sharp pain on his head and an image came to his mind.

The young fairy was in danger; he had his shield on his back; they were both just children; something threw an attack towards the fairy; she couldn't avoid it…

248

"Navi... NO!" the lad screamed and jumped to cover her. The fairy just looked at him.

"Link... Link? Are you still there?" the little fairy asked, flying around the lad, "It seems that we've lost him," she said to Fado while trying to catch the lad's attention, unsuccessfully.

"No... no. I just had a memory from my past... when we were young, Navi," said the lad, coming back into his senses.

Everyone was silent, but the old man, "I see that the bond that unite you two, fairy and protegee, is so strong that it can't be easily erased,".

The fairy noticed Hood's presence. She flew towards him and checked him thoroughly.

The little fairy seemed shocked, "You..." she started saying. "I've played the Ocarina of Time more than once," interrupted the old man, "that's why you know who I am and trust me and him," he added as he pointed at Link and winked at the fairy, "But he isn't fully aware of who I am. And it must remain so if we want to keep this delicate timeline intact,".

Then, the old man spoke to everyone in the room, "More important, right now, is Saria's health, which is severely compromised. We need the power of the fairies to save her,".

Another fairy flew in, this one, with a lilac-reddish shine, covering it. It was a male fairy.

"Tael!" Mido received the fairy.

"Mido!" the winged lad responded, "I'm so happy that you're ok!".

The fairy looked as it hadn't had a good night's sleep in days, even its flight showed its tiredness.

"Navi, I see that Link has returned after so long, I guess you're really glad," Tael said.

"Yes, of course!" the little fairy responded.

Tael than proceeded to greet everyone. Navi updated him on the situation with Saria, just as Hood told her.

"So, you're saying we must take Mido with the Great Fairy?" Tael asked Navi.

"No," Hood interceded, "He had just arrived from an unsavory adventure for his health and we got him into another one, not one day apart one from the other. Besides, you haven't slept well for a while either. The most logical thing to do would be for the two of you to catch up and rest, while Navi takes us with the Great Fairy," explained the old man, talking about him and Link. Everyone agreed that it was indeed the best option.

"That's settled then. Moving on, I guessed you'd be hungry so I told Saria's cook to have a few sandwiches ready for your arrival. They should be waiting for you at the guest house. You can eat and resupply there. All your stuff is in the closet next to the coat rack," Fado informed the group.

The hylian lads and Navi headed over there, they snacked briefly and, once they were done, Hood grabbed some oil and refueled his lantern, "It's not goron oil, but I'll be enough to light a fire or two,".

Then, he headed to the sink and cleansed the wound on his forearm, "Link, pass me the thread and needle on that sack over there,". The lad did as he was requested and then oversaw the old man sewed his own wound, "I'll be only two stitches at each side of the forearm," explained the old man to the disgusted lad and, once the task was fulfilled, he applied some sap over the sewn area.

"Don't worry lad, this is just temporary. By tomorrow there will be no sign of it," he told Link.

The young kokiri grabbed his sword and shield, "No, boy. You can't take those," The old man warned him, "Only take the wooden sword, the boomerang and the two blowguns that, If I'm not mistaken, should be in that closet. I'll teach you how to make the darts for those along the way. Navi, could you go and ask Mido for those wooden shields he uses for training?".

"How do you know he's training? That's supposed to be a secret between Mido and Teal," Navi said.

"And which one of those are you? Mido or Teal?" the old man jokingly asked the fairy, showing her that, if it was a secret, there would be no way for her to know about it. The young fairy blushed as she realized she'd been discovered and, with a smile on her face, flew off.

"Ok, Link, we have around a day's worth of trip ahead of us. We'll camp halfway through but, most likely, one of us will have to mount guard. The swamp can get tricky," said the old man.

"Wait... did you say swamp?" enquired the lad.

"Yes, if I'm not mistaken, the cave where the Great Fairy lives, is located southeast, across the swamp," Hood clarified.

"How could you know that?" wondered Link.

"It doesn't take a huge load of knowledge to be aware of basic topology. All it takes is reading a map, lad," replied the old man.

Hood took his saddle and so did Link. They both exited the guest house, all restocked, and headed towards the stables. Once there, they prepped their horses and, once the deed was done, they mounted up and got set to ride.

While they were at it, Fado arrived with Navi. The kokiri lass had two wooden shields in hand, each one with a carved logo, painted red, in the center of it.

"I see it's not just Tael and Mido's secret," said the old man as he laid eyes on Fado, who smiled.

"A snitch is better at keeping secrets than my brother," Fado joked, "Here, Link, this one for you. And this one for you, Hood," said the lass as she handed over the shields.

"Thank you! I'll try to return it unscathed... at least I hope so," laughed the lad.

"This is a nice shield. Thank you," said the old man.

Fado stood still, analyzing the old man, "I might have an idea about who you are..." she told the old man.

A brief silence got hold of the room, "I believe congratulations are in order, that is one outstanding wound treatment. Who taught you that?" Fado asked the old man.

The old man laughed quietly, "I think you and I know who taught me," replied the old man as he set his horse on motion.

Fado laughed and headed towards the village door to open it for them and bid them goodbye.

"Come back soon! Saria's condition is stable but she really needs the medicine as soon as possible," the lass told the raiders as they left.

"Two days tops," Hood claimed as his horse started to gallop, "Navi, get inside Link's hood, we need to hide your light. You tell him the way and I'll follow," the old man instructed the fairy.

"Ok. Just to be sure, we're taking the short road, right? The swamp road?" the fairy asked.

"Yes, that one," the old man replied.

"Ok... as you wish," answered the fairy, getting inside the lad's hood.

For a long while, they both rode, following the fairy's directions. Night had fallen and it was too cloudy for the moon to light a path. Hood got besides Link and passed him his lit lantern.

"Here, hook it on your horse to see where he's stepping. I'll follow in your footsteps," the old man said.

The lad obliged and kept on galloping. From time to time, he looked back to check if Hood was still there. Although, most of the times, it was unnecessary, since he could hear the old man's horse galloping right behind him.

About three hours went by. Link realized the ground was starting to get rather muddy. The sound of the horseshoes splashing in puddles was more frequent. Link slowed down and located himself besides the old man.

"I believe we've reached the swamp," claimed the lad.

"Yes, about half an hour ago, to say the least, we've entered the grounds of the southern swamp. You're a bit tired, aren't you?" asked the old man.

"To be honest... I'm exhausted. We've spent most of the day riding, walking, running, digging, fighting... more than once," said Link.

The old man started to laugh, "I understand, I've been there, remember? Hand over the lantern, I'll go ahead and search for a place to camp. Sounds good?" he asked.

"Sounds excellent," replied the tired lad.

Link handed back the lantern and put himself behind the old man, who rode a bit further ahead until he reached a slightly higher ground.

"This looks like a good place," the old man said.

"No puddles here?" asked the lad.

"Looks like a fine high ground. No puddles, spider nests, deku drools, holes or…" the old man was checking but was interrupted by the lad, "Deku drools?" Link asked.

"Yes, Deku drools. They're a kind of carnivore plant which can move their stem. That allows them to feed from a longer distance," the old man explained.

"Hmm… I think I saw one. Forgot to add it to the "Things I did today" list," joked the lad as he unmounted, "This morning, when I was chasing the demon, one of those things… bit me, I guess? I had to cut its… head? off," he told the old man.

"It's called chalice. It's a shame I wasn't there… would have been a great chance to teach you how to make darts," explained the old man.

They started to mount the encampment while Navi checked the surroundings.

"How is it that you make darts with those… what was is, deku drools?" asked the lad.

"Yes, deku drools. With them you can make a nice array of darts: Poisonous, narcotics or even healing," the old man explained.

"you can heal while doing damage?" asked Link.

"Well… kind of yes. The damage is minimal, of course. You can apply a potion and improve health through a dart," answered Hood.

"And which part of the deku drool you use to make the darts? It's teeth?" Link tried to guess while assembling the tent.

"Precisely, Link, it's teeth are hollow," said the old man who was helping the lad with the tent, "When they die, the plant loses its teeth and they get absorbed by the ground after a few days. If you pick them up and cleanse them, they can last quite longer. The reason why you need to wash them it's the glue. Deku drools produce a sticky sap that comes out through these hollow teeth. If you wash them, you're left with some hollow needles that you can fill with any substance, then, at its thickest part, you make a plug with mud and you stick a tiny feather to it and let it dry," Hood explained the method as if he was a botanist.

Link was paying close attention while digging a ditch around the tent. While they were at high ground, the area was rather damp and the ditch would prevent a flooding, should it rain.

"What's the feather for? Is like in the arrows, to improve stability?" asked the intrigued lad.

"Yes… and no. You see, it is necessary for stability but, in darts, the feather fulfills a more essential role. Once the dart lands on its target, the momentum carried by the feather helps with the injection of the fluid contained by it. In short, the feather pushes out of the needle whatever is inside the dart," detailed the old man.

Link analyzed it for a second, "Interesting… That way the whole content of the dart is injected, and not only what's on the tip of it," he summarized while he started digging a hole.

"What's that hole for?" asked the old man.

"this one? For the fire," the lad replied.

"No, wait. We're making a reflector fire this time. Do you remember how to make one?" asked the old man.

"Sure. It's like a normal fire, locked with stones so that heat and fire head towards one direction," answered Link.

"That's right. In this kind of terrain, a normal campfire will probably get humid in the bottom of the hole and that would make starting it more difficult," Hood explained.

"That makes sense… Ok then, I'll go gather some stones," claimed the lad.

"Remember! Preferably big stones with a plain side to them," the old man told the lad.

"I know, I know," said the lad, "Navi, want to join me?... Navi?" right then, the lad noticed that it was a while since he last felt the fairy's presence and couldn't find her anywhere, "Hood, I can't find Navi," he warned the old man.

Hood looked at him. Link could see how the expression on the old man's face suddenly changed.

"Let's go," Hood said, without hesitation.

Both men were calling for the fairy, shouting her name out loud. Suddenly, behind a tree, they saw the tiny fairy lying on the floor, her body barely shining. Link hurried to her side and kneeled on the floor.

"Navi? Navi?... Hood, what is it? What's wrong with her?" the worried lad asked.

The old man touched the water on the floor with his fingers, and smelled it, "Link, I know you're tired, but we need to unmount the encampment and move on... Navi is in bad shape. This is wrong... the water was poisoned".

CHAPTER 19

WILD NATURE

The men run towards their horses. In a brief time, they disassembled their encampment and rode away.

Hood, who was carrying the lantern, hurried his horse and Link Followed him. The lad, whose face was showing signs of tiredness, was wide awake now, as if he had received a bucketful of cold water straight to his face. The horses seemed to feel their master's worries since they were galloping at full speed, dodging roots, jumping over puddles and avoiding different kinds of obstacules while making their way through the swamp.

"Hood!!" shouted the lad.

"What, Link?" He replied, without slowing down.

"Where are we heading?" Link asked.

Still at full speed, Hood answered "We're looking for the secret cave!".

"And how are we going to find it, if it's secret?" the lad suspected Hood knew something else.

"I think I might have a clue of its location," He replied, without further detail.

Suddenly, a screeching noise, followed by a black stain, hit Hood, throwing him off his horse.

"Hood! What was that?" Asked the lad.

"Damn it! It had to be now!" cursed the old man as he got up on his feet.

"What's going on?" Link once again asked.

"Badbats!" answered Hood.

"Bad... what?" the lad asked again, but Hood spared further explanations "They're bats. Really, really, big bats,".

The huge animal came back for a second round and Hood did a barrel-roll to avoid its attack. Link was able to catch a clear view of the bat for a brief moment.

By the size of its wings, it seemed as a furry hawk, with two red blood-shot eyes. It possessed an agility worthy of a night hunter.

The old man run towards his horse, which stopped a few meters after he fell, grabbed his wooden shield and sword, and, lantern strapped to his belt, he readied himself for a new ramming from the bat.

"There it comes!" Link pointed out, listening to its wings flopping through the branches of the trees.

The old man swung his sword but the bat dodged it. "Damn bat!" cursed Hood.

Link climbed down from his horse and grabbed his weapons to aid his partner. He had Navi into a flask, with its lid open, hanging from his belt. He put the fairy there for safe travelling but now decided to put her under the root of a nearby tree for the time being, before joining the old man.

"Back to back, Link!" shouted the old man.

The lad run towards the old man and got himself in position. As the beast flew by, Link was the first one to spot it. He tried to hit it but unluckily it was yet another miss.

"It's too fast," said the lad.

"The bat isn't the problem," replied the old man, "what worries me is that, where there's badbats, there's wolfos. They fight each other for turf and prey for their respective packs,".

"Wolfos? What are those?" asked Link.

"It's a kind of wolf, a bit bigger than normal, with thicker paws," the old man explained.

The flying animal rammed again, furiously. This time, Hood faced him, covering with his shield. The beast smashed his feet against it and, with the tiny claws that were on its wings, grabbed it. The old man hit it, strongly, a few times with his wooden sword and the now dizzied animal flew away with difficulty.

"This is going to be tough. With this wooden weaponry, it's going to take us ages to leave them out of combat," claimed the old man.

Then, as if they weren't having enough trouble as it was, another predator showed up.

"Damn it... it's two of them now," Link shouted as he saw both bats circling over their heads.

The old man looked troubled, "Link... I have a bad feeling about this,".

In a coordinated attack, both bats came down at the same time, fighting against the shields and receiving swords slashes but the wood wasn't hard enough to knock them out. Each time the men tried to hit them, the bats flew away, and every time the bats launched their attacks, the brave heroes barely managed to defend themselves and counter-strike briefly. The lad's mind was running wild, trying to make a plan to get themselves out of that hard place.

"Fleeing is not an option, right?" asked Link.

"I'm afraid they would catch up rather quickly and, without our shields, we'd be easy prey," Hood answered.

As if they were trying to split them apart, one of the bats attacked Hood, grabbing him by his injured arm, which was rather painful for the old man.

Link looked at the old man, the bat attacking him and lastly the other bat, which he was fighting against. He felt that everything was up to him but he didn't know how he could help.

Then, in a risky move, turning his back on his enemy, Link did a barrel-roll and passed by the old man, ending up behind the bat that was grabbing his arm and, without dropping his sword, he used his arms to apply a lock to its neck.

Hood took advantage of the lad's move and released himself from the bat's hold, "Damn beast!" he shouted as he freed his arm. His wound seemed to have opened again, this time, worse than before. The old man was losing a lot of blood, but still, he landed a nice shield bash to the head of the bat that the lad was holding.

The animal was stunned by the hit, but Link didn't release his lock, "Hood, get the other one!".

The old man turned around and hit the other one, again, with his shield. The bat rolled on the ground and got back up.

"Link… I can't use this arm," said the old man, referring to his injury.

"What do we do now?" asked the lad.

"You'll have to handle both of them by yourself. And you must do it before this gets any worse," answered the old man. But, as if it was bad luck, a sharp howl was clearly heard which let the men know that at least one wolf was nearby.

"I think it won't be long before this gets worse, right?" said Link.

"No, it won't," replied the injured old man.

The lad had the bat firmly grabbed, but it still fought him, trying to catch his face or arms.

"Put it on the ground and stretch its wings," ordered Hood.

The lad threw himself on the ground without releasing the bat and did as he was told.

"An eye for an eye!" shouted Hood while wielding his sword with his shield hand.

While the sword was made of wood and didn't have an edge, it did have a sharp tip. The speed with which the sword descended into the bat's wing, and the thinness of its skin, helped with the task at hand. The sword passed through it, like it was some kind of stake and buried itself on the ground beneath the bat. The animal let out a rabid screech and its eyes were focused on Hood.

"This will ground him for a while," claimed the old man.

"I think it will… but just in case," said the lad as he grabbed his shield by its end and hit the bat square on its head, knocking it out. "Well thought!" the old man celebrated the lad's idea.

One bat was down. The other one, while it was flying erratically, he was still able to do so and that made it a hard target.

A new howl was heard in the distance, but this time, it was interrupted, as if the animal was wounded by something.

"Did you hear that?" Link wondered.

"The howling? Asked the old man, "Yes, I did,".

"What do you think happened to it?" wondered the lad.

"Heck if I know," answered the old man, more concerned about his current foe and pressing his wound with his shield-holding hand, "Most likely they're fighting amongst themselves…

260

so it won't be long before they arrive,".

"We need to take this bat down quickly... I just can't find a way," admitted Link.

The flying beast hovered above them but didn't attack. It seemed to be sizing them up, or maybe, waiting for his partner to wake up.

"Link... I'm losing a lot of blood. I need to reach my horse," claimed the old man.

"Ok, go. I'll cover you," affirmed the lad, valiantly.

Hood swiftly headed towards his scared-looking horse. Stumbling, he reached it and, without wasting time, the old man threw his shield on the ground. Then, he pulled the thread and needle from his saddlebag, luckily, he had everything set up beforehand.

"This won't leave a nice scar..." said to himself the old man, on the brink of losing consciousness.

"Go on, Hood! Just a little longer!" encouraged the lad.

The old man did a few more stitches on his skin. He was suffering while he was at it, but still it wasn't enough to fully awaken him.

"You've got to be kidding me..." Hood complained out loud as he sat down and leaned on a tree behind him.

"What is it now?!" asked the lad, completely focused on the bat swirling over their heads.

"I really thought I would be able to last longer..." answered the old man, throwing his head backwards and bumping the crust of the tree.

"Come on, Hood! Don't say that. We can still find a way out of this," said Link, trying to keep the old man awake.

"Ja! Well... we should," answered Hood.

Link guessed that Hood started to become delirious, after checking through the side of his eye and seeing that the stitches he made on himself were crooked and he was still losing blood, he realized that the blood loss was probably the cause.

"Don't worry, Link," said the old man while he covered his wound with his hand, "Everything's going to be fine," and after that, he fainted.

The lad started to scream at the old man, trying to wake him up, but the bat charged against him once again. Link arrived at the conclusion that the animal, seeing how the tables had turned, felt like it had the upper hand now.

The bat descended over him and targeted the lad's wooden sword. He held it, tightly, with its paws and then, after being able to rip it from the lad's grasp, threw it a few meters away.

"Damn it! Is everything going to go sideways for me?" he asked to himself.

Link was panicking and started to get desperate. But then, he looked at the old man and remembered his first lesson.

"Look, Link, in my opinion seven out of eight is not a miss, but seven rights. You have to start seeing the positive side of things, I mean, give it your best shot, but don't expect everything to go your way. Otherwise, when things go wrong, you'll panic, as you did with the last goat," he remembered.

The lad looked at his own arm. He only had his wooden shield. He then looked at his other hand, which was now empty, but...

"I've got it! He shouted. He then focused on the bat, "Let's go for a fly together,".

As he looked at his empty hand, he realized he completely forgot about the bracelet he was wearing. Without delay, he removed the safety and aimed towards the flying beast, waiting for a perfect shot chance.

The bat charged once again, but the lad seized this moment to reduce the error margin and took his shot. The claw left his bracelet and flew at full speed towards his foe.

As the claw hit it, the bat let out a cry filled with pain. It was now hooked by its abdomen and was frantically batting its wings, trying to get loose.

Flying with difficulty, it dragged Link, who rose from the ground like a feather. They were about three meters above the ground when the lad realized he had to pull the claw back to him.

"Let's see who can hold on for longer," the lad claimed and then squeezed his fingers to call back the claw.

As the claw retracted, both of them were getting closer to each other in the middle of the sky. Link, who had one hand busy with the bracelet, was only carrying his shield on his other hand and was seemingly planning to attack with it. The bat, which was being dragged towards the lad by its abdomen, was completely subjected to the will of the lad.

It was, probably, the hardest someone ever hit anything with a shield. After landing his blow, the lad realized he had to do something right then, or the fall might kill him. Then, in a quick display of skill, he reached out and grabbed the fainted animal by its fur. He held tightly to it and then free-fell the last remaining meters to the ground.

The bat was the best, and only, thing he could find to break his fall. Both of them hit the ground and rolled a few meters, parting away one from the other.

There they were, lying flat on the ground, both of them, with their extremities outstretched. Link with his arms and legs and the bat with both its wings, which occupied almost twice as Link's body did.

It took the lad around ten seconds to be able to move again. He was exhausted. His body screamed for some rest. Every spot of his body was aching and his bones felt as if they weighted a ton. The lad lacked the will to stand up and, if it would've been up to him, he would have stayed there, lying on the ground and closed his eyes, leaving himself to the will of the nature. "… but… what about Hood…" he thought. Suddenly, he remembered the young kokiri lass who wouldn't recover if they didn't return with the tear from the Great Fairy… even if he still didn't know how they would get it, "… and what about Zelda?". The lad opened his eyes and twitched his fingers, "Zelda needs me!" and then he slowly sat down where he was, "… Hyrule needs me…" he thought as he leaned on his knee, trying to stand back up, "… Ganondorf can't win. We can't make it this easy for him…" the lad staggered to his feet, "… I can't die, not until that bastard pays for his crimes…".

263

"And I'm not going to!" screamed the lad out loud.

Suddenly, he turned his head to his side. He was feeling watched over, and he wasn't mistaken, since he caught a glimpse of a figure, many meters away from him, hiding behind a tree. The darkness and his dazing didn't allow him to guess who or what it was.

"Who's out there!?" the lad screamed in anger, but no-one answered.

Then a wolf howled many meters away from where he stood. Link heard it, but couldn't move his sight from the tree where the mysterious someone was hiding.

"Come out, you coward!" Ordered Link, realizing then that he didn't have his shield with him anymore.

The lad headed a few steps in the direction of the tree, knowing that, if that someone ended up being a foe, he would be completely lost. Then, he remembered his crossing with a mysterious someone a few nights ago, when he was hunting for dinner for him and his companions. That guy back then didn't seem hostile, still, what was his purpose? Why was he following him? Was he being studied?

Link couldn't stop the thoughts coming at him while he neared the tree where he thought this wonderous spectator was hiding. But then, he found a giant wolf, at the side of another tree nearby, lying on the ground, dead, bled out.

Link realized that its partners were close by and he thought that, while this one was dead, the others might very well be alive and ready to attack. This made him desist from the idea of facing the guy in hiding. "Stop following me! I won't be always in a good enough mood to let it slide!" He claimed, even if he knew he was at disadvantage and, turning around, he started to wonder where the rest of the wolf-pack might be.

Since he flew some good few meters, he was not quite sure where he was. Nevertheless, he ran forward, guided by his instinct. He hadn't taken more than ten steps when he stumbled and fell, hitting his knee. He closed his eyes in pain, held back an insult and, when he opened them up, he was being faced by some sharp fangs, filled with drool. A snout, black as night, a pair of furry cheeks were over those fangs and a pair of black eyes, with dark-green splashes. The lad quickly fell back, dragging himself face-up on the ground as he realized the animal was ready to attack. Link's mind was racing trying to find a way to get out of that situation, when he realized than the animal wasn't in fact preparing an attack but, far from it, it was dead, just like the last one, but with it eyes open and in a position that was certainly easy to mistake.

"This is unbelievable… Who could have handled such a beast?" wondered the lad.

Link couldn't find what killed that huge wolf. Still, amidst the mud and the lack of light, he was able to realize that there was a puddle beneath the animal and he concluded that this puddle wasn't made of mud, but blood. He got closer, leaned over and touched it, to then take the fingers to his nose and sense the smell of it.

"As I thought… You've been sliced wide open," he said to the dead wolf, "… I don't really have time for this,".

The lad got up on his feet and started to run once again. He was looking at his surroundings, trying to find some track that could lead him to his friends. Suddenly, he came across a set of hoofprints and recognized the road they had previously taken. He knew that a few meters ahead, Hood was knocked down from his horse by the first bat, which still remained there, with its wing staved to the ground.

The lad followed the marking made by the hooves of the horses and finally arrived to the place where the old man was lying unconscious alongside with the fairy under the root.

"Thankfully you two are fine," claimed the lad, "Well… I'm not sure if fine is the word, but at least you're not worse than you were when I left," he thought out loud.

Behind him, a loud batting noise sounded.

"Damn it! This never ends!" he screamed without even turning to check what made the noise.

Once he did, he saw the trapped bat, swinging his loose wing, trying to release itself from the sword that kept him staved to the ground. The animal had regained consciousness and was frantically moving.

Link checked his surroundings and found the old man's shield, lying beside him.

"I'm going to need to borrow this," Link claimed while grabbing the wooden shield from the ground, "although I don't think it's going to be of much help,".

The bat pulled hard and unearthed the sword which went flying to a side. Link realized he had to get it since, even if it was made of wood, it was better than having nothing.

The bat got its two tiny claws on the ground and squealed loudly as he got ready to tackle the lad, but, as he was about to, a huge wolf jumped over the furry bat and sank its fangs on its neck.

The bat didn't stand a chance against the wulfo. While it's true that both species compete for turf and pray, once on the ground, the wolfo has a huge advantage over the winged animal.

Link watched as the wolf broke the bat's neck and realized he was now in trouble. Then, he focused back on the wooden sword, about two meters away from the beast and remembered that, behind him, was his horse and, in its saddlebag, his boomerang.

Subtly, he walked backwards, until he hit his saddlebag. The wolfo looked at him, analyzing his movements. Link grabbed the boomerang and, without taking his sight away from the beast, started to cautiously walk sideways. The wolf looked at the lad and did the same as he did. Both of them were checking each other's moves.

The wolf then howled and threw itself against Link, who threw his boomerang and then rolled sideways. The wolf avoided the lad's attack and the boomerang got lost in the bushes. The beast turned around to once again face the lad who now held the wooden sword in his hands.

Link screamed as he ran towards the animal and jumped towards it, lunging forwards, which the wolf dodged.

Link landed near Hood. His nose was a few centimeters away

from the flask which contained the tiny fairy. Navi had both her glowless hands against the glass. She looked at him with squinting eyes.

The little fairy mustered as much strength as she could to scream loud enough for the lad to hear her, "Keep it close to you and watch its movements closely! Attack when its guard is down!" and then she fainted once again.

"Hold on, Navi," said the lad. He got on his feet and, following his friend's advice, he stepped away from his friends and waited for the wolf to get near.

The animal came closer bit by bit and, once he was close enough, it jumped towards its prey.

The lad dodged it and gave it a strong blow with the side of his sword on its back-left paw.

The wolf howled in pain. Now he had trouble putting that paw down, still, Link needed more than a little blow to be able to escape from that situation. The beast attacked again and, again, Link dodged and riposted. This time, he missed the target. The wolf dodged the attack and this threw the lad out of balance. The animal took this chance and got the lad's leg on its jaw.

Link answered again, this time, he hit the animal's snout with his sword. The beast released his leg and fell back, but Link couldn't stand up anymore, his leg was bleeding profusely and the amount of strength he had left wasn't enough to let him move as he desired.

The wolf ran towards the lad and jumped over him. He rolled like a log to a side and sunk his sword on the wolf's ribs. Regretfully, the wound wasn't deep enough to completely stop the beast.

Both were injured and Link couldn't stop thinking, "Why on earth doesn't this damned beast leave me alone and just leaves? I'm not even interested in this damn fight...". But the wolf didn't seem to feel the same way and charged once again. Link rolled over once more while he shield-bashed the animal. That, was the last big effort Link could afford. He hardly managed to drag himself backwards, heading towards Hood, as if dying besides his friend was the best he could hope for right now.

"Hood... Navi... I'm sorry," he said with as little strength he had left, "I've let you down...".

The wolfo, limping but still quite swiftly, charged and once more jumped over the lad.

Everything was lost. Then, suddenly, another wolf came out of thin air and bit on the lad's opponent. This one was a majestic white wolf, it seemed to be covered with a silver mantle on its back. The two wolfs battled it out, biting their paws and necks. The lad looked the fight with the only eye he could keep open. The two wild animals were intertwined but then, the black wolf was able to repel the white one, kicking it back. The white wolf rolled a few meters, closer to Link. Without giving it a break, the black wolf charged against its foe. The white wolf dodged and the dark beast kept on running towards Link. The lad was unable to move and therefore, dodge. He just open both his eyes, looking at his predator one last time as it jumped towards him with its eyes filled with rage and fangs covered in drool. He closed his eyes and waited.

Then he felt it. The weight and warmth of the body of the wolf over him. A heavy pressure, sure, but... no pain? Link opened his eyes and saw two arrows stuck on the neck of the black wolf, which laid dead over him.

"What the heck?" claimed the lad, shocked at the scene. He tried to move the dead wolfo off of him but it was too heavy and impossible to move in his current state. He looked at the silver wolf, roaming around, "I'm afraid I'm not getting out of this one on my own," he thought as he realized he was trapped and, while looking at the blood that was coming out of his leg, he just closed his eyes and fainted.

The lad was lying on the ground, with the black wolf, bleeding out through its neck, on top of him. Beside him, under the root of the nearby tree, into the glass flask, the fairy laid, motionless. On the other side, the old man was sitting, with his back leant on the same tree and with his head tilted forward.

Two men approached the group.

"Is he dead?" one asked.

"Yes, he is," replied the other.

268

EPILOGUE

THE SOUL TRIP

As if he was levitating, Link was traveling laying down. He didn't feel his legs, arms or even chest nor head. It was as if something took the sense of touch out of him.

Some images came to his mind in a storm of confusion, but still, he was at peace. He flew over the valleys of Hyrule, a breeze he couldn't feel was caressing the grass, making it form waves as if it was a blanket. The morning dew left behind thousands of drops on top of the green leaves of the big trees and bushes of that place. A rather familiar smell overcame him. "Roasted meat... Dad used to cook that from time to time, when the weather was nice,".

But he didn't remember his father... nor his mother. How long did Astor take care of him? Was it since he lost his memory or maybe he was already under his tutelage when it happened? So much to remember...

The lad flew over the stable and saw a few beautiful, well groomed, brown steeds. He didn't need to touch them to realize how soft they would be.

Beside the stable, a pen with sheep, springy as pillows, still not sheared, were covered in white and shiny wool.

A Few meters ahead, still inside the farm, he could hear the cuccos cackle. He trembled while remembering the pecking those birds had given him throughout his life. Nevertheless, he couldn't check if he was getting goosebumps, since he couldn't see any part of his body. The weird thing was that he could actually see everything else. Everything was crystal clear, although at times, things did get a bit blurry and sped by, but mostly, he could catch a good glimpse of everything. Was he really there or was it only his mind? What time was that? Past, present or future? So much to think about...

As if he was weightless, he rose even higher and looked at the whole forest from above, descending only to pass amongst many branches and move a few sleeves, as if he was wind itself. He filled every hole, squeezed under every elevated root, dodged every stone and rose again to contemplate everything.

Entangling himself with the clouds, Link moved, completely devoid of weight. The forest ended and he could see the shore of lake Hylia. As a bird of prey, Link submerged. The water was a bit cold, "The water is… cold?" he thought. Could he now feel his body once again? Was this all a dream or only his spirit transcended? So much to feel…

He dived a few meters, many fish of many colors came by, curious, and then fled. The light started to abandon him, the depth difficulted his sight and let him see less and less, "Breathe… I should breathe," reasoned the lad, as he felt the pressure on his chest.

"I think he's waking up," Link heard.

The voice came from everywhere, as if it was an absolute being.

"He's lost a lot of blood, I don't think he's going to wake up for a while," said another voice, which sounded in the vast darkness of the lake.

Both voices could be heard clearly, but distant. Deep and slow, as if every syllable was being dragged. His eyes didn't allow him to see anything. Was it his eyes, or the water? The depth, or his eyelids? Because… His eyes were open… Right? Out of sheer willpower, the lad opened his eyes. They were closed after all. Now he was traveling, laying down on a horse, tied to it. It was raining… heavily. His eyelids were heavy… He was so tired. He felt as if more than one horse was riding along him, "Three… maybe four," he thought, by the sound they made.

Was he awake or was it another dream? Every part of his body ached. Was this the real thing, or what he felt before? Where was he going? How? Why was he tied? So many things to ask…

Every cell in Link's body wished to fade away and, as if his brain knew that he shouldn't be there to feel pain, he fled again.

Once again, he was in the deeps of that lake, he felt a bit cold, but at least he wasn't in pain, "I wish I could stay here, peacefully, until the end of time," he meditated.

The water was getting warmer, "This is getting better," he thanked, relaxing. He was floating in that fluid with no worries in mind. What was that which tormented him before? Who was waiting for him? Zelda? Hyrule? …Yes, it was them. What might have happened to Zelda, Astor and the rest of the hylians if Link didn't return to help them? What would happen to Saria and the kokiris? What about Hood and Navi? So much to live for…

"I forgot to breathe again… I should do it," remembered the lad.

Link so himself, once again immersed on all that water, and the surface appeared above him, "Out… I must get out… and return…" he thought as he swam upwards… Was he swimming? Yes, he was. He could see his arms again and they were paddling upwards, in search for fresh air to breathe. He was getting near to the light, faster every time, he could almost touch it. The shining light covered him completely and everything became white.

CONTENIDO

(ANCIENT ALPHABET)

A	a	B	b	C	c	D	d
E	e	F	f	G	g	H	h
I	i	J	j	K	k	L	l
M	m	N	n	O	o	P	p
Q	q	R	r	S	s	T	t
U	u	V	v	W	w	X	x
		Y	y	Z	z		

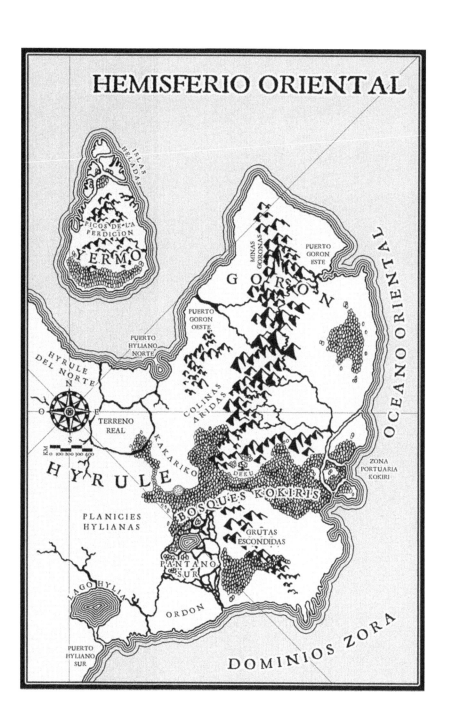

HEMISFERIO ORIENTAL

ISLAS HELADAS

PICOS DE LA PERDICIÓN

YERMO

GORON

MINAS GORONAS

PUERTO GORON ESTE

PUERTO GORON OESTE

PUERTO HYLIANO NORTE

HYRULE DEL NORTE

TERRENO REAL

COLINAS ÁRIDAS

KAKARIKO

OCÉANO ORIENTAL

ZONA PORTUARIA KOKIRI

DEKU

HYRULE

PLANICIES HYLIANAS

BOSQUES KOKIRIS

GRUTAS ESCONDIDAS

PANTANO SUR

LAGO HYLIA

ORDON

PUERTO HYLIANO SUR

DOMINIOS ZORA

KM 0 100 200 300 400

N O E S

Printed in Great Britain
by Amazon

21195457R00161